Clover Covered Corpse

Clover Covered Corpse

A
Texas Flower Farmer
Cozy Mystery

Jackie Layton

LEVEL
BEST BOOKS

I dedicate this book to Tim. We've enjoyed gardening together for many years, and he's always up for listening to my book ideas.

Praise for the Texas Flower Farmer Cozy Mysteries

"I was blessed by Author Jackie Layton to be one of the first to read her new book *Weeding Out Lies*. It is always fun to start a new series right at book one. Jackie gives us some charming characters to live with, the kind that just charm their way in…"—~My Readying Journeys

"*Weeding Out Lies* has set the Texas Flower Farmer Cozy Mystery Series off to an exceptional start with some charming characters, an intriguing mystery, and a small town filled with possibilities for more mayhem and murder."—~Escape With Dollycas Into A Good Book

"*Weeding Out Lies* by author Jackie Layton is a cozy mystery set in small-town Texas, and my interest was held from the first page to the last. I couldn't wait to see Whodunnit, which surprised me."—~Novels Alive

"*Weeding Out Lies* by Jackie Layton is a layered cozy mystery that introduces readers to a quaint Texas town (complete with an equally quaint town square) and a bevy of colorful residents. The mystery was well-plotted, and I immediately got a good sense of the setting. I look forward to seeing where the series takes Emma from here!"—
~Reading is my Superpower

"I enjoyed the first book in this debut series. The pacing was nice, and I liked the comfortable tone that made it easy to follow along. I also liked the fact that Emma had a good relationship with the police, which helped in her search for clues. There were a few twists and turns that kept me in the game, and I especially like that big one when it was apparent who the killer was. Good job. Boasting an eclectic cast of characters and engaging dialogue, this was a fun book and I look forward to more adventures with Emma and her friends."—Dru Ann Love, https://drusbookmusing.com/my-musing-weeding-out-lies/

Chapter One

My good friend Brett Tirabasi sat across the wood table from me at BBQ Hut. Our little town of Lutz, Texas didn't have a wide variety of eating establishments, but the ones we had were excellent. Barbecue was one of my weaknesses, and it was the thing that prevented me from becoming a vegetarian.

Shelby Penn, our waitress, refilled my Dr. Pepper and removed our dirty plates. "Can I interest you in banana pudding for dessert?"

I smiled at the teenager. "None for me, but thanks. Everything was delicious."

Brett waved his hand in a way that indicated he wasn't in need of dessert. "I'm good."

"Okay, I'll bring your bill in a minute." Shelby's black hair grazed her shoulders, and it bounced as she turned away. Shelby was in high school, and her uncle, Houston Turner, owned the restaurant.

"She seems like such a nice girl, but there's always something sad in her eyes." I stirred my straw in the carbonated drink. Did she want to waitress for her uncle, or would she rather hang out with friends on a Friday night?

"It's fear. Maybe a touch of anger." Brett was a veteran who suffered from PTSD, and he'd seen a lot in his thirty-six years.

"Oh, no. Poor, Shelby." I glanced around the restaurant. The regular Friday night crowd had gathered. Loud country music played in the bar, children laughed and cried, and the more the beer flowed, the noisier the place grew.

"Let's get down to business." Brett took a paper napkin and dried our table before opening a file of papers. "These are the new smoothie recipes I've created for Anytime Coffee House. What do you think about supplying the herbs for me?"

I was Lutz's local flower farmer. After a nudge from Sophie Becker, my best friend, I'd been trying my hand at growing herbs. She owned Sophie's Bakery and used herbs in some of her recipes. "Tell me what you've got on your list."

"Mint and parsley."

I placed my arms on the table and leaned forward to hear him above the restaurant's noisy patrons. "Not a problem. What else?"

"Basil? I've come up with an interesting blackberry smoothie with a hint of basil."

"I have some basil and can grow more if the drink is popular."

Brett laughed. "You sound doubtful."

"Probably because I am. It seems like basil should be used in Italian dishes. I'm not sure about smoothies, but you're the expert." Brett was one of the few Black business owners in Lutz, but we were a small town without a lot of independent businesses. Brett and I first met, when I'd been a pharmacy tech at the local drug store.

"I'll make it for you the next time you're in the coffee shop." He glanced down at his notes. "Turmeric?"

"I hate to be negative, but don't you think turmeric will make your drinks bitter?"

"I'm going for the health benefits. It's an anti-inflammatory and goes well with mango." His eyebrows lifted higher with each word. "I've been watching Houston Turner sell his health drink—"

"Good Life." Despite the name of the drink, I hadn't heard many good reviews.

"Right. The locals are excited about it, because of the health benefits, but he buys it from a supplier. I can make healthier and fresher drinks right here in town. The fresher the ingredients, the better the benefits. Don't you think?"

"Yeah, but you're not competing with Houston. His product is a health drink, not smoothies."

Brett's head jerked back. "Mine will be healthy."

"I know, but his drinks are, like, in a different market, and he sells multiple processed bottles at a time. I don't know who he hired to produce the drink, but he claims it's his own creation." I lowered my voice. "Isn't he running the product as a pyramid scheme?"

"I hope not because pyramid schemes are illegal here."

Police Chief Matt Young appeared and tapped on our table. "Howdy, folks."

I met his gaze, and my face grew warm. He didn't look happy. Had I said anything to earn a lecture from him? I didn't think so. "Hi, Matt."

"Chief." Brett nodded. "How ya doing?"

"I'm doing great. Got the night off and decided to join some of my guys for dinner." His gaze bounced from me to Brett then back to me.

"Have fun. We're having a business dinner." I pointed to the file folder.

"I best shove off then. See y'all around."

Brett stared at me. "That was weird. Is he sweet on you? I thought you were interested in my man Jake."

"I've known Matt for years. Our kids had after-school activities and dance lessons together." I avoided sharing my feelings about his good friend, Jake Hunter. "Any other herbs you're interested in?"

"Naw, let's start with the mint, parsley, and basil. I'll take your word and hold off on the turmeric for now."

"I'm growing peppermint and spearmint, and I'll bring both to you. The Lutz Farmers Market is open tomorrow, so it'll probably be Monday morning before I can stop by. Is that soon enough?"

"It'll be perfect."

"Hey, I've also got some lavender. You might try it with tea or lemonade. I'll bring some stalks of it for you, too."

"Thanks. Lavender is super popular these days." He reached for the check. "Dinner's on me tonight."

"I can't let you pay for mine." I dug a twenty out of my purse.

"It's a business expense." He retrieved a credit card. "Let's get out of here."

I waited by the restaurant's door while Brett stood in line to pay.

Buddy Hewitt, the owner of the hardware store, entered with Paige Booker, the owner of our local bookstore.

"Hi, y'all." Were they on a date, or was it business, like Brett and me?

"Hey, Emma. Are you waiting on someone?" She hugged me.

Buddy said, "Excuse me just a moment. I want to get our names on the list."

After he moseyed over to the hostess, I focused on Paige. "Are you dating Buddy?"

She shrugged. "He was nice to me when the cops thought I was guilty of committing murder, and we've always been friends. For now, we're hanging out more. Are you here with Jake?"

"Actually, Brett and I had a business dinner." I didn't want to spoil the surprise about his smoothies. That was his news to share at his designated time.

"Cool."

Brett joined us. "Hi, Paige. Emma, are you ready to split?"

"Yeah, I'm fixin' to go to bed early because tomorrow will be an early day. See ya later, Paige."

"Bye." We gave each other a quick hug before Brett and I exited the restaurant.

Brett drove me home in his red sports car and walked me to the door. "Thanks again."

"We never finished our conversation about Houston Turner's business. Do you think the drinks are part of an unofficial pyramid scheme?"

He shook his head. "I don't have any proof, but the stories I've heard make me wonder."

"It just seems sketchy. Something to think about another day. I'll see you later." I entered my house then locked the door.

My golden retriever mutt barked, and I hurried to release him from his crate. Cowboy had been abandoned and survived on the streets for several weeks before I rescued him. The vet said my dog was part mutt, but the dog seemed mostly golden retriever to me. He was well-behaved and a good companion, but he tended to forage for food in the garbage or on my kitchen counters. When he wasn't eating, Cowboy seemed to like the security of his crate and often took himself there.

"Hey, boy. How ya doing?" I rubbed each side of his neck before leading him to the backyard. I settled into an Adirondack chair while Cowboy sniffed around the fence. A mix of purples, blues, and oranges filled the evening sky as the sun set for the day. The beauty was like a warm hug, and as much as I'd enjoy watching until it was completely dark, I needed to get to bed.

I'd be up before dawn to prepare my flowers for our local farmers market. I mentally reviewed my to-do list. This was my first year as a flower farmer, and the excitement for every Saturday in Lutz, Texas, thrilled me.

Cowboy returned, and I petted him. "It's an early night for us. One day, when you've learned more manners, I'll take you with me."

He released a happy bark, and we headed inside.

The weatherman predicted Saturday would be a perfect day to be outside, and I couldn't wait for the market to begin. What was more exciting than a spring Saturday, spending time outside?

Chapter Two

Saturday morning dawned warm, with only a slight breeze. I dressed in shorts, a T-shirt advertising Emma's Flower Farm, and my wide-brimmed straw hat. I drove my truck, Ms. Daisy, to the market with plenty of supplies. Each week more people were buying flowers for spring parties, wedding showers, and even weddings.

My yard had been ransacked in March, and I'd had to begin again with the help of neighbors and friends. Instead of a wide variety of flowers, I focused on dahlias, lilies, coneflowers, and daffodils. Every few weeks, it'd be time for other flowers to bloom. Then, I'd add zinnias, daisies, and black-eyed Susans to my offerings. My focus was to grow and sell flowers that'd make beautiful flower arrangements that would be popular with the shoppers.

I carried the supplies needed to set up my booth and arranged the flowers in the buckets situated in flower stands. Tissue paper, ribbon, a credit card reader, cash, and flower arrangements were my basics.

I kept watch for Paula Jones who'd asked to assist me at my booth. She worked in the high school office, and she was interested in getting more involved in the community.

"Good morning, Emma." Houston Turner appeared, carrying a cup of coffee from Anytime Coffee House.

"Morning, Houston." For a big man, he sure moved quietly. He owned BBQ Hut, a food truck, and his Good Life drink was his most recent business venture. That was the thing causing friction between him and Brett. The drink was supposed to help you gain muscle, lose fat, and get healthier all around. "How can I help you this morning?"

"I'd like to buy some of your purty flowers, like a bouquet. Let's say a dozen. What's the best price you can give me on a dozen of them yellow daffodils?"

I quoted a price to him. "It's the same for everyone."

His nostrils flared, and he swiped a hand over his mouth. "Fine."

I pulled out the flowers and dabbed water droplets with a towel. Then I wrapped the daffodils in colorful tissue paper and tied it with a ribbon. "What do you think?"

"She'll like them." He handed me the exact amount of money and left as fast as he'd appeared.

My curious side had wanted to ask about the lucky lady, but Houston's swift departure made it impossible. I recorded our transaction, then glanced around the market. Food trucks formed a semicircle across the way. BBQ Hut, Fiesta Mexico, Lemon Squeeze, and Anytime Coffee House were today's offerings. Oh, how I wished I could run over to get a green tea or coffee.

A gray-haired man stopped by and bought a small arrangement of coneflowers in a Mason jar for his wife, who was going through rehab from a hip replacement. He was quite talkative, and I listened, giving him my full attention. At last, he said, "I heard one of the farmers is selling homemade cinnamon rolls. I think I'll buy one to share with my wife. Have a good day."

"I hope you have a good day too."

I smiled at people shopping. Some took their time and studied every booth. Other people appeared to be on a mission, heading for their favorite vendors.

"Sorry I'm so late." Paula shoved her keys into a big leather purse and pushed the bag under my table. Her slicked-back ponytail was cattywampus, and Paula never stepped out in public unless she looked her best.

"Is everything okay?" Her jerky movements surprised me. Paula was usually more composed.

"Not really." She ran her hands over her thighs. "I ran into Houston Turner. He played me, big time."

"How?" I joined her behind the table of wrapping supplies and noted she wasn't carrying the daffodils I'd sold him a few minutes earlier.

"He acted like he wanted to date me. We even went to Dallas once. I got all dressed up, but we only picked up bottles of his new drink. On the way home, we drove through a burger place and ate in his truck. I was aggravated but pretended everything was fine. Because that's what I do. It's probably why people feel like they can walk all over me. Anyhow, Houston asked if I'd ever done any modeling. He suggested I could drink Good Life and lose weight."

I gasped. "No way. That's terrible."

Paula shrugged. "I'll be fifty soon, and it wouldn't hurt me to shed a few pounds. What really got me was when he wanted to take before and after pictures. For some reason, I agreed to let Elijah Barnes take some pictures, but I refused to wear a swimsuit."

"Good for you, but I think you look great." Poor Paula.

"Thanks, but the drink doesn't work. At Houston's insistence, I started drinking it, but I haven't lost any weight. This morning, I told him I wanted a refund, and he laughed in my face. That stuff isn't cheap, and I bought a lot of it. Thank goodness I was smart enough not to invest in his company."

"Invest like how?"

"He wanted me to sell it. In order to sell Good Life, you must invest a certain amount of money. On top of that, you buy your own supply and sell from it."

"Isn't that how pyramid schemes work?"

"Who knows? I am so mad at him. The stuff doesn't even taste very good." She bent down and pulled a bottle out of her purse. "You try it. Just don't expect to lose weight."

I twisted off the plastic top and sniffed the drink before taking a small sip. Ugh. My throat closed, and I had to force myself to swallow. "Bleck. It's too sour. I wasn't sure if I'd be able to swallow it."

Paula laughed. "See what I mean?"

"Yeah. How does he get people to buy it?" I screwed the top back on.

"There are testimonials for the product, and I'm not the only sucker to give it a try. People are convinced it'll turn your life around with healthy benefits."

Two ladies approached and studied the display of cut flowers.

Paula touched my arm. "Let me try. I need to get my mind off Houston and onto something nice."

"Go for it." I waved her toward the flowers.

A young man appeared with his camera. "Hi, I'm Elijah Barnes. Mr. Johns asked me to take pictures of vendors, because he wants to update his website."

"Give me just a minute." I adjusted my wide-brimmed straw cowgirl hat, reached for a tube of lip gloss, and swiped it on my lips. "Okay, this is as good as it gets today."

He chuckled. "Act natural. I'll take some shots of your flowers and your interactions with customers. Pretend like I'm not even here."

Easier said than done, but I'd give it a shot. "Sure. Let me know if you need me to do something different."

"Yes, ma'am."

A man walked up, holding a little girl's hand. The child met my gaze. "My mommy just had a baby. He's my new little brother."

I knelt beside her. "Would you like to get flowers for your mommy and baby brother?"

She nodded. "Yeah, but I don't know what to get."

"I'll be happy to help you." I looked at the nodding father, and we went to work creating a flower arrangement.

The next couple of hours flew by, and I forgot all about Elijah Barnes.

"Looks like the market is hopping today." Jake Hunter held out an insulated cup toward me. "I brought you my April Sunshine brew."

Before meeting Jake Hunter, I'd mostly drunk tea. From the first day, he'd challenged me to try different coffees. To my delight, I enjoyed most of his creations. I wrapped my fingers around the cup. "April Sunshine?"

"You bet, because it's April, and you are the Sunshine."

My heart may have skipped a beat. Jake had a habit of calling me Sunshine. I avoided looking into his brown eyes and sipped the coffee. Notes of lavender danced over my tastebuds. "I like it. Do I detect a hint of lavender? And you sweetened it with honey."

A big smile split his face. "Yes, thanks for noticing."

"It's delicious, and it smells nice too."

Paula cleared her throat. "I heard there's a lady who makes jewelry with health benefits, and she's a Texan. Do you mind if I look for her?"

"Take your time, Paula." It seemed as if Paula was a sucker for anything with healthy benefits. When she disappeared, I faced Jake. "It feels like I haven't seen you in a long time."

He shrugged. "I get it. Without a murder to solve, you didn't need me."

"Oh, no. That's not it at all. I've been busy working on my gardens and marketing. I just haven't had time for much of anything else. I figured you were working hard too."

"Brett doesn't need me as much. If he wasn't so focused on his smoothie business, I doubt he'd need me at all." Jake crossed his arms. "Did you hear that Houston Turner threatened to sue Brett?"

"No way. Oh, hold that thought." An elderly man stood looking at a display of flowers I'd already arranged in vases. "Can I help you?"

"My wife is in a memory care community. She still loves flowers, and I want to take some to her."

I discussed his options, and he chose a green plastic vase of dahlias before walking away. I returned to Jake. "Please, continue."

"Houston told Brett that only one of them could sell healthy drinks. Houston created Good Life first, so Brett needs to stop selling smoothies."

"Whoa, how'd Brett react?"

Jake chuckled. "He was cool as a cucumber and told Houston to try and sue him. Then Houston stormed off, yelling threats all the way out the door. Once he left, all the customers in the coffee shop cheered. It turns out Brett's not the first person Houston has tried to bully in town."

"I'm glad Brett stood up for himself. Spring is a perfect time for smoothies. It's heating up in Texas. Good for Brett to try creating new drinks on his menu for the scorching hot days."

"Definitely. You got to be aware of your customer base and what they enjoy. It's a smart move—

A scream interrupted Jake's sentence, and chills ripped up my spine.

Chapter Three

I grabbed my cash box and credit card reader before hurrying toward the scream.

Miranda Penn, Houston Turner's sister, stood in the field of clover behind the food trucks, pointing at the ground. "He's dead! My brother is dead!"

Jake took off and beat me to the body. When I reached them, Jake was checking for signs of life. His cheek was near the man's mouth; then he moved his fingers to Houton's wrist.

Others stood around the body, talking on cell phones. A middle-aged man wearing a Texas Rangers ball cap gripped a phone next to his ear. "The operator said to start CPR."

Two women dropped to their knees and began the life-saving procedure. They elbowed Jake to the side.

Houston had been alive and rude only a couple of hours earlier. What had happened?

I avoided looking at the big man's body and studied the grassy area full of clover. The yellow daffodils I'd sold him lay scattered by the body. There was also a bottle of Good Life, a crushed paper cup from Anytime Coffee, and a bracelet on his thick wrist. He hadn't worn it earlier, but maybe he'd bought it from the same jewelry booth Paula was interested in. I hoped they hadn't been there at the same time.

A siren wailed. Woo-woo-woo. Whoop. An ambulance parked near the picnic tables for the food court. Two EMTs hopped out of the vehicle and dashed to Houston Turner's body.

Jake joined me and slipped his arm around my shoulders. "How are you holding up?"

I could feel his racing heart thump against the back of my arm. "Okay, I guess. What about you?"

"I'll be fine, but Houston won't." Jake's voice trembled.

"I was afraid of that. Do you think he had a heart attack?"

"Nope." He pressed his lips together into a flat line.

Two police cars pulled next to the ambulance, and four cops ran to the body.

I watched the people who had gathered around the tragic scene. Elijah Barnes took pictures from a discrete distance. "If I was a cop, and if this turns out to be a murder, I'd ask the photographer to share his pictures with me."

"Oh, Emma. You're not a cop, so please don't ask to see the pictures."

Officer Steve Koch approached the crowd, waving his arms. "Everyone git back. This here is an official crime scene." His Texas twang rang out.

The crowd gasped. It was followed by murmuring, but nobody moved away.

"I said to git back." Officer Koch's voice had turned into a growl, and the crowd began to disperse.

Jake said, "He surely means us too. We best bounce."

As much as I wanted to watch and maybe overhear a clue, I did need to sell flowers. "You're right. Hey, thanks again for the coffee. It's delicious."

"You're welcome."

"Jake, if you see anything from your coffee truck, will you tell me?"

"Umf." He thumped his chest. "I knew it. You're only interested in me for my investigative skills."

"That's not true. I've really been busy with my business."

"Just kidding. See ya later, Sunshine."

"Bye." I walked back to my booth. Everything looked just like I left it. Nothing stolen, but I was still glad to have remembered to take my money with me.

Paula raced up to me and placed a death grip on my arm. Her face was pale. "Can you believe it? Houston Turner's dead."

"It's a shock. Do you suppose you cared more about him than you realized?"

She shook her head. "No, that's not it. What if the police learned I'd been arguing with Houston this morning? They might believe I'm a suspect."

"One argument doesn't mean you murdered Houston. I think you're overreacting."

Paula gulped. "We also argued earlier this week. Emma, you've got to help prove I'm innocent. You need to catch the real killer."

This time I gulped. There'd only been one time when I'd helped a friend out by proving she didn't commit murder. It'd been dangerous, and I'd almost been killed myself. How could I agree? Paula's wide, water-filled eyes implored me. Dag gum it. How could I not agree? "Fine. I'll see what I can do."

"Thank you so much." Paula hugged me tight.

A sense of dread filled me. I was a flower farmer, not a detective. By agreeing, I'd lessened my friend's stress. On the other hand, it was doubtful I could really solve another murder.

Chapter Four

The only way to take a stab at solving the murder was to gather some evidence. "Paula, if you'll run my booth, I'll try to find some clues."

"Yes, I'll do anything you need." Her face was pale, and her mascara had smeared. "Show me how to work the credit card machine, and I'll take care of business here."

"Um, first, you might want to check your face."

Paula reached for her purse and looked in a small mirror. "Oh, dear." She took a tissue and repaired the damage. "Okay. I shouldn't scare you customers now. Show me how to work that machine."

I explained to her what to do, then dug through my backpack for a notebook and a pen to take notes.

Caution tape blocked off the crime scene, and the crowd had dwindled to mostly family. Miranda Penn, Shelby Penn, and the photographer huddled together. I knew Houston's sister and niece, and I was becoming a little better acquainted with Elijah Barnes. What was his relationship with the family that he felt close enough to hunker down with them during a crisis? "Hey, y'all. I'm so sorry for your loss. What can I do to help you?"

Shelby was crying and wiping tears with a paper napkin. Miranda looked to be in shock. Nobody answered.

"Can I get you coffee or tea?"

Miranda blinked as if coming out of a trance. She was a strong woman, but she looked pitiful. She took a deep breath and squared her shoulders. "Do you think coffee will replace my brother?"

"No. Absolutely not." My spirits sank. "I just thought it—I'm sorry. A hot beverage usually gives me a small amount of comfort."

Shelby sniffed. "I'd like hot tea, please. And bring Momma a coffee with sugar only."

"I'll be right back." I virtually ran to Anytime Coffee's van at the food court. "Jake, I've got an order for you."

The corners of his mouth turned downward. "Don't think for a minute that I didn't see you back at the crime scene."

"I'll explain later. Right now, I need drinks for Miranda and Shelby." I gave him the order. "Oh, let's add your special spring coffee for Elijah."

Jake sighed. "I've got a better idea. He usually orders a sweet Texas pecan blend with cream and sugar."

"Perfect. That's what I'll get."

Brett stepped out of the shadows and joined me at the order window. "Emma, what do you know about the murder?"

"Not much, yet. Why?" I took in his knuckles, gripping the counter.

He lowered his voice and leaned closer. "Houston and I've had a couple of altercations this week. He also stopped by the coffee shop when I opened today, and he threatened me. Again. All over some stupid drinks."

The hairs on the back of my neck lifted. "Oh, Brett. That's terrible."

He shrugged. "You never know what direction a murder investigation will take. There are a lot of innocent men in prison for crimes they didn't commit. It happens."

Jake placed my drinks in a cardboard tray on the counter, and I passed him my credit card. I met Jake's gaze, then turned to my friend's. "Brett, I've already been asked to investigate the murder by someone else. I'll keep you posted."

"Hold up, Jake. Her order is on the house this time. It's only right, with them grieving, and Emma's investigation will help me." Brett tapped Jake's arm, then turned his focus back to me. "Don't put yourself in danger for my sake, but I'd appreciate it if you'd share any clues with me."

"You know I will. Thanks for the drinks."

Jake returned my credit card. "Like my friend said, be careful."

I picked up the coffee caddy. "I'll let you guys know when I learn anything important."

"Thanks, Emma." Brett nodded.

I returned to the others and passed out the hot beverages. "Anytime Coffee didn't charge for the drinks and sent their condolences. What are the cops saying?"

Miranda was a tall woman, and she lifted her chin. "They say it's murder."

More tears streamed down Shelby's flawless teenage cheeks. "Who would murder Uncle Houston?"

Elijah paused, lifting his cup to his mouth. "Hey, no offense, but your uncle wasn't the nicest person around. He had enemies."

Shelby cried out. "Elijah, how could you say such a thing?"

Miranda patted her daughter's shoulder. "Shh, baby girl. He's not wrong." Miranda's gaze shifted from her daughter and zoomed in on the young photographer. "He wasn't the easiest person to get along with, and you speak the truth. My brother did have enemies, but how do you know this?"

He held his paper coffee cup in one hand and lifted the other hand. "Sorry, Shelby. You're not going to want to hear this. Miranda, people tend to ignore the photographer in the background. I heard stuff."

It made sense to me. "What kind of stuff?"

He shook his head. "I won't speak any more ill of the dead in front of his family."

Miranda said, "His ex-wife and their sons should be notified. I guess that's my job. Excuse me." She walked to the BBQ Hut food truck.

Shelby shivered, then sipped her hot tea. "I can't believe it."

Elijah took a step toward the teen but backed away. He met my gaze.

I understood it wouldn't be appropriate for him to comfort her because of the age difference. I moved close to the young lady and slipped my arm around her shoulders. If my daughter found herself in a similar situation, I would want someone to reach out to her, especially since her mother wasn't offering comfort. "It's going to be okay, Shelby."

"Uncle Houston gave me jobs so I could save up for college." She leaned into me.

"My daughter Abby started college in January, and she got some scholarship money. I thought you'd be attending school on a tennis scholarship."

"That was my original plan, and Momma wanted it to happen too. Uncle Houston had other ideas, though. He used me as a model for a lot of his advertisements, and I worked at the restaurant. He demanded so much of me, and I wasn't allowed to play in tournaments. That's the best way to get your rankings up."

It didn't escape my notice that she said Houston used her.

Elijah cleared his throat. "Shelby pretty much was only playing high school matches."

I turned to the young man. How'd he know about Shelby's tennis? "Really?"

"Hey, nothing creepy going on here. I'm the photographer for the high school yearbook, and Houston used me for his advertising."

"Makes sense."

Miranda returned. "I just learned something very interesting. Leigh, Houston's ex-wife, is here in Lutz. She came to insist Houston catch up on missed child support payments. If he refused, she planned to take him to court."

It sounded like a motive to me, but I didn't know much about Leigh Turner. "What are you saying?"

Elijah said, "Money is always a good motive for murder."

Miranda's nostrils flared. "My point exactly."

Chapter Five

Police Chief Matt Young approached the four of us with determination in his stride. "Emma, not sure you have any business here. Miranda and Shelby, I'm sorry for your loss. I'm afraid I don't know you." The police chief pointed to the young man.

"Elijah Barnes, sir. I'm a photographer, and Mr. Turner was one of my clients."

"Give me a call later today. We need to talk." Chief Young pulled a business card out of his shirt pocket and passed it to the young man. He turned his focus to the mother-and-daughter duo. "The market is over for the day, but I need to ask you some questions. You probably know Houston better than anyone else. Hopefully, you'll be able to give us some leads on where to begin our search to catch the killer."

Miranda crossed her arms. "I worked for my brother at the restaurant, and I always ran the food truck for him. He was fourteen years older than me, and we weren't very close."

I found her comment odd. If she worked for him, they must've had a fairly good relationship.

Chief Young raised his eyebrows. His next question revealed he might have the same thought as me. "But you did work for him. It seems like you may have been closer than you realized."

"My brother was involved in many business ventures. Take Good Life, his drink to improve your health. I know nothing about it."

"I disagree. You just told me the name of it." The police chief adjusted his cowboy hat. "One of my female officers will take you and your daughter to the station for questioning. My gut tells me you'll be more helpful than you think."

"What about my food truck? I need to move it before it gets towed." She leaned toward Matt and frowned. Miranda was almost as tall as Chief Young, and she had good posture. She had shed her sorrow, at least for the moment. The woman appeared to be a force to be reckoned with, and I decided it wouldn't be smart to get sideways with her.

Chief Young raised his hands. "You have my word that it won't be towed."

Miranda pointed to the turquoise blue food truck with red lettering. "If it stays too long, the food might spoil. The generator won't run forever. Cold food needs to stay cold, and hot food should remain hot."

Another valid point. Still, it almost seemed like she was coming up with reasons to avoid talking to Chief Young.

"Ms. Penn, would you like me to have it moved for you while we discuss your brother at the station?"

She huffed. "It's more involved than that. The food needs to be secured before it's moved."

I waved my hand, and they both glanced my way. "Miranda, would you like me to drive your truck to the restaurant? I'll take good care of it."

Elijah said, "I can help."

The woman's shoulders drooped. "I guess I don't have much of a choice. If it's okay with the police chief, I will call the sous chef to help you unload everything when you get to BBQ Hut."

Matt looked at all of us. "Sounds like a plan. Make your call, and I will send one of my officers over here to drive you to the station."

"Here's my set of keys to the food truck." She fingered the lanyard around her neck and removed two keys, then explained in detail what she needed me to do.

In a short time, we made arrangements for me to return the truck and food to the restaurant. Elijah was going to BBQ Hut first and let the staff know what had happened to Houston. He planned to stay and help unload the food truck.

Chief Young touched my shoulder. "Emma, I'd like a word with you."

Uh-oh. "Okay."

"Let's go to your booth where we won't be overheard."

"Paula is there. If you want a private conversation, we need a different spot."

He glanced both ways before pointing to his official car. "Over there then."

We walked in silence to his Charger. Once there, he leaned against it. "There's a possibility Houston was poisoned. Would there be a good time to discuss plants and poisons? I figure with your background in plants and drugs, you'll be a good source of information."

"Sure. I'll help as much as possible. What time?" The pharmacist would know much more than me, but it was probably convenient to ask me questions.

"I'll pick up a pizza and shoot to arrive at your place around six thirty."

"See you then." I hurried to my booth to check on Paula. "Hey, it looks like you heard the market has been shut down by the police department."

"Yeah. I'll help you get all of this to your house."

"I have a huge favor. Do you mind to take this to my place by yourself? Chief Young asked me to drive BBQ Hut's food truck to the restaurant. I can meet you at home in a little while, but you can drop everything off if you have other things to do."

"I'll wait. I want to hear what you've discovered about Houston's murder."

"Perfect." I gave Paula my house key before snagging my backpack and jogging to the food court.

Jake and Brett were closing the coffee truck. Actually, it was a VW van. Still, they were shutting down.

"Hi, guys. I'm supposed to move the BBQ Hut truck for Miranda. Any tips?" I gulped. "I've never driven anything bigger than my pickup."

The men looked at each other.

"Never mind. I know to secure the food so it doesn't slide around."

Jake said, "I'll help you. It's not like driving Ms. Daisy."

Brett stepped closer. "Have you picked up any clues?"

I looked in each direction before motioning for the men to huddle up. "Chief Young is coming over tonight to discuss poisons with me."

Jake's eyes widened. "I'm surprised he didn't call you into the station."

"He's bringing pizza with him, so I guess it's like a work dinner."

"No way." Brett shook his head. "It sounds like a date to me. What you and I had last night was a work dinner."

"How's it different?"

"First, we've been friends a long time. Second, I'm dating Celia. Third, by the time we were both free to talk, we were starving, and that's how we ended up at the restaurant." He ticked each point off on his fingers.

I wasn't sure I saw the difference, but Brett seemed adamant. I trusted his gut instinct, and he'd been dating Jake's sister for about a month. "I'm not interested in dating Matt, but I might be helpful. What should I do?"

Brett said, "Jake can be your buffer. He'll help you deliver the food truck, and he'll be there when Matt arrives with the pizza and the questions."

"Um, Jake, how do you feel about this plan?" I tried to gauge his reaction.

"You can call me a willing participant." He winked at me like the first day I'd met him. "You ready to leave?"

"Yeah. Paula is taking my stuff to the house, and I don't want to take advantage of her generosity." We broke the huddle and left Brett to close his van.

Once Jake and I were inside the food truck, it was easy to understand the storage system and directions I'd been given. "Wow, Miranda really has this organized."

"I'm impressed. It won't take long to pack up and head out." Jake lowered the service window awning, and I turned off the burners. Together, we secured all the food.

It appeared as if we'd done everything necessary that I remembered Miranda telling me. I looked at Jake. "Have you ever driven one of these trucks before?"

"As a matter of fact, I have. Would you like me to drive?"

"Yes, I want to write down some thoughts in my notebook. I mean, that is, if you don't mind." My face warmed.

"No problem. Buckle up." Jake settled into the driver's seat. "Do you have the keys?"

"Yes. Sorry." I handed Miranda's keys to him.

Jake inserted the first key, and the truck started. "Success."

I slid into the passenger seat and removed my notebook from the backpack. First, I wrote down what I'd seen at the crime scene.

"Emma, tell me something." Jake waited in a line of vehicles, trying to exit the market area.

"What?"

"If Matt had asked you out on a date, what would you have said?"

My heart dropped. I didn't like where this conversation might go. "I would have politely turned him down."

Jake cleared his throat. "What if I ask you out on an official date?"

My face burned. "If you ask? Or are you truly asking me? You know, to go out with you?"

He edged up in the line of cars, then looked at me. His expression was sincere and maybe even vulnerable. "Emma, would you go on a date with me?"

As much as I'd like to be cute and sassy, this wasn't the time. I answered with sincere honesty. "Yes, I will."

A smile lit his face. "Nice."

Chapter Six

Fifteen minutes later, Jake parked the food truck in the back parking lot of BBQ Hut. Benito Carlos rapped on my window with his knuckles. I opened the door and hopped out. "Hi, Benito."

"Ma'am." He nodded. "Miranda called and said that kid, the photographer, was going to help. I convinced her it'd be easier to deal with the food by myself. I will help you unload the truck. It's a terrible thing that happened to Mr. Turner."

"Yes, it is." How was it possible another murder had occurred in our little town? "I'm sure you're busy. Let's get this unloaded."

"Ma'am, can I ask you a question?"

"Absolutely." I hoped he wasn't going to ask me about Houston's body.

"The photographer. Do you trust him?" Benito was younger than me, but it seemed like he was in his thirties.

"I barely know him. Why?"

"I'm a people watcher, and I'm not sure he respected Houston. But what do I know?"

Jake met us at the back door of the truck. "Emma, would you like to clean up in here while Benito and I carry the food inside?" His gaze met mine, then darted toward the garbage can. "Might take that with us."

"What a brilliant idea." I took a few pictures with my phone, and then I gathered cleaning supplies and wiped down all the prep surfaces, the grill, and the refrigerator. It seemed curious the police chief had let the food truck leave. He must not suspect Miranda of murdering her brother. How competent was Matt? Would he have solved Willow Moore's murder if I hadn't jumped into the investigation? Had he not hired Jake because he was afraid people would discover his weaknesses?

Jake and Benito made two more trips, then we were finished.

I lifted the bag of garbage. The clinking glass rattling and the heaviness of the bag assured me there must be empty bottles of Good Life inside. No doubt, there were also paper plates, plastic cups, and food scraps. Had the garbage can been located outside of the truck for people to throw their trash away? Or was it inside for Miranda's use only?

Benito said, "Thank you for your help. I need to get back to preparing food for dinner."

We waved goodbye and began walking home.

"Here, let me since it was my bright idea." Jake reached for the trash bag.

"Keeping the garbage was a brilliant idea. It seems to me like I'm not the only citizen interested in solving Houston's murder."

"Don't forget, I've had training. I'm a Marine, and I went to the police academy."

"Oh, touché."

A red Accord honked and pulled to an empty space on our side of the street. Brett lowered the passenger window. "Can I give you a lift?"

"You bet. Do you mind if we put this in your trunk?" Jake hefted up the bag.

"Naw. You're good." He popped the trunk. "It's not leaking, right?"

"Right, and I'll set it upright."

I got into the backseat, and we waited for Jake. "How'd you move the coffee van so fast?"

"It's smaller and easy to load and unload, which enabled me to get to the front of the line of people leaving the farmers market. And that, in turn, allowed me to give you guys a ride."

Jake shut the trunk and soon slid into the passenger seat. "Thanks, man."

"Anytime." Brett pulled back onto the street. "Why'd you bring the garbage sack?"

Jake leaned his right shoulder against the door. "I learned from Emma during her investigation of Willow Moore's murder, there's an opportunity to find clues in a garbage can. Benito didn't question what we were going to do with the garbage, so I figure we can give it to Matt after we look through it."

His words made me proud of myself. "Thanks for the compliment."

He pushed his dark Oakley sunglasses to the top of his head. "You're welcome."

I said, "You guys know Chief Young wants to discuss poisons. Do y'all think someone poisoned Houston? If so, I'm not sure what I can tell him."

Brett signaled to turn right. "You and I've discussed herbs. Use your handy dandy flower book or phone app if you don't know the answer."

"Right. I sold daffodils to Houston this morning. They can be toxic but not deadly." I thought about it. "I mean, it might be possible to vomit lying on your back, then possibly suffocate."

"Girl, stop." Brett pretended to gag. At least, I thought he was pretending.

Jake snapped his fingers. "I noticed the flowers beside his body."

"Along with a bottle of Good Life, a cup from Anytime Coffee—"

"Yes. I did sell him a cup of black coffee. It was during my most crowded time. Right after him, I helped the Nelle sisters. I love those ladies, but it does take a little longer to handle their orders." Jake rubbed his chin.

I laughed. "Yeah, because the sisters like to flirt with you."

Brett snorted. "Man, you been holding out on me. I had no idea."

"Don't start." Jake shook his head.

His warning didn't deter Brett one little bit. In fact, he teased Jake about the octogenarian sisters until we pulled into my driveway and parked behind Ms. Daisy.

Paula had managed to park Ms. Daisy in the driveway and her RAV4 in front of my house. She must've run back for her vehicle, but at least I lived close to the market's site. I needed to hurry inside.

A red-faced Jake hopped out; then he opened my door for me.

I patted Brett's shoulder. "Thanks for the ride. I'll get the herbs to you soon."

Once again, he popped the trunk. "I always got your back."

"Right back at ya, my friend."

Jake pulled out the trash bag. "Emma, what time would you like me to come over tonight?"

"Matt said he'd be here around six thirty. I want to dive through the trash before he arrives, in case there's a clue. If you want to go through it with me, why don't you come about an hour earlier.?" I reached for the black bag.

He released it into my grip. "Sounds like a plan. See you then."

I placed the garbage bag behind a rocker on my front porch and hurried inside to check on Paula. Part of me felt guilty for allowing her to close the booth and transport the flowers by herself. Another part of me was excited to have collected the garbage from the food truck.

Chapter Seven

"Hey, Paula. I'm home. How'd your car get here? I hope you didn't walk back for it. I would've taken you back." I paused to take a breath.

Paula stood in my kitchen with her hands on her hips. Her brown hair with blonde highlights had been pulled into a messy bun, but it looked better than the lopsided ponytail from earlier. Minor dirt stains appeared on her shirt. "It's a short walk, so I drove it over after I got your truck here. I was afraid the police might tow it because of the murder. But boy, I'm glad you're here."

"What's going on? Are you okay? Did Cowboy give you any trouble?"

"No, he's fine." She lifted her chin. "I wasn't sure what to do with the flowers to keep them looking nice."

I studied the leftovers. "Not having a full day at the farmers market really put a dent in my sales. I can take some to the retirement community, the church, and Heart of Texas Bed and Breakfast. Faith and Zig are my best customers, and I should share with them." The Meiers owned the bed-and-breakfast, and we'd become friends.

"Won't it hurt your business, if you give away flowers for free?"

I pulled vases from the pantry and placed them on the kitchen counter. I reached for the daffodils and put them in a solitary vase. "It seems like the right thing to do. Thanks so much for your help today."

"Should I add other flowers to your daffodil arrangement?"

"No. They need to be alone for a bit so the toxic sap will release. If there are other flowers in there, they'll die faster. Except irises. They live longer when paired with daffodils. Weird, isn't it?"

"Yeah. If they have toxic sap, could the daffodils have killed Houston?"

"Toxic isn't the same as deadly. Some people get skin irritations from the flowers, and even if Houston had eaten a bulb from the plant, he would've only gotten sick."

"Okay. When you took the food truck to the restaurant, did you find any clues about Houston's murder?"

"Maybe." I wasn't sure how private to keep Matt's theory on poison. Even though we'd just discussed the flowers he'd bought from me, I wouldn't mention Matt's suspicion about a poison possibly killing Houston. "Tell me more about the Good Life drink."

"Houston said he created the special drink to help increase muscle mass, decrease fat, and be nutritious and tasty. Trust me. It's not tasty."

"Understood. You made me taste it earlier. Remember?"

"That's right. It's hard to think straight after—well, you know."

"Death is never easy." I arranged the daffodils, then pulled my notebook out of the backpack and took notes. "You said the drink didn't help you lose weight, right? Not that you need to lose any weight."

Paula blushed. "I knew a few pounds had crept on over the winter, and Houston preyed on my fears. In the summer, I swim every day, and the pounds come right off. I don't know why I let him get in my head. He was a sweet talker, and I bought his drink because he said there was a money-back guarantee."

I wrote fast to keep pace with her flow of words. "Didn't you say you two argued about getting your money back?"

"Yes. He refused. The man claimed he never made that promise." She sighed. "I shouldn't speak ill of the dead. If I wasn't so scared the cops would pin his murder on me, I'd probably accept the loss of money and move on with my life. Although Good Life is expensive. I know I wasn't confused about the money-back guarantee. If it wasn't for that promise, I wouldn't have bought the drink. Listen to me rattle on. I had better pull myself together, or that handsome Chief Young would arrest me. Please don't tell him what I said."

"I won't blab about your experience with Houston. I know from my sip earlier that it is sour, but I'd like to study the list of ingredients. Do you, by any chance, have more of the drink bottles?"

"Ha. I've got enough to throw a party." She covered her mouth with both hands. "There I go again. I'm just so conflicted. I'm sorry a man was murdered today, but he caused me a lot of harm."

"Do you know anybody else who might hold a grudge against Houston over Good Life?"

"Not over the drink, but his sister wasn't happy with him. I overheard an argument between them. Miranda didn't like how Houston treated her daughter. Shelby had dreams of going to college on a tennis scholarship. Houston wouldn't give her time off to practice or play in local tournaments."

"I heard the same thing. Do you think Shelby could get angry enough to murder her uncle?"

"I don't believe so. She's never gotten into any trouble at the high school. Her grades are good, and she's in the academic clubs and plays on the tennis team. Also, Houston was much bigger than Shelby. I don't know if it would've been possible for her to get the upper hand and kill him."

"What about her science classes?"

Paula's eyes grew wide. "Why science? Why wouldn't you want to know about her athletic activities? There's a self-defense class."

"Just curious. Did Shelby take the self-defense class?"

"I'll find out."

Cowboy barked at the back door, and I moved to let my golden retriever puppy inside. "Hiya, boy. I missed you. Do you need some water?"

Paula said, "He paced by the back door when I got here, so I let him out. I hope that's okay."

"It's terrific. He's got a lot of energy to burn."

Cowboy trotted straight to his water bowl and lapped it dry.

I refilled it before turning my attention back to Paula. "Where were we?"

"Science. Shelby. I know she takes organic chemistry, because we didn't have enough students register for the class at first. Shelby asked if they'd keep the class on the curriculum this year if she got a total of twenty-five students to register. The principal agreed, and the next day, there were twenty-eight students signed up for organic chemistry."

"I'm impressed. Why do you need a minimum?"

"Because there's a lab. That makes it two classes. If you're going to book a teacher for both classes and order supplies, you want to make sure it's economically worth it." Paula looked both ways. "If it was a physical education class, there'd be no problem."

"Gotcha."

She released the bun, ran her hands through her thick hair, and rubbed her scalp. "So far, you've asked all the questions. Have you learned much of anything yet?"

"I brought home the trash from the BBQ Hut food truck, and I'll sift through it later."

"Oh, that's wonderful. What do you hope to find? The murder weapon?"

I met Paula's gaze. "A confession would be nice, but I honestly don't know what I'll find. Probably nothing, but I still want to look. By the way, Houston was wearing a bracelet when he died. I'm wondering if you saw him at the jewelry tent."

She shook her head. "No. Sorry."

"When you spoke to Houston earlier this morning, did you notice if he was wearing a bracelet? Like the one sold at the market?"

Paula closed her eyes. "Houston was wearing a black polo untucked over jeans. His bifocals were tucked into the opening of his shirt, and he wore those reflective sunglasses where you see yourself. And he had a black and white ball cap advertising BBQ Hut. I really don't remember seeing a bracelet or a watch."

Her attention to detail impressed me. "When I sold him the daffodils, there was no bracelet, but he was wearing one when he was murdered in the field of clover behind the food court area."

"What did the bracelet look like?"

"It was brown. Probably leather. It fit tight against his arm." Could it have been too tight? Was it possible Houston was poisoned by a gel or something applied to the inner bracelet? "It was probably an inch wide."

"Braided?"

"Yeah, how'd you know? I think there was a turquoise stone and silver too. Did you see him wear it?"

"No." Paula crossed her arms. "The jewelry booth I visited had braided unisex bracelets as well as bracelets with beads. Can we get a list of vendors from Wayne Johns? There may have been multiple people selling jewelry, but if there was only one booth selling jewelry, we've got a lead."

"Good idea. If that doesn't work, I have another idea too. I'll deliver these flowers and try to track down information about the bracelet."

Paula looked at her watch. "I have a yoga class at four. How can I help you now?"

The retirement community was the farthest away, and the pastor was usually chatty. "That gives you two hours. Would you like to take flowers to the Lutz Village Retirement Community and maybe the church?"

She nodded. "I'll go by the church first, and my class is near the retirement community."

"Isn't the one on the square closer to your home?"

"No offense if you are a member there, but the uppity women go to Yoga House, and I feel too intimidated to relax. Yoga Love is much better for me."

I raised my hands in surrender. "I've never tried yoga, and I'll take your word for it. Let's get you loaded up so you're not late to your class."

We secured vases of flowers in the back of Paula's SUV, and she left with a wave.

I let Cowboy out in the backyard while I took a quick shower and dressed for my errands. April was warming up, and I decided to drive in hopes of not breaking a sweat.

Chapter Eight

Faith and Zig Meier were delighted with my gift of flowers for the Heart of Texas Bed and Breakfast. They had already heard the news about Houston Turner's death. Neither knew the man very well, so I gathered no clues from them.

After our visit, I sat in my truck and texted Wayne Johns. **Can I get a complete list of vendors at the farmers market today? Thanks.**

I also sent a social media message to Elijah Barnes, the photographer, asking if he could meet me at Anytime Coffee, my treat.

I drove to the coffee shop on the square but stopped at Sophie's Bakery first. My best friend, Sophie Becker, was the owner. Inside, I stood to the side, waiting while she rang up an elderly customer.

When the place was empty, I hugged Sophie. "How's your day going?"

"Better than yours, I imagine. Have you had lunch?"

"Oh, you know me so well. I'm famished."

"Let me fix you a Toast Hawaii sandwich. I heard there was a murder this morning." She pulled fresh white bread from the bread rack along with ham, pineapple, and Gouda.

"I'm afraid so." My phone vibrated. "Hold on a second."

Wayne Johns replied with an attachment. I thanked him and turned my attention back to Sophie. "You're bound to know it was Houston Turner. Paula Jones was in a heated argument with him early this morning, and she's afraid the police will suspect her."

Sophie came around the counter with a plate. My sandwich, carrot sticks, and fresh fruit filled the dish. "Sit down and eat."

I obeyed her because if your best friend can't boss you around, then who could? Plus, I was salivating over the food. I chose a seat facing the window. "There's quite a bit of traffic on the square this afternoon."

"It'll be worse next weekend with the festival, er the Lutz Antique and Vintage Market. The mayor said to call it by the appropriate name. Ha." Sophie sat with me. "It's almost closing time. When Chief Young shut down the farmers market, my business picked up. If Tara hadn't come in to help, I'm not sure how I would have survived. I've got her scheduled for extra hours for the upcoming event."

"I'm glad you finally got some help." Tara Thompson was a young mother, and working part-time at the bakery seemed to fulfill her.

"Me, too. Building a business takes time, and I didn't want to hire staff before I knew I could afford to pay them." Her eyes widened. "I can't believe I forgot a drink for you. What would you like?"

"Just water, please. I'm hoping to meet Elijah Barnes at Anytime Coffee. Have you ever used him to take pictures of the bakery for social media or other marketing?"

Sophie walked behind the counter and fixed a glass of water for me. "No, but I have his business card. It's on my one-day-wish list. For now, I'm content with the pictures you and I take to post on social media."

Being practical, not tightfisted, with our money was one of the many things Sophie and I had in common. "I get it."

She placed the glass of water on the table and sat down again. "Please tell me that you won't let Paula rope you into another murder investigation."

I gulped down the bite of the delicious sandwich. "Too late. She asked for my help earlier. That's why I need to speak to Elijah. He was taking pictures at the farmers market this morning."

"You got lucky last time, and Chief Young isn't going to be happy if you barge into another murder investigation. And let's not forget you almost got yourself killed investigating Willow Moore's murder."

"Trust me. I learned my lesson. If Paula is arrested, I will be more discrete. I'll be better organized and not just run all over town asking everyone I see questions. I think this time will be different."

Sophie frowned. "I hope different doesn't mean you get hurt or killed this time."

Another comment only a close friend could make. I understood her point. I didn't want to put myself in danger either.

Chapter Nine

Elijah agreed to meet at Anytime Coffee. I got there first and found the vendor list on my phone from Wayne Johns. I squinted and tried to decipher the small print.

"Whatcha looking at?" Jake sat beside me in a booth at the front of the coffee shop.

"I'm trying to read this list of vendors, but it's pretty small on my phone."

"How about I print it off for you?"

"That'd be terrific. Elijah Barnes is heading this way. When you see him, I'll pay for his order."

"Okay." Jake tilted his head. "Why?"

"I plan to pump him for information on the pictures he took this morning."

"Oh, Emma. Is he trustworthy?"

"Funny you should ask. Benito doesn't think Elijah respected Houston. He didn't go into much detail, though."

"So why meet him?"

"Mr. Johns hired him to take pictures for the website of the farmers market. Houston paid him to take pictures of his niece for BBQ Hut advertisements and Good Life ads. Oh yeah, he also takes pictures for the high school. They would've surely done a background check before allowing him around the students."

"You're probably right. That makes me feel a bit better. Give me your phone, and I'll print off your list."

I handed it to him with the file open. "Thanks, Jake."

"No problem." He sauntered away, humming a tune.

I pulled out my notebook and reviewed the limited notes. Not much yet, but maybe I'd learn more from the photographer.

"Here you go." Jake returned my phone and handed me four pages. "Mind if I join you? We're not busy, and Brett will let me know if he needs assistance."

"Sure." I scootched over and held the first page so we could both read it.

"Is there any particular item we're looking for?" His breath tickled my neck.

"First, I want to look for people who might be selling jewelry. Early this morning, Houston wasn't wearing a bracelet."

"And there was one on his wrist when he died."

"Very observant, Mr. Hunter."

"I've been told I have a good eye for details." He winked. "There was leather or something woven with turquoise."

"It might've been a strand of linen, and you're right about the turquoise. There was also a glint of silver."

"It sounds like we've identified three components of the bracelet, but where did it come from?" Jake tapped the paper. "Jewels of Texas is the first one to jump out at me."

I reached for my phone and searched for the name.

Elijah entered the coffee shop and strode to us. "Hi, sorry for running late. My parents taught me better, but I was consoling Shelby about her uncle."

I waved off his apology. "Perfectly understandable. Elijah Barnes, this is Jake Hunter. Do you mind if he joins us?"

"We've met before. I guess it's fine, considering I'm not sure why we're meeting. But if you offer free coffee, I'm showing up."

"I can handle your order. Do you want your usual or are you going to be adventurous?" Jake stood and led him to the counter.

While they stepped away, I found a website for Jewels of Texas. I jotted down some notes, then sent a link to my email and Jake's email. I placed my phone to the side and was ready to chat when the men returned.

Elijah sat across from Jake and me. "So, I'm curious. What would you like to discuss?"

I leaned forward. "You took pictures this morning. Can you share them with me? Or can you tell me your impressions of the market this morning?"

He scratched his head and glanced at the ceiling. "Mr. Johns might not appreciate me sharing them with you, since he paid me and all."

"That's understandable. I'd never try to use them for my personal marketing when he was your client." I flattened my hands on the table and hoped to give the impression of being relaxed. "Did you notice anything unusual?"

"You mean besides a dead body?" Elijah grimaced.

"Well, yeah." His lack of tact startled me. He wasn't going to make it easy for me to get information.

He reached for his coffee with a shaky hand. Maybe he wasn't as cool, calm, and collected as he was trying to appear. "I saw Houston arrive early. He went to the food truck and got into an argument with his sister. Not long after that, he and that woman helping you—"

"Paula Jones. Long dark hair and average height. She's very pretty." I smiled and tried to look relaxed.

"That's the one. I photographed her for the Good Life drink. She was on the shy side."

No surprise there. "What about Paula and Houston?"

"They got into a big argument." He took a drink of his coffee. "There was also a man he evidently fired last night at the restaurant. His name is Eddie Hayes. I know because Houston made some social media posts about Eddie, the great barbecue master. I took his picture, too, at the time he worked for Houston. Anyway, Eddie had established an area for cooking beef behind one of the tents this morning. A local farmer hired Eddie to cook, so the farmer gave out samples. Houston appeared and made some rude comments about Eddie. That didn't fly, and the farmer had to hold Eddie back until Houston left."

Jake whistled. "Would it be easier to ask who Houston didn't get into an argument with?"

"Maybe." Elijah laughed.

"I dread asking, but is there anyone else?"

He did the head scratch and looked at the ceiling again. "The jewelry chick."

"Who is she?"

"She's the gal who travels in her camper van and sells jewelry made by Texans. Her gimmick is that her jewelry has healing properties, *and* it's all made by people who live around here." He scoffed.

Jake said, "You don't sound like a believer."

Elijah lifted his eyebrows. "I may be young, but it doesn't seem possible to me. No siree."

I wouldn't debate it with him. "Do you know what they argued about?"

"She was trying to convince Houston to try her plan. It's some business structure to make more money with his drink."

"A Ponzi scheme?" I was aware that I tended to be suspicious of anything claiming to make easy money. "Or maybe a pyramid scheme?"

"Yeah, maybe the last one."

To my knowledge, they weren't legal in Texas. Although, it didn't mean people weren't running them. They just weren't getting caught. I opened my notebook. "Elijah, I need to write this down so I don't forget later."

"You're not a cop, so why are you taking notes?"

"Um, I always like a good mystery. Not that I'm happy Houston was murdered."

"Cool, cool, cool." He raised his cup to his mouth and drank.

Three cools did not sound like it was cool. "It seems like you were tight with Houston. Did you respect him?"

He took a deep breath, and his chest puffed out. "I could respect he was a good businessman, but I didn't appreciate how he treated his family."

"If he was mean to his family, I imagine he was mean to other people. Do you have any idea who might have murdered him?"

"Best guess? And you can't go around saying I told you."

"Trust me. Your name will never come up."

"Deep down, I believe it was the ex-wife, his sister, or Eddie Hayes, the barbecue master."

He had given me three possible suspects, making me think he didn't know much more than me.

Jake said, "What about the niece? I heard Houston tended to take advantage of her."

"Nah, Shelby is too sweet to harm anybody. No way she killed her uncle. No. Not Shelby." He glanced at his watch. "I've got to head out. Thanks for the coffee."

I smiled. "You're welcome, and thanks for the info."

"You bet." Elijah hurried away.

I looked at Jake. "That was one hasty retreat."

"If you grilled me that hard, I probably wouldn't have lasted as long as he did."

"You've got to admit that I got some useful information." I ran my hand over the notebook. "I find it interesting how much Elijah observed Houston's activities this morning. It's almost stalkerish."

"Yeah, but maybe photographers are trained to stand back and watch in order to get realistic pictures. Or maybe Houston wanted Elijah to take his picture with the others. Who knows?"

"I guess it doesn't matter since he shared it all with me." I stuffed everything into my bag. "I can't believe it's almost five. Do you want to come on over? We can review my notes before Matt arrives with pizza."

"Sounds like a plan. Let me tell Brett."

I also needed to check out poisonous plants. All parts of a daffodil could be toxic from the bulb to the bloom, and I'd sold a bunch to Houston. It'd be a good idea to double-check my facts before talking to the police chief.

"Emma, you can't leave yet. We've got to talk." Brett joined me at the table and pounded a fist on the table. "Sorry, but we've got to talk about this morning."

My heart leapt pert near out of my chest. "What on earth's wrong with you? I've never seen you so distraught."

"I'm not sure you're taking me serious enough. I might be accused of harming Houston."

Chapter Ten

"There's no way you'll be accused of murdering Houston Turner." I patted Brett's fist with my cold hand. I tended to forget how cold my hands were until I touched someone or something warm.

He sat across the table from me in Anytime Coffee Shop and leaned forward. "Emma, listen to me. Houston was all up in my gills about the shop's new smoothies. He threatened to ruin me and my business."

The lights dimmed in the coffee shop, and the front door lock clicked. Jake joined me in the booth again, and we both faced Brett.

Jake said, "Our business, and we would've fought him every step of the way."

I needed to support Jake's declaration. "Houston wasn't the first person to create a smoothie, plus his health drink was completely different. Good Life isn't a smoothie, and it's not sweet. In fact, the taste is so sour that it's hard to swallow."

Brett's head snapped back. "You bought Good Life?"

"No, but I tried one of Paula's drinks. Houston convinced her of all the benefits, and she bought quite a bit of it. In fact, this morning, she told him she wanted a refund."

"How'd that go?" Brett relaxed his fists.

"In the beginning, he promised a refund if she didn't achieve the desired results. This morning, he flat out refused to return any of her investment." I paused. "Elijah and I discussed the possibility that Good Life is more of a pyramid scheme than a legit health drink. Before y'all say anything, I'm aware it's illegal to run a pyramid scheme here. Fines, and or jail time, are possible repercussions if you're caught."

Brett's shoulders drooped. "I don't see how this helps prove I'm innocent."

I said, "Did you know Houston fired Eddie Hayes last night?"

"No, but I was aware of a commotion coming from the kitchen. Again, I don't see how that helps me."

"My point is that there are plenty of people with stronger motives for murdering Houston. For instance, his sister, his niece, Eddie Hayes, and Paula Jones are more likely to have done the deed than you."

Jake smiled at his friend. "I saw Coop Henderson earlier today. He was sorry to hear about Houston, but he knew the man had anger issues. Last night, Houston accused him of trying to skip out on paying for his dinner. Coop had merely left his wallet in his truck and ran outside to get it. Houston followed him to the parking lot and threatened him. You just need to stay chill. If you act all nervous, the cops might look harder at you."

"I'll try, but it won't be easy." Brett slumped in his seat.

"Paula asked me to help find the killer, because she's also afraid she'll be under suspicion. I know you're innocent. Trust that the killer will be caught."

Brett rolled his head. "Okay, just don't get yourself hurt because of me. It helps to hear you know I'm innocent."

Jake stood. "We're supposed to see Chief Young at Emma's place in a little while. You know, it's possible I'm crashing his plans for date night."

"I hear ya." Brett nodded. "I'm on Team Jake."

I got up and gave Jake a playful punch in the arm. "Stop that. He said he only wanted to discuss—" I'd almost revealed a possible secret.

"Poison. You already told us."

"You're right. If I can't keep up with details better than that, I have no business trying to solve a crime." It must have been the shock muddling my thoughts. "Brett, we're on your side. Try not to stress."

"You two warn me if I need to grab my go-bag and Rufus. We'll run for the hills. One of my buddies has a cabin that's pretty well hidden overlooking the Brazos River." Brett followed us to the door and let us out.

Jake gave Brett a man hug. "Don't worry, and don't do anything crazy.

We've got your back."

"Thanks, man." He waved, then locked the door.

I looked at Jake. "Do you want a ride to my place?"

He did a double-take. "You drove to town instead of walking? Are you hurt?"

"I wasn't sure if I'd have to drive somewhere to talk to Elijah Barnes, and I wanted to be prepared."

"Okay, then I'll ride with you."

I unlocked my white Silverado with a tap on my fob, and we got in and buckled up. "Is Coop Henderson the construction guy?"

"Yeah. I've been working for him some the past few weeks."

I backed out and headed home. "Have you given up on Chief Young hiring you?"

"Pretty much, but it's all good."

"Do you feel like your police training was a waste?" I signaled to turn into my driveway. "Education is never a waste, but it hasn't turned out like I'd planned."

"I'm sorry about that."

He raised his hands. "Who knows? Maybe I needed the training to help you solve mysteries."

"Aw, that's a terrific attitude." It was good to know Jake wasn't bitter about not getting hired at our local police department. I didn't know if it was a budget issue or a personal issue coming from the police chief. I parked in my driveway, and we headed inside to prepare for Matt's arrival. "I'm glad you're on my side."

He winked. "You haven't been accused of murder yet. I might have to change my tune then."

I laughed. "Then let's hope Matt doesn't come up with a reason to add me to the suspect list."

"I'll always have your back, Emma." He squeezed my hand before we went to the house.

Chapter Eleven

My phone vibrated with a text message from Chief Young. **Emma, I need to reschedule. Maybe tomorrow we can get together.**

I wanted to make certain Matt knew this was not a date. After a quick glance at my favorite flower reference book, I considered my reply. **No problem. I'll have more time to look up poisons. BTW daffodils are toxic and not deadly.**

The back door opened and closed. Cowboy appeared, ran circles around me, then raced to his water bowl.

Jake laughed. "Man, I wish I had his energy."

"Me, too." I smiled at my puppy. Having a fur baby hadn't been planned, but when I'd found him the previous month, malnourished and abandoned, I was a goner. He was homeless, and I adopted him. In a short time, he'd added laughter and smiles to my life. "I just heard from the police chief. He can't come over tonight. What would you think about us walking over to the farmers market in hopes of finding a clue?"

Jake crossed his arms. "If we take Cowboy with us, it'll seem less suspicious."

"Good idea. I'd like to take my sketchbook. I feel like drawing the scene might trigger a memory."

"Why didn't I know you're an artist?"

"Because I'm not, but that doesn't mean I can't sketch out a crime scene. It'll be like when I plan my flower gardens. I'll be right back." I walked into my office and gathered my pad and pencils then met Jake in the kitchen.

"I've been working with Cowboy on heeling, so I need to take some beef dog treats. He's better behaved every day."

"He's always been a good boy."

I entered the pantry and found the bag of treats. After stuffing a few in my pocket, I harnessed Cowboy, and we headed outside.

Jake walked on my right side, allowing my dog plenty of space on my left. Cowboy matched my pace and didn't tug on the leash until a cat slunk out from under an old black pickup. The gray and white striped tabby hissed.

Cowboy growled.

"Easy now." I ran my hand along the dog's back. "Behave yourself."

The cat's tail swished back and forth.

My dog stiffened.

Jake said, "Take Cowboy to the market, and I'll keep an eye on the cat. It's probably harmless, but no need to risk either animal attacking the other one."

"Cowboy, come." I snapped my fingers and drew his attention away from the cat. When we reached the empty parking lot of the farmers market, I knelt beside him. "Good boy." I rubbed his head and gave him a treat.

Jake joined us. "As soon as you two disappeared, Alley Cat took off."

"Alley Cat? You already named him?"

"Or her, but yeah. I feel like I've spotted the same cat near the bookstore." Jake lived in the apartment over Paige's Turn Bookshop, and his front door was in the alley.

"Well, well, well. I didn't picture you being a cat person."

"I like all animals."

"I believe it. You've always been nice to Cowboy." I stood and looked around the deserted area. All the vendor booths had been dismantled. There were no food trucks or any other signs of life.

Jake propped his fists on his hips. "Seems different when the area is deserted."

"Yeah, it does." I spun on my toe and tried to imagine the area like it'd been that morning.

"The body was found in the field of clover over there. Shall we?"

"Yeah." This had been my bright idea, but I questioned the wisdom in my actions. My eyes watered, and a sense of loss overwhelmed me. A man had died today.

"Would you like me to take the leash?"

"Thanks." My voice was barely a whisper. I passed the leash to him, and the three of us walked across the deserted parking lot. I took slow breaths, trying to compose myself.

The place was empty. Even a tad creepy. There were no people, cops, or crime scene tape. "This was probably a dumb idea."

"We didn't come this far for nothing. Draw. I'll play with your dog over in the food truck area."

"Okay." With shaky fingers, I opened the pad and sketched the field. Green grass and clover. Some areas had been trampled, probably by the authorities, or maybe by the killer and Houston. I drew an X in place of the body, then gave attention to my memories of the daffodils, the crushed Anytime Coffee cup, and the Good Life drink bottle.

I lost track of time until Jake reappeared. "How's it going?"

"Matt has questions about poison. The flowers came from me, and they were not deadly. So how was he poisoned? It seems to me that someone could've slipped a fatal substance into either drink somewhat easily. If Houston was poisoned with the new bracelet, it would've needed to be a transdermal application."

"Explain."

"There are pain patches, and medication is absorbed into the body through the skin. I think it's possible a poison could've been applied to the bracelet somehow. It would need to be fast acting, though, and I could be way off base. Hopefully, the police will test the drink containers."

Jake spread his feet shoulder-length apart and crossed his arms. "It might not help Brett's cause though. Despite the contract we signed at the startup of Anytime Coffee House, he's the owner."

"You mean the face of the shop, but you help when he needs you."

"True, and he might need me now. Houston threatened him about his healthy drinks. If either drink was spiked with something deadly, the police might look hard at Brett."

"It's up to us not to let that happen. Paula's worried about herself being a suspect. If not for her, I might have refused to investigate the murder."

"What's your next move?"

"It seems like we should swing by BBQ Hut and see if they're open for dinner. The cook was fired last night. It's possible we can discover another disgruntled employee or a customer with an ax to grind."

Jake relaxed his stance. "Let's rock and roll."

Chapter Twelve

We arranged for Brett, Paula, and Sophie to meet us at Houston Turner's barbecue restaurant. The line was out the door, and I chalked it up to morbid curiosity.

We were eventually given a booth in the middle of the room. Taped on the front of the menu was a flyer announcing a percentage of the evening's proceeds would benefit the high school girls tennis team. Had the fund raiser possibly been planned before the murder?

I leaned forward. "Our table is in a good location. Everyone, keep your eyes open for a potential disagreement or anything suspicious. We'll be able to focus on almost all areas of the restaurant."

Elijah Barnes walked to our table. "Howdy. What can I get everyone to drink?"

I met his gaze. "Do you work here?"

"Nah, I was discussing a photo shoot with Shelby earlier. She got a message from her mom that this place was packed and they were already short-staffed. I volunteered to pitch in. Lucky for you, she accepted my offer. Now, how about those drinks?"

We placed our orders, and the photographer ambled away.

I sat between Sophie and Jake, and Sophie was on the outside. She elbowed me. "I'll be right back."

Paula wrung her hands. "It's hard to believe the restaurant is packed. I understand people wanting to pay their respects, but it also seems like the family would've closed the restaurant."

Brett said, "Maybe they need the money for the memorial service. It'd be hard to turn away this much business."

I kept my eyes on the action. "They'll most likely close for the service."

A George Strait song played on the old jukebox.

Sophie returned and motioned for us to listen. "Not only did Shelby get called in to work, but Miranda is running the kitchen."

Elijah appeared with our drinks. "Your waitress will be here soon to take your order."

Officer Steve Koch walked through the restaurant wearing neat jeans, an official police shirt, well-worn cowboy boots, and a black Stetson. He stopped by most tables and spoke to the occupants. When he reached us, I stared.

"Evening, folks. Brett, Chief Young would like you to stop by the station tomorrow afternoon."

"Why?"

Officer Koch frowned. "He's got a few questions for you. Trust me. It'll be easier if he doesn't have to track you down."

"I'll be there, but do I need an attorney? Am I about to be charged with something?"

"Not to my knowledge. I believe the chief just has a few questions for you about that drink Mr. Turner was peddling." He looked both ways. "You do what you think best about bringing an attorney."

Brett gave a two-finger salute, and the policeman moved to the next table.

Jake said, "Hold it together, man. It's probably nothing."

"Easy for you to say. If I get arrested, tell your sister I'm crazy about her. Take care of my dog, Jake. You know what Rufus means to me."

"Whoa, Brett." I raised my hands to stop his depressing words. "You are innocent. Quit worrying."

Paula shrugged. "I understand his sentiment. None of us is safe from the Lutz Police Department. Those people—"

"Shh, Paula. It won't help your cause to get sideways with the local law enforcement." I looked at her and Brett. "You two need to walk around with your heads held high. You are both innocent, and the truth will conquer lies and misconceptions."

Sophie clapped. "Great lecture and you should both listen to Emma."

A screech from the kitchen area brought our conversation to a halt. The restaurant grew deathly quiet.

"Houston never trusted you. And here you show up around the time of his murder, demanding money from my brother."

"You know I didn't lay a finger on your brother. He was supposed to pay me twenty-five percent of his income every month. He's way behind on what he owes me."

"I don't believe it's a coincidence that you're in town when he's murdered. Somebody, call the cops." Miranda's voice rang out.

"I'll hire a forensic accountant and an attorney."

Sophie shot me a look. "I'd say this is going to be newsworthy in regard to your murder investigation."

"No kidding. It's a good thing Officer Koch is around, but who is Miranda yelling at?" I held my breath, wanting to hear more.

"It sounds like someone who got tired of waiting for her money. Possibly a female loan shark?" Sophie's eyes widened.

The unknown woman's words were indistinguishable. There was a crash like a pan hitting a concrete floor, followed by an *umph*.

The police officer ran to the kitchen. "Break it up." His commanding voice would've stopped me in my tracks.

My heart raced in anticipation of seeing the woman behind the commotion.

So far, I had considered Miranda, Shelby, and a female jewelry maker as female persons of interest in Houston's murder. Could this be the mysterious woman who sold jewelry for health benefits and lived out of her van? If not, it sounded like there was a new name to add to my list.

Chapter Thirteen

I couldn't have been more wrong with my guess about who had been arguing with Miranda. It wasn't the jewelry lady. Nope. It was Houston's ex-wife, Leigh Turner. She was the person fighting in BBQ Hut's kitchen with Miranda.

Officer Koch dragged both women to a corner table and pointed to the sturdy wooden chairs. "I don't want to hear another word out of either one of you, or else we're going to the station. Understood?"

Miranda removed her hairnet and crushed it into a small ball. Thick dark hair spilled onto her shoulders. She frowned, but didn't utter a word.

Goosebumps popped out on my arms. The sight of Miranda's anger made me shiver and confirmed my earlier theory. I didn't want to get sideways with Houston's sister. I'd be extra cautious when looking at her as a suspect.

I shifted my gaze to Houston's ex-wife. Leigh looked the same as I remembered from the days before her divorce. She was tall, thin, and had curly blond hair. She currently lived in Austin with her sons. If I remembered correctly, one son was in high school, and the other was in college.

Earlier in the day, Miranda had informed me Leigh was in Lutz to collect back child support. Their loud conversation involved money, so it was possibly the reason for her appearance.

Yet, it didn't make sense for Leigh to murder Houston, unless she or their sons were named in his will. Could Leigh have begun with a civil conversation? Maybe somebody lost their temper, and the talk turned deadly. Or was there more to her arrival in Lutz besides child support? Had she hoped for a reconciliation? Maybe he rebuffed her advances, and she killed him.

No, that didn't make sense.

If Houston died from poisoning, it must've been premeditated murder. If Leigh was guilty, she'd come to Lutz intending to murder her ex-husband.

The Western swing music ended.

Chief Young entered the restaurant. With hands on hips, he did a slow visual sweep of the scene. His gaze paused when he met mine, then he strode through the crowded tables and stopped beside his officer.

The room remained quiet. All eyes were on the policemen and the two women. At last, Matt faced all of us. "Carry on with your meals, y'all. Because of the tennis team's fundraiser, we're not gonna shut the restaurant down. Be generous with your donations and your tips tonight. It's been a long day for everyone." Matt's gaze landed on me again, and he compressed his lips.

Officer Koch spoke to Matt, ending our visual connection. They turned to the women and ushered them out of the room.

The noise gradually grew in volume, and Shelby appeared at our table. "I'm sorry for your wait. What can I get y'all tonight?"

Sophie said, "I'd be happy to help in back if you think your mother and the police will allow it."

The teen shook her head. "I couldn't ask you to do that."

"You didn't. I offered. That's what we do in Lutz. Help each other." She slid out of the booth. "Emma, I'll catch you later."

"Sure."

"Thank ya, kindly." Shelby watched Sophie stride to the kitchen before turning her attention to us. "That's right nice of her. Momma will trust her in the kitchen because of the bakery. She'll know all the food rules, er laws, or regulations. This isn't really my jam, but you probably already guessed that."

I said, "Shelby, would you rather for us to come back another night?"

"No, ma'am. The tennis team needs your donations, and my family needs your business. What would you like?"

"I'd like a veggie plate. Cole slaw, potato salad, baked beans, and corn."

The men ordered brisket with sides, and Paula ordered a Caesar salad.

After Shelby walked away, Paula propped her arms on the table. "I know better than to fall for diet gimmicks. Losing weight comes down to consuming fewer calories and increasing my exercise. Good Life is such a joke."

I patted her hand. "Don't be so hard on yourself. Lots of people believed Houston."

Jake said, "I've been thinking about Houston's ex-wife. How long ago did they get divorced."

I tried to remember exactly when Leigh moved to Austin. "Probably five years. Why?"

"Good Life is a recent development. It's possible Leigh thought she deserved more than the original divorce settlement. Do you think alimony is involved?"

Paula said, "She's a dental hygienist, and I never heard rumors about alimony. You might be surprised how much gossip I hear working in the high school office."

"No doubt." I considered where Jake was heading with his thoughts. "From what we heard earlier, Leigh came to town for missed child support payments."

"True." Jake turned on the seat to face me better. "We can run with two theories here. One is that Leigh only wanted the money Houston owed her for their sons. Another theory could be she wanted more money because Houston was making more than when they got divorced."

"In the argument, didn't she say she was supposed to get a percentage of Houston's earnings for child support?" The others nodded. "Most people get a flat amount every month. Getting a portion of his income seems weird."

Brett raised his hand. "We should consider Houston may have been losing money on his drink, which resulted in him missing payments to Leigh. It's possible he was embarrassed to admit the truth."

"Good point." I leaned back in my seat. "Here comes our food."

Shelby passed around the plates of food, and we dug in. Despite the morning tragedy, the food tasted delicious.

By the time we finished, the crowd had dwindled. Brett and Paula left, but I wanted to wait in case Miranda returned. "I'd like to stay a little longer. You know something else might happen."

"Makes sense. I'll hang with you."

I switched sides of the booth to see different things than Jake would observe from his side.

Jake said, "What are you thinking?"

"As far as persons of interest?"

"Yeah."

"After tonight's scene, it'd be silly not to include Leigh Turner and Miranda Penn. Brett and Paula may be on Matt's radar, but I don't believe either one of them is guilty."

"No way Brett is guilty." Jake frowned.

"Yeah, sorry. That's what I meant." This conversation was getting stickier than a taffy pull.

"All right then. Keep going."

"There's also Eddie Hayes, the cook Houston fired last night." I pulled my sketch pad out of my purse and flipped past the drawing I'd made at the farmers market. "When I heard the argument tonight, I wondered if the mysterious jewelry lady is a serious suspect."

"The person who suggested Houston should use a pyramid scheme to sell Good Life? At least that's according to Elijah." Jake rubbed his chin. "You know he's an interesting kid."

"I agree. He said being a photographer gives him the ability to observe people and see what they do when they think nobody's watching." I made a note to call Elijah and see if he'd gotten permission for me to look at the photos he'd taken at the farmers market. "Can you believe it's still Saturday? So much has happened."

"It's for sure been a busy day and a long one." Jake turned when a man appeared at the end of our table.

"Howdy, folks." Matt pointed to my seat. "May I?"

My face warmed, but I scooted over. "How's the investigation going?"

"It's going. Were y'all here for the altercation between Miranda and Leigh?"

He removed a notepad from his shirt pocket.

"Yeah. We heard Miranda loud and clear." I glanced from Matt to Jake. "She accused Leigh of coming to town to murder Houston, but earlier today, Miranda thought Leigh came to collect back child support. I don't see how Houston could have financial problems. He had a successful restaurant, a food truck, and Good Life." Although, Brett had wondered if Good Life had drained Houston's finances.

Jake propped one arm along the back of the booth. "The appearance of wealth isn't the same as being wealthy. Unfortunately, I know lots of men who neglect their families when they experience financial woes."

Matt jotted something on his paper. "I have to agree with Jake. Houston's wealth could've been a show. It's possible he was too poor to paint and too proud to whitewash."

It'd been years since I heard his expression. "How did he begin a new business venture if he was so poor? Was he good friends with a banker?"

Jake drummed his fingers on the table. "Maybe he convinced his sister to borrow the money for him."

Matt said, "Or he could've gotten backing from an unscrupulous sort."

I made bullet points of their theories. "What else?"

"Home equity loan. Pawnshop." He raised a finger with each possibility, counting off the ways of securing money. "Borrow money from a friend or family member. Borrow against your 401K. And there's the possibility Houston paid with a credit card or got a cash advance with his credit card."

"Some of those sound costly." I remembered a time when my daughter was an infant. We'd both gotten sick, and I'd resorted to using my credit card. The interest rate had been staggering, and it'd taken me longer to pay off than I'd expected. The lesson learned then was to always save for a rainy day.

"I'll dig into Houston's finances." Matt wrote a word and underlined it three times, creating a small tear. He licked his fingertip and tapped on the rip.

Interesting maneuver, but I didn't believe it'd fix the page. As far as the investigation went, studying Houston's assets might reveal a motive for his murder. Even Leigh had mentioned hiring a forensic accountant.

55

Chapter Fourteen

"Emma, do you have time to discuss plants and poisons?" Matt followed Jake and me to Ms. Daisy, in BBQ Hut's nearly empty parking lot.

Before I could answer, Jake said, "Matt, we discussed it some this afternoon. Why don't the three of us talk about it tomorrow?"

The police chief's body stiffened. "I don't recall inviting you into the discussion."

Jake lifted his chin. "Emma did."

Matt glared at me. "What'd you do, Emma? Spread it all over town I was interested in poisons?"

" No, but you know Jake and I are close—"

"Actually, we're dating." Jake slipped his arm around my shoulders.

Parking lot lights shone on Matt's face and revealed his puckered brow.

I elbowed Jake. He could've been a little more tactful. "So, you can understand why I shared the information with Jake. Time got away from me this afternoon, but I will be prepared to have a conversation with you later tonight."

"Call or text me first." Matt strode to his Charger and sped away.

Jake rocked back on his heels. "Okay, Sunshine. Let me have it."

I turned on my toe and faced him. "Jake, you might've hurt Matt's feelings. That wasn't very nice."

"Sometimes it's easier to rip the bandage off than to slowly peel it away."

"Are you accusing me of being too nice?"

He tilted his head. "You're not being too nice to me, but I wasn't sure how long it'd take you to get to the point with Lutz's beloved chief of police. Hence, I butted into the conversation and revealed the truth."

I stepped back, unsure if he was teasing me, or if he was serious. "Jake, I'm sorry if I wasn't nice to you just now. You know I want to date you. Not Matt. To be blunt, there's nobody else I want to go out with." In fact, I hadn't really dated since my husband died when Abby was a newborn. At thirty-eight years of age, a person should know more about romantic relationships. Was it possible I was too old for romance?

Jake reached for my hands. "That is very good news."

I placed my hands in his comforting grip. Maybe I could do this. "Are we good?"

"Better than good. Maybe great. Should we celebrate by going through the bag of trash from the food truck? And aren't we supposed to research poisons?"

"Ugh. I forgot about the garbage."

He wrapped me in a hug. "I'll do it as an apology for my bad behavior. Emma, I'm not going to be a jealous boyfriend. Either you want to date me, or you don't. My reaction tonight wasn't jealousy. Something about Matt just rubs me wrong. It's probably a good thing he hasn't hired me yet."

"Why?" I could get used to Jake's embrace.

"Working with Matt could turn out to be like trying to bag flies."

I laughed and pulled away. "That would certainly be difficult. Shall we head to my place and tackle this mystery?"

"Yep, and when we finish, we can enjoy being together." He kissed my forehead.

"I could go for some uninterrupted you-and-me time."

I drove us to my house, hoping for quality time with Jake. Too bad there was a car on the street and a woman sitting on my front porch. I swallowed hard. "It looks like Paula. Why can't we ever get a break?"

"It'll happen." Jake's phone signaled a call. "And Celia's calling. Let me get this."

"Come on inside when you finish the call. I'll make sure Paula knows you're not leaving." I crossed the yard. "Hi, Paula. Is everything okay?"

She stood. "I'm too antsy to stay at home doing nothing. How can I help with the investigation?"

I unlocked the door. "When Jake finishes his call, he's going to come inside. We were planning to work on Houston's murder."

She nodded. "Okay. I can sleuth with you, or take care of the dog, or wash your dishes. Just please, don't make me go home alone."

"Come in." I led her to the kitchen and let Cowboy out of his crate. "Tell me more about Shelby Penn."

He barked a friendly greeting and licked my face when I bent over to love on him.

"Good boy."

Paula said, "Shelby's nice and has a lot of friends. She's athletic, but her uncle kept her busy with his businesses. It made Miranda furious."

I retrieved my notebook from the office and took notes at the kitchen counter. "Furious enough to murder her brother?"

Paula paced. "Do you remember what I did concerning Nick?"

My friend had recently shared that she'd left her abusive husband to have their baby without ever telling him that she was pregnant. Her parents changed their names and were raising the teenage daughter in Louisville, Kentucky. After recovering from the pregnancy, Paula returned to Lutz and gave Nick one more chance. He hadn't changed, so she moved out and filed for divorce without ever revealing her secret baby. "Yes, I remember."

"I was desperate to protect my child, and I believe Miranda would go to great lengths to protect Shelby. I even believe Houston could've provoked her into murdering him."

I inhaled deeply. What lengths would I go to in order to protect Abby? I'd go far. I'd give my life for hers, but hopefully, I wouldn't resort to murder. "Paula, in your opinion, who had the most to gain by Houston's passing?"

"Miranda will be able to run the restaurant and food truck now that her brother's dead. Leigh may get money for her sons in the will. Shelby will gain freedom."

"Can you elaborate? I thought she needed to work to help pay for college."

"Shelby and Miranda always believed she could get an education if she combined athletic and academic scholarships instead of working for tips. They often came into the school office, asking about scholarship applications. If there was a chance she'd win a scholarship, she applied for it. Both mother and daughter are determined that Shelby will go to college."

"Good for them, but what about her working for Houston?"

"Houston never really asked his niece to work for him. He demanded it."

"Why'd she agree, if she was applying for scholarships?" I sat on a barstool and added this to my notes.

Paula leaned against the counter. "He dangled the offer of a car in return for her employment. But the day Houston insinuated he'd fire Miranda if Shelby didn't work for him was the day she agreed. There was really no choice. She had to work for her uncle, but there's no way she's involved in his demise. Shelby is sweet and innocent."

"If anyone gets it, I do. When you're a single mother, money is tight." It broke my heart that Shelby worked to protect her mother. I would've hated it, if something like that had happened to my daughter.

Jake entered the house and joined us in the kitchen. He knelt beside my dog. "Cowboy, how's it going?"

I smiled. Jake was so natural with the golden retriever puppy. He was the first dog I'd owned. I'd rescued him, but some might say he'd rescued me. Jake would've been a better owner, but I was learning, and goodness, I'd fallen in love with the sweet pooch.

Jake stood. "Catch me up to speed before I search through the garbage bag."

"You didn't miss much. I've decided Houston was a big ol' bully."

Paula said, "He definitely bullied his family."

"Can't say I'm surprised. Emma, where would you like for me to go through the garbage?" He quirked an eyebrow. "Don't suppose you want to assist."

I rubbed my hands together. "You know me. I want to help, and I'm used to working in dirt."

He laughed. "That's my farmer girl."

I smiled at him. His brown eyes sparkled, his cowlick fell forward, and my knees went a little weak. "Um, let's head out to the back patio. There's some landscape ground cover in the shed, as well as gardening gloves. We can sort through it together."

Paula's eyebrows rose. "What are we looking for?"

"Clues. This is the garbage bag I told you about from the BBQ Hut food truck. Would you like to take pictures of what we find?" I didn't want her to ruin her nice clothes in case there were gross items. From the atrocious odor, there'd be an abundance of disgusting stuff." I turned on the outside flood lights and opened the door.

"Sure. I've got plenty of storage on my phone, and I can forward the pictures to you."

Cowboy followed the three of us to my backyard. My raised beds were well organized. The unfortunate incident back in March had almost destroyed my business in one night. The locals had rallied around me though, and Emma's Flower Farm survived.

I grabbed gloves from my shed for Jake and me, and I also pulled out a tarp. The dog sniffed around, while we went to work. We arranged the cover on the patio, then Jake poured the contents from the bag onto the tarp.

"Gag." The stench snapped my head back. "It wasn't so bad when the bag was closed."

Jake laughed. "I've smelled worse."

Paula sighed. "Well, I haven't. Emma, you can't get sick, because I'm a sympathetic vomiter. Can you hurry?"

"Doing the best I can." I held my breath and opened a clean garbage bag to discard the items after we studied them. "One half-eaten taco. Dirty napkins. Empty cups. Straws." We moved non-suspicious items into the new trash bag.

Cowboy nudged me.

"Paula, can you take him inside and give him a treat? Then you can come back out if you want, but don't let him back outside."

"Be right back." She snagged the golden retriever's collar and led him inside.

Jake pointed to an empty bottle of Good Life. "Let's set that to the side for now."

I met his gaze, unsure of his motive. "Sure."

Paula returned and snapped pictures with her phone. "Just look at that peach, would ya? Why would it be in the garbage of a barbecue restaurant? Did Houston have a peach barbecue sauce? Or maybe peach cobbler?"

I glanced at the browning fruit. "If he used it in the sauce, it didn't take much. The fruit has barely been touched. There wasn't peach cobbler in the food truck today."

Jake said, "The peach pit is missing."

"I'm not much of a cook, but can you get some flavor from the pit that you can't get from the rest of it?" Paula looked at me.

"No, but I think the pit can be poisonous. Once a woman came into the pharmacy with her young son. The child had swallowed a peach pit, and she was convinced he'd die from cyanide poisoning. He was fine, though." I raked my hand through the dregs of the garbage. "It must be in here."

Cowboy joined us and barked.

"Sorry," Paula giggled. "He slipped past me when I came back outside."

"Stay away, boy." I signaled him with my hand like the dog training book suggested. If there was the possibility of any poison in the trash, I needed to protect my dog.

He whined but moved to a shadowy spot near the back door.

"I don't see a peach pit either." Jake held up an empty cup from Anytime Coffee. "This is all from the garbage can inside the food truck. I don't recall selling coffee to Miranda this morning."

"Brett said Houston stopped by the coffee shop early. He probably bought it then." I shut my eyes and tried to remember my morning encounter with Houston. "Yeah, I remember now. Houston did have a cup."

"I sold him a cup of coffee—"

"Yeah, you told me it was super busy when he stopped by the food truck, and the Nelle sisters were in line."

"Right. It makes me think the crumpled coffee cup I sold him was at the crime scene. But there's no way to prove it. We use the same paper cups at the coffee shop as we do our food truck." Jake sighed. "The barbecue food truck wasn't using a grill or smoker. There was a warmer, and I imagine the ribs and other meat were prepared at their restaurant. The burners probably kept the beans warm. The fridge wasn't very big. I pulled banana pudding and coleslaw from it when we got to the restaurant."

I said, "I bet that's why they sell canned drinks from large coolers."

"Probably so." He opened a crushed carryout box. "Empty. You know, I'm surprised Matt allowed us to return the food truck for Miranda. It seems like he'd want the crime scene to do their thing."

"He must not believe Miranda's a legit suspect." I picked up a glass bottle with no label. "Do y'all think this is the same as the Good Life bottles? It's the same shape."

Paula took pictures from different angles. "It looks like the ones I have. It's easy to peel off the label. It's a pretty good stress reliever when you're trying to finish drinking the contents."

Jake said, "Why'd you drink it if it tasted bad?"

"I'm a sucker. Houston promised it'd make me thinner and healthier, but I dreaded drinking it."

I placed the empty glass bottle beside the other one Jake had asked me to set aside. "I know Good Life isn't a smoothie, but did Houston mention his concerns that Brett's tasty drinks would decrease his sales?"

"Not really." Paula shrugged. "Was Brett marketing his drinks to be fun or healthy?"

"Both." Jake wadded up pieces of plastic, including large plastic bags that had held buns.

A glimpse of bright red caught my attention. "Wait, is that a food service glove?"

"Looks like it." Jake separated the glove from the other plastic items.

"There's something red inside." I pointed to the object.

Jake turned the glove so we could get a better view of the item. "I see what you mean." He turned the glove upside down, and the item fell out.

A broken red fingernail plinked onto the table.

Chapter Fifteen

Jake, Paula, and I stared at the red fingernail. It was both gross and mesmerizing. I envisioned a woman pointing at me and mocking me for believing I could help solve Houston's murder. I swallowed hard. How had I allowed myself to agree to Paula's request? The red nail taunted me.

Jake was the first to speak. "Did either of you notice Miranda's hands today? Is this possibly her broken fingernail?"

I glanced at my non-manicured hands. "To be honest, Miranda usually wears her nails long. Way longer than mine. I've kept my nails on the short side for years."

Paula took a photo of the nail. "I remember being surprised the day she told me she buys her nails at the dollar store. They attach over her real nails. Looks like it popped off."

Jake raised the glove that had contained the potential fake fingernail. "Wonder what she did to make the nail fall off inside the glove? And why didn't other nails fall off?"

"I've seen her wear gloves in the food truck." I glanced back at the garbage. "I don't remember a time when she didn't wear food service gloves while handling food."

Paula sat in a chair and yawned. "It's been a long day."

"Why don't you go home? Jake and I can handle the rest of this."

"Okay. I'll text the pictures to you later."

Jake said, "Let me walk you to your car."

The two of them disappeared, and I picked through the remaining garbage.

Nothing seemed newsworthy, but I'd keep it for Matt. I pulled the black bag with the yellow plastic drawstring closed.

"Did you finish?" Jake opened the back door. Cowboy moseyed inside; then Jake joined me.

"Yes. Why did you have me save the Good Life bottle?"

"Matt insinuated Houston was poisoned. What if the drink was contaminated? It'd be potential evidence against Miranda. We should also give the coffee cup to Matt in case it's contaminated."

"Won't that look bad for you and Brett?"

"It's possible, but we're innocent. No good can come from hiding the truth."

Jake's integrity shone through. "Okay. I'll put each container in a separate sealed plastic bag so there's no cross-contamination. Be right back." I removed my gardening gloves and jogged into the kitchen. After grabbing the bags, I returned to Jake. "Here you go."

He went about sealing the evidence. "What are your thoughts on peach pits?"

"Not sure. Let me do the math." I swiped my phone and looked for the answer. Jake whistled a song, and I tuned him out during my search. When I found an acceptable answer, I searched for Jake. He was in the kitchen, playing with Cowboy. "Listen to this. Peach pits, or stones, can be crushed. They contain amygdalin. It changes into, are you ready for this?"

"Don't keep me in suspense."

"Hydrogen cyanide. The stones need to be ground up and disguised by placing the mixture in a smoothie. Now, we just need Matt to tell us what poison killed Houston."

"We only found one peach in the garbage. Is that enough to kill a man?"

"One second." I returned to the article on my phone and read it again. Math was a strong subject for me. "Would you suppose Houston weighed about two-hundred pounds?"

"Sounds about right. Why?"

"Let me calculate this." I swiped to the calculator app and began by converting pounds to kilograms. It didn't take too long to find the answer.

"One peach pit won't provide enough hydrogen cyanide to kill a person the size of Houston. It'd take roughly one-hundred-thirty-five peach pits."

Jake whistled. "That's a lot, but let's not get discouraged. The peach in the garbage could have nothing to do with Houston's death. In fact, I kinda hope that if he died from a poison it wasn't in a smoothie."

"Why does it matter?" It seemed like Jake would be more concerned about the coffee.

"Brett is currently promoting healthy smoothies."

I gulped. "All the more reason for us to solve the murder."

"Exactly. He joked about me taking care of Rufus, but I'm not sure how he'd survive in jail. Prison would be even worse with his PTSD. He's come a long way since we got home, but it wasn't an easy journey."

"Poor Brett." I'd seen a subtle sign of distress with Jake in the past, and my heart broke for all veterans. "We'll catch the killer. You should head home, and I'll keep studying poisons."

"I'll swing by Brett's place and check on him."

I walked Jake to the front door. After a quick hug, he took off. I locked the door and set my alarm system. There was nothing to be afraid of. I was locked inside, and Cowboy and I would protect each other if someone breached my security measures. I plugged in my phone and led my golden retriever to my home office.

Miranda Penn, possibly Shelby Penn, Leigh Turner, Eddie Hayes, and the mystery jewelry lady were on my suspect list. Brett and Paula were persons of interest to the police chief, but I wouldn't waste time with them. They were innocent.

If Houston died of a poison, alibis would be hazy. Each poison had a unique time to react. How had the toxin entered Houston's body? Food? Drink? Inhalation? Or could it have been absorbed through his skin?

I powered up my computer and settled down to investigate deadly plants.

Chapter Sixteen

Midnight approached, and I yawned. It'd been an early morning because of the farmers market. The stress of Houston's murder weighed on me. I was exhausted.

My phone beeped a security alert, and my pulse skyrocketed. "Cowboy, come with me." I tiptoed to the kitchen and snatched my phone from the charger.

The rattle from the gate in my sideyard reached my ears.

I texted Jake. **Someone's in my yard.**

The dog sprinted to the back door and growled.

"Shh. Let's go in the pantry where it's safe." I headed for my secret pantry. Very few people knew of its existence, because it blended into the woodwork. We would be safe in there. "Come, boy. Treat."

The magic word caught his attention. After only a slight hesitation, he joined me in the safe space.

I shut the door, gave Cowboy a dog biscuit, and then, with a cold finger, tapped the security app on my phone.

The front motion sensor picked up an SUV, parking behind Ms. Daisy. Jake stepped out of the vehicle and looked in each direction before moving to the side of my house.

My knees grew weak at the sight of help. I decided to text Chief Young in case the intruder got the jump on Jake. I shot off a short message and grabbed my Louisville Slugger before returning to the kitchen. Cowboy followed me.

There was a knock at my back door.

Through the shadows, I saw Jake's silhouette. I disarmed the alarm and went to let him inside. "Are you okay?"

He motioned for me to allow him to enter the room. "I was going to ask you the same thing."

"Yeah. How'd you get here so fast?" I backed away.

"Brett was at Anytime Coffee House, working on a new smoothie. I was helping, so it didn't take me long to hightail it here. What's going on?" He turned and locked the door.

Cowboy jumped onto Jake. His tail wagged in what I assumed was joy. It could've been relief.

Jake rubbed his head. "Good boy."

"The security system picked up motion and beeped." I snapped my fingers. "Cowboy, sit." To my surprise, he obeyed.

Jake pointed to the baseball bat gripped in my left hand. "Nice to see some things never change."

"I've gotten more comfortable with it after practicing at the batting cages." I set it to the side.

"Have you looked at the motion library on your phone?"

"I only saw you arrive. Let me go back farther to previous alerts." I tapped the controls and studied the different devices. "Oh, Jake. It's probably a false alarm. A truck drove by, and the front camera alerted."

"May I see?" He held out a hand.

"Sure. Right here." I passed the phone to him.

Jake watched then turned his gaze to me. "Do you mind if I scroll other alerts on this camera?"

"Go for it, but why?"

"I'm curious why tonight it notified you of traffic on the street." His eyes focused on the screen.

I shivered. "Do you think someone changed the camera angle to conceal themselves?"

"I sure enough reckon it's possible."

The doorbell rang.

A squeal, make that a little scream escaped my lips.

Cowboy barked.

"Hold on. Let's see who it is." Jake tapped the screen. "Well, well, well. What do you know? It's the chief of police."

My body relaxed. "I contacted him in case you ran into trouble."

Jake shook his head. "Oh, Emma. I wish you had a little more faith in me."

I reached for his hand. "You were the first person I contacted. I have all the faith in the world in you. It's me I didn't trust to help in case you ran into trouble."

The bell rang again, followed by pounding on the door.

"You better let him inside. I'll gather the trash and drink containers."

"In my defense, I wanted you to be safe."

"It's all good, Emma. No worries."

I walked to the door with lead feet. Maybe I truly didn't know how to act around men, and maybe I was too old to begin a romantic relationship. Life had been simpler before I started my business and solved my first murder. Of course, it'd been boring and not as fulfilling, too. I opened the door.

Matt's hand hovered over his gun. "Emma, are you okay?"

"Yeah. Sorry to have bothered you." I waved him inside and explained what happened.

Jake reentered the house carrying the big trash bag along with the two sealed bags and the plastic glove with the fingernail. Oh, so many bags. "Matt, thanks for coming. We have some potential evidence for you."

"What is it?" The police chief frowned.

I said, "You're aware we drove Houston's food truck to the restaurant while you spoke to Miranda. In fact, we had permission to do that. Jake carried food inside with the help of Benito Carlos. I remained in the truck and cleaned the prep area and stuff. It seemed smart to take the trash with us, and we looked through it tonight. We didn't want to waste your time in case there was nothing worth your attention. And we wore gloves while examining the garbage."

Matt reached for the three clear zippered bags. "What did you find?"

I rubbed my cold hands together. "You mentioned poison, so we saved these in case—"

"In case what? My people gathered the items spread out around the body."

My heart beat faster. Despite my desire to find the killer, I didn't enjoy confrontations. I held the two bags with drink containers high. "Is it possible one of these containers has poison in it? Could the killer have gone to the food truck expecting to connect with Houston? Maybe he—or she—pulled a switcheroo, and Houston ended up with the tainted drink."

Matt raised the bags with a sarcastic expression. "Then these would be clean."

I sighed. Why was he so difficult?

Jake said, "Do you want the fingernail? Or would you like me to toss all of this?"

"I don't see how it can be connected to the murder, but I'll take it in as potential evidence. Anything else?"

I crossed my arms. "There was a rotting peach in there, but no peach pit. In case you're wondering, one peach pit, or stone, isn't enough to kill a person. In fact, if my math is correct, it'd take one-hundred-thirty-five peach pits to kill Houston."

Matt whistled. "That's a lot of pits. Why do you think the peach was in the garbage?"

"I have no idea, but nothing on the menu required peaches. The food truck served barbecued meat, buns, banana pudding, macaroni and cheese—"

"I get the picture. Is this all you two have got for me?"

Jake stuffed his hands in his pockets. "That's it. Shall I dispose of this?"

"No, I'll take it with me." He held out his free hand.

I was aware he was tired, but I had a question. "Matt, you mentioned poisons. Is there a specific one you'd like me to focus on?"

"How about giving me a rundown on fast-acting poisons?"

"Tonight?"

"May as well. I'm already here."

Jake said, "Should I start a pot of coffee?"

Matt nodded. "Why not? I doubt any of us will get much sleep tonight. I'm going to run this out to my car." His disappearance gave me a moment alone with Jake.

"I am so tired. You should probably give me a double shot of espresso, and I'll round up my notes." I dragged my weary self to the office and gathered my notes. My daughter had begun college in January and often joked about pulling all-nighters. I'd have to inform her I was also pulling my one, except it was for a murder case and not a test.

Chapter Seventeen

Matt, Jake, and I sat around the French farmhouse table in my breakfast room, drinking coffee. Cowboy snoozed at my feet. "As nice as it is to catch my breath, I need to stay focused on Houston Turner's murder." Matt leaned forward, placing his arms on the table. "Whatcha got for me, Emma?"

"According to my research, some of the deadliest poisons are digitalis, botulinum toxin, batrachotoxin, ricin, abrin, amanitin, and aconitine. Was the poison inhaled, injected, absorbed through the skin, or ingested? When was it administered? Last night at the restaurant? This morning at the farmers market? Or another time? If I had more information, I could narrow down the selection."

Matt took notes as I shared. "It's too soon to answer your questions until I hear back from the medical examiner. I asked him to put a rush on it."

"How long will that take?"

"At least a week, maybe two. I'm only playing with a hunch based on my observations."

"Two weeks seems like a long time to get results in a murder investigation." Growing flowers took time, and I had learned to be patient in the process. Matt had probably learned to make allowances in an investigation's process.

"There's not much I can do about it."

Jake said, "How can we help?"

Matt pointed to my sketch pad of notes and drawings. "This is all I need. Don't tell anyone I asked about poisons, and don't interfere with my investigation."

My feathers had officially been ruffled. If it wasn't for me, Willow Moore's killer could be roaming the streets of Lutz, Texas. I wrapped my hands around the warm coffee mug. "Matt, this is the second murder in two months. Will you be able to hire more officers soon to help with these kinds of investigations?"

"That is none of your business. There are people I answer to concerning budget issues, but you're not one of those people. If you'll excuse me, I need get back to work." The force from which he stood caused the chair to bump into the wall.

Jake remained seated.

I followed Matt to the front door, and Cowboy trailed along.

Matt yanked the door open, then glared at me. "Emma, I shouldn't have involved you in this case. You got lucky with the last murder investigation, but I shouldn't have allowed you to assist. Houston has a lot of enemies, and you might not survive this time."

"Good night, Matt." I shut the door on his retreating figure without agreeing to his command.

Jake appeared in my front gathering room and sat on the couch. "That probably could've gone better."

I collapsed next to him and held a throw pillow against my stomach. "Yeah. We didn't learn anything. Despite drinking coffee, I think sleep won't be a problem."

"I fixed us decaf." He looked around the room. "You know we're always so busy, and I don't remember sitting in your family room before. We're usually outside or in the kitchen."

Cowboy looked at us, then moseyed away.

I cleared my throat. "Welcome to my gathering room. Before you ask, that's what the agent called this room, and I've followed suit all these years."

He rubbed his jaw. "Sounds a tad old-fashioned to me, but gathering room it is. Say, I don't have to work tomorrow. Do you want to do something together?"

I rested my head on his shoulder and yawned. "Yes."

"Let's touch base after church."

I nodded. "Sounds good. Are you prepared for anything?"

"Like tracking down clues?"

I giggled. "Exactly."

He reached for my hand and laced our fingers together. "If it makes you happy, let's solve this mystery. For now, let me go home so you can get some sleep."

I walked Jake to the door and kissed his cheek. Once he left, I secured my house and fell into bed.

If Matt wouldn't get lab results back on Houston's murder for at least a week, why had he asked me for information on poisons? Was there an odor near the body? Dilated pupils? Foam coming out of his mouth? What hadn't I observed in the few minutes I'd seen the body? I pulled the covers tighter around me. Soon, I'd ask Elijah again to look at his photos. They were bound to contain a clue.

Chapter Eighteen

Technically, I wasn't late to church, but on a whim, I'd brought flowers for the foyer. Driving made it possible to bring more than an armful of flowers, and I still had plenty left over from the farmers market being shut down yesterday. I'd included daffodils because, for whatever reason, Houston purchased them from me before his death. It seemed like a fitting remembrance. I put the finishing touches on an arrangement sitting in the large windowsill.

Miranda Penn entered the building surrounded by family, including her daughter Shelby. I scootched to the side to give them a private moment. Miranda was taller than me, and at five-feet-nine, I felt tall. Miranda wore a black blouse, black slacks, and black flats. She wiped her tears with a red bandanna.

Shelby rubbed her mother's shoulder. "Momma, we can go back home if you're not up to this."

"No, it's best for us to be here in honor of Houston."

"Okay, then we should go in before the preacher begins. We don't want people to stare." Shelby held her mother's hand, and they entered the sanctuary, followed by more than a dozen others.

Music began, and the ushers closed the doors. I tweaked the flowers once more before entering the service. Pastor Chisholm was making announcements, and I slipped into the back pew, hoping not to draw attention to myself.

Too late. Across the aisle and in a pew ahead of mine, Jake sat with Celia and Brett. He winked at me, and I smiled. Music played again, and everyone stood to sing. Jake came back and joined me.

I whispered, "You didn't have to sit with me."

"I wanted to."

"Thanks." I'd raised Abby in Lutz Community Church, and when she left for college in January, I discovered the fun of picking out who to sit by. Today, it was nice to have Jake go out of his way to join me.

The pastor's topic centered on doubts. Boy howdy, did I have doubts. Would my business survive? Was it possible for me to help catch another killer? Was I truly ready to date Jake? Or was I comfortable being single for the rest of my life? Before I knew it, the service was over, and people rose to file out.

In the foyer, Leigh Turner clomped down the steps from the balcony; then she dashed outside in her chunky heel sandals.

"Jake, I want to speak to Leigh. Will you wait for me?"

"Yeah. Go on."

I hurried as fast as possible, wearing my dress sandals. In the parking lot, I caught Leigh opening the door of a sporty sedan that had been backed into a space. "Leigh, wait a second."

She whipped around and faced me. "Do I know you?"

"I'm Emma Justice."

Leigh nodded. "Oh yeah, you work at the pharmacy. Sorry, I'm a little on edge, what with Houston's murder and everything."

I wasn't sure what else had her on edge, but that wasn't my objective this morning. "I'm a flower farmer now, and I saw Houston yesterday morning before he died. Can we talk?"

"Not here." She scanned the parking lot. "Nope, definitely not here."

Miranda stalked toward us.

"Okay. How about the dog park? In an hour?"

"Fine." She hopped into her car and sped away. I scurried out of her path to keep from getting run over.

"Emma, what are you doing talking to the enemy?" Miranda shook her finger at me. "I thought you were on my side."

"Oh, Miranda, I am your friend. Does that mean I can't speak to Houston's ex-wife? There are a lot of people grieving your brother's death."

"Are you trying to help her get away with murdering my brother?" Her flaring nostrils gave the impression of a bull about to charge.

"Whoa, we don't know who committed the murder. Everyone is innocent until proven guilty." I didn't want to share who was on my unofficial list of suspects.

Shelby joined us. "Momma, what are you doing? The family is ready to go back to the house with us."

Miranda pulled the wrinkled bandanna from her pocket and blew her nose. "This one is not our friend any longer."

"Momma, you can't mean that. Of course, Ms. Justice is our friend, and Abby is my friend."

"She was talking to Leigh. I caught her." The bitterness in her tone alarmed me.

I said, "I'm sorry, Miranda. I never meant to offend you."

"Momma, let's go before you say something you regret." Shelby tugged on her mother's hand, and they walked away from me and toward the family.

I met Jake standing beside his SUV. "Hey, Leigh agreed to meet me at the dog park."

"Then it sounds like we need to get Cowboy and head in that direction." He waved to Brett. "What time are we meeting her?"

"We've got an hour."

"Do you want to ride with me?" He made no attempt to move, looking rugged and handsome where he stood.

"I drove today, and I'd like to run home and change clothes. How about I meet you at your apartment, and we can ride to the dog park together?" He lived over Paige's Turn Bookshop, and it'd be easy to swing by.

"I don't mind to drive. I'll pick up you and Cowboy in plenty of time to meet Leigh."

"Sounds good." It'd be nice to slip into something cooler, like shorts and a T-shirt.

In less than an hour, we were ready and waiting at the park with Cowboy. Soon, I'd be able to learn more from Leigh Turner. With a little luck, I'd keep her firmly on my list of suspects or move her off so I could focus on the others.

Chapter Nineteen

In the dog park, my golden retriever puppy ran around the fenced-in area for big dogs all by himself. Cowboy was growing and full of energy. I sat on a bench with Jake, and we waited.

Jake stretched his long legs and crossed them at the ankles. "What do you plan to ask Leigh?"

"I find it interesting the very weekend Leigh arrives in town is the same weekend Houston is murdered, but I won't ask her if she did it. Instead, I plan to fish for who she thinks is guilty."

A white Subaru car pulled into the parking lot and parked by Jake's vehicle.

Leigh stepped out and looked our way. The wind whipped her wavy blond hair into her face, but she ignored it and walked to us. "I didn't expect anyone else to join our discussion. I'm tempted to leave."

I stood. "Leigh, this is my friend, Jake Hunter."

Jake rose and stuck out a hand. "Nice to meet you, and I'm sorry for your loss."

She pushed her sunglasses to the top of her head, and they held back her hair. "We weren't married anymore, but I thank you for the sentiment. He was my first love, and they say you never get over the first person you give your heart to."

"I've heard that before. Why don't I go play with the dog? It sounds like you might be more comfortable with just Emma." He turned on the toe of his well-worn sneaker and left me alone with Leigh.

"Would you prefer to sit?" I pointed to the bench.

"Walking might be better. I feel like there's a target on my back after what happened to Houston."

I shivered. "That's terrible. How about I follow your lead?"

She looked around us. This area of the park was basically deserted. "Let's take the walking trail."

"Okay." I trusted Jake to keep an eye on us, but the woman did make me nervous. To be fair, I'd been fooled before by a killer, so I sent him a quick text in case he lost track of me.

We walked along the concrete path, and Leigh said, "Why did you want to get together?"

"A friend of mine is concerned the police will arrest her for Houston's murder, because they had an argument yesterday morning. She asked if I could help find the real killer."

"How can a pharmacy tech turned flower farmer expect to catch a killer?"

I pulled my loose hair into a ponytail and adjusted my sunglasses. "I read a lot of mysteries, and I'm pretty good at solving puzzles. Leigh, who do you believe killed your ex-husband?"

"If I had to guess, it'd be his sister."

I wasn't shocked at her announcement. "Why?"

"Houston worked Miranda to death, and he wasn't fair to her. He'd make promises like promoting her to top chef and restaurant manager. The promotion didn't include a raise. My sons told me that Houston roped Shelby into working for him as a model and waitress."

"Why was that bad? Wouldn't the pay for modeling be good?"

"Not if you're working for Houston." Leigh shook her head. "Plus, Shelby longed to go to college and play tennis. Miranda and Shelby would do almost anything for Houston, including laundry. Although, I think they drew the line at cleaning his house. The man is a pig. My ex-husband stole Shelby's ability to be a normal teen. If she wasn't such a sweetheart, I might suspect her."

"That seems to be a unanimous sentiment around town."

"I imagine the rumor mill has been going nonstop."

"Yeah. It's part of life in a small town."

"It's one of the many reasons I live in Austin."

The walking path took us out of Jake's sight, making me glad I'd texted Jake. "Did Houston pay Shelby enough to save for college?"

Leigh snorted. "Not likely. My youngest son, Seth, is Shelby's age. They were close when I was married and living here. Ryan is twenty and attending college, so he's older. Shelby's an only child and treats my sons like brothers."

"Let me get this straight. Houston didn't deal fairly with Shelby, and she told her cousin how his dad treated her. Did that put Seth in a bad predicament?"

"You need to understand this. The only person Houston was nice to was himself. If I know Seth, he dragged the truth out of Shelby."

"Hunh. Your son sounds like a good kid."

The tension seemed to ease from Leigh's shoulders. "Both of them are good, despite their father."

"Did Seth ever confront Houston concerning Shelby?"

"No, she asked him to let her handle it. She confided in him because she knew he could be trusted not to spread rumors."

"Okay. That makes sense. Protecting her child makes a good motive for Miranda to have committed the murder. Any other thoughts?"

"Fear, envy, anger, and desire are all motives for murder. Miranda was afraid Shelby wouldn't get to attend college if Houston didn't let up on her. She was envious of his success while she worked for him. She was also angry at how Houston treated her and Shelby. As for desire, Miranda desired a better life for herself and Shelby."

None of her theories were focused on money. Interesting. "I'm still not ready to accuse Miranda. Can you think of anyone else?"

"The list of people with a grudge against Houston is probably long and ugly."

"Leigh, I'm going to come right out and ask. Do you find it odd that the weekend you come to Lutz to have it out with Houston over unpaid child support is the same weekend he's murdered?"

She huffed and turned on me. "How'd you know why I came here?"

"Like I said before, Lutz is a small town, and word gets around." I smiled. "You didn't answer my question."

"I didn't murder Houston, but I can see how it looks bad for me. In fact, Police Chief Young asked me to stick around town until he could speak to me. I had already reserved rooms at the Heart of Texas Bed and Breakfast for the next few days because of the funeral. One room for my sons and another room for myself. We'll be in town until after Houston's celebration of life service."

I didn't want to feel sorry for Leigh. In order to crack the case, I needed to stay neutral.

"So, no funeral?"

"Houston has donated his body to science. One of the colleges will study or dissect it. Leave it to my ex-husband to find a way not to completely leave this earth."

"One of the pharmacists I worked with had an anatomy class where they studied cadavers." I shivered. "Leigh, do you have an alibi for yesterday morning?"

"Unfortunately, no." She looked both ways. "Let's go back."

"Still feeling the target on your back?"

"I'm afraid so." She began retracing our steps.

I matched Leigh's pace. "Why do you feel like a target?"

"It's hard to explain. I'm not sure if I'm afraid the killer will come after me next, or if the police are going to arrest me. Either way, I feel vulnerable."

"But you believe Miranda killed Houston." I refrained from repeating the possible motives. "Suppose Miranda is the killer. Why would she come after you next?"

"Houston's will. He claimed he left the bulk of his estate to my children."

"That makes sense to me, so why come after you?"

"I'm in charge of their money until each son turns twenty-five. If I die before they reach that age, Miranda oversees the money. So, you can see why it's possible she'd come after me next."

Indeed, I did. It was also possible to flip the scenario. Leigh could have murdered Houston for the money. What if she was lying? Maybe Miranda was in charge of the money? If Leigh had murdered Houston for the money, maybe she planned to knock Miranda off next.

Chapter Twenty

Jake followed me around my backyard as I analyzed the flower crop. Plenty of lilies, dahlias, daffodils, and coneflowers were available for beautiful arrangements. Cowboy rested in his crate, and I told Jake what I'd learned from Leigh.

"Miranda, hunh. For Shelby's sake, I hope it wasn't her. Did Leigh suggest anybody else who might have had it out for Houston?"

I plucked a weed out of a raised bed of dahlias. "There wasn't anyone specific, but she said there were probably a lot of people who would prefer not having to deal with her ex-husband. In fact, she said something along the lines of it'd be harder to find people who liked him instead of vice versa." I moved down my path to the next raised bed and shared my notion about Leigh being guilty.

"That would be a twist for sure. Are you providing flowers for the service?"

"No. I'm not sure if you've met Yarrow Martin yet, but she's the town florist. She's back at work after recovering from her hip surgery, and I'm sure she'll handle the arrangements for the church and cemetery. No, wait. There's no burial because he donated his body to science. But back to your question. I might get lucky if Yarrow can't get enough flowers from her supplier. She might need to buy some of my stock."

"I imagine that's not as profitable for you."

"True, but being a flower farmer is more about growing flowers and selling to customers. I'm not in the business of creating the arrangements myself."

"I don't get it, Emma. You bring flowers to the coffee shop and some other businesses in town."

"It's different. You've heard of farm to table." I met Jake's gaze.

"Of course."

"Think of me as farm to consumer. I sell stems to consumers for their everyday flower needs. I also have orders for weddings this spring and summer. Brides who don't have a big budget often shop from flower farmers and make the bouquets and other arrangements on their own."

"I think it's finally sinking in. When you bring flowers to Anytime Coffee Shop, you put the stems into vases and make them look nice."

"You got it, but making them look nice is more of a favor to Brett. Mostly, I only deliver flowers." I moved to the patio. "Leigh said she is staying at the B and B. She also booked a room for her kids. They'll stay here until after the service. Do you think she's in any real danger? Should I warn Faith and Zig?" The Meiers had moved to Lutz from California, where Zig had made his money as a big movie star. These days they ran our local bed-and-breakfast. Faith had once confided to me that Zig had been careful with his money. He'd invested wisely, and while they enjoyed working together, they didn't necessarily need the money.

"It couldn't hurt. They should probably keep their eyes open for danger." Jake rubbed his jaw. "When I stayed with them, they were the most laid back people. Should we pay them a visit?"

I surveyed my land. All seemed in order. Not everyone agreed that my big backyard was a little flower farm, but I knew better. Years ago, when I'd begun to research flower farms, I learned there was more than enough land for my business. "Yes. I'd like to wash up and grab my sketch pad. Give me five minutes."

"Take your time, Sunshine."

* * *

Thirty minutes later, I knocked on the front door of the bed and breakfast. I glanced at Jake. "I never know whether to just walk inside or knock first. They live here as well as host guests, but it is their home."

The door opened, and Leigh Turner greeted us. "Oh, hi, Emma. I was hoping you were going to be Ryan and Seth. Are you here to see me?"

"No, we stopped by to see Faith and Zig. Are they here?"

"I know Faith is in the kitchen fixing afternoon tea. I can take you to her." She opened the door enough for us to enter.

"Thanks. Do you remember Jake?" I pointed my thumb at him.

"I'm sorry, but I had forgotten your name. Hi, Jake." She shut the door behind us.

Jake said, "Don't worry about it. You're dealing with a lot, and we only briefly met earlier."

"Thanks." She leaned outside and looked in each direction before closing the door. "You probably think I'm the most paranoid person around."

I patted her shoulder. "It's not paranoid if someone really is out to harm you. I feel like we should alert the Meiers. They can help look out for your safety."

A nervous giggle escaped Leigh. "That's too much to ask of them."

Jake said, "They have big hearts. My sister and I were staying here last month. After my sister experienced a terrible shock, Faith took great care of her. She's more than a host; she's a true caretaker."

Jake's sincere words impressed me. "For everyone's safety, we need to warn them."

Leigh stopped at the doorway to the kitchen. "She might decide to kick me and my sons out of here."

"Don't sell Faith and Zig short." I pointed to the large kitchen. "We're right behind you."

We stepped into the kitchen, and Faith looked up. "Hi, Emma. Jake. What a nice surprise." She enveloped us in warm hugs. Her blond hair was pulled into a messy bun, and she wore a short-sleeved dress. Faith would've probably enjoyed living in the fifties.

"Faith, it's good to see you. Leigh needs to tell you something."

"Sure. Why don't y'all have a seat at the table?"

Leigh said, "I want to keep watch for my kids, but there is something I should say. You know Houston Turner was my ex-husband."

Faith took Leigh's hands in hers. "Yes, and we're sorry for your loss."

"Thanks, but here's the thing. I'm a little worried that my sister-in-law, Miranda Penn, may be the killer. And if she murdered Houston for monetary reasons, she might come after me next."

"Oh, no." Faith gasped. "How can I help you?"

A tear trickled down Leigh's face. "If you see Miranda, please don't let her near me. At the very least, please give me a warning."

"Absolutely. I'll talk to Zig, and we'll change the codes on the keypads. We'll alert the other guests and just ask them not to share the code. This way, in case Miranda learned the code from someone else, it won't work. Zig and I will also be extra careful if we see her. No, we'll call the police if she shows up here."

I said, "That's really nice of you, Faith, but we don't know positively that Miranda is the killer." If Leigh had murdered Houston, she would have done a marvelous job of making Miranda look guilty.

Faith looked from Leigh to me. "Okay, but until the killer is caught, we'll do our best to protect our guests."

A knock at the door ended our conversation. Leigh pulled her phone out of a pocket. "It's the boys texting that they're here. I'll let them inside." She hurried away.

Jake crossed his arms. "Faith, we don't know who the killer is. If you and Zig don't feel safe, I can camp out here and help keep watch."

She squeezed his bicep. "I appreciate your offer, and I'll mention it to Zig. However, for now, I don't want to overreact. Know what I mean?"

"Yes, ma'am. I sure do. We'll shove off for now, but holler if you need me."

"Thanks, you two." She gave us parting hugs.

I walked out of the kitchen and hoped nothing bad transpired at the Heart of Texas Bed and Breakfast. Faith and Zig were good people, and it was important for them to be aware of the danger.

Chapter Twenty-One

Jake walked me home from the B and B. We stood on my front porch, and he ran a finger down my shoulder. "It's still early. Do you want to do something fun?"

"Fun? Is that allowed when there's an unsolved homicide in Lutz, Texas?" For a change, I winked at him.

His eyes grew wide, then he laughed. "Nice one."

"I'd like to look on social media and see if anyone posted pictures from the farmers market yesterday. You never know. We might get lucky." I opened the door, and he followed me inside.

"Have you abandoned hope that Elijah will share his pictures?" Jake crossed his arms, and my gathering room seemed to shrink with his presence.

"Not a chance, but until he agrees, I thought using a hashtag followed by Lutz Farmers Market might reveal something."

"It's worth a shot, but it's such a nice day. Can we do it outside?"

"Absolutely. Come on." I led him through the house to the back door and grabbed a straw hat off the hook. Cowboy moseyed out of his crate and followed us to the patio.

"Hey there, boy. Did you recover from all the fun you had at the park with Jake?" His tail wagged, and I rubbed his head. "How about some fresh water?"

Jake said, "I'll get it so you can start your search."

I sat in the shade. Red hair and a fair complexion had led to more than one sunburn. I started on Instagram and searched for Lutz Farmers Market.

There were posts featuring baked goods, fresh produce, free-range eggs, jewelry, pickles, and my flowers. Nice. There were also posts of people eating at the food trucks. A photo of a large cinnamon roll made my mouth water.

I screenshot several photos.

"Any luck?" Jake sat beside me.

"Maybe. Let me send you some pictures." I texted him the screenshots of the posts I'd saved. "Can you look for Houston in these? I'll continue searching."

We spent the next hour sifting through social media. At last, Jake stood and stretched. "I need to move around."

"Fair enough. What should we do?"

"Let's go to the batting cages at the park. Something tells me you may need to practice your swing."

"Okay. I'll fix some water bottles." I didn't want to use my Louisville Slugger for protection, but my brother had given it to me for that very reason. If it became necessary, I'd swing it to protect myself from an attacker.

"Don't forget quarters for the machine."

"I've got a stash in the pantry." It only took a few minutes to gather my supplies and drive to the park. I batted first, then Jake took a turn.

After our batting practice, we stashed the bat in Ms. Daisy and grabbed our water bottles. I took a deep drink and reached for a ball cap. "Would you like to walk on one of the trails?"

"Yeah, and we can review what we learned from social media about the murder." We walked on a public trail that wound through the park. Kids played soccer, baseball players practiced with their teams, and toddlers ran around one of the playgrounds.

"I saw Houston in the background of some pictures, but it could be nothing. He was talking to a lot of the locals. It's a good thing Paula warned me about her argument with him, because one photo has them in the background. There's nothing friendly about their interaction."

"Is it possible she killed Houston?"

I reflected on what I knew about Paula. She'd left her husband and hidden her child from him in order to protect their daughter from potential physical abuse. "It seems like Paula is more of a planner who runs from her problems instead of confronting her enemy."

"Hear me out. If she's a planner, and if Houston was poisoned instead of getting himself shot or pushed off a cliff, wouldn't it fit Paula's personality?"

"I see your point." I paused when a soccer ball headed straight at us.

Jake kicked it back to a little boy.

"Thanks, mister."

"Anytime." He caught up to me. "We also need to remember Matt is only guessing he was killed with poison. It could've been something else."

I glanced at him. "Wouldn't it be terrific if he died of a heart attack or a stroke or something natural? We wouldn't have another murder to deal with."

He reached for my hands, and we faced each other. "Emma, you don't have to solve another murder. You're not in law enforcement. Just because Paula asked you to help her, it doesn't mean you should."

My stomach clenched. "Brett is also worried."

"Yes, but Brett is a Marine. He understands chain of command, and my guess is he trusts the Lutz Police Department to catch the real killer."

I wasn't so sure about Brett. He'd seemed shaken. "What about you, Jake? Do you believe Matt can lead his people to find the guilty person?"

"Ouch." He grimaced.

"There are innocent people in prison for crimes they didn't commit."

"I hear ya. Celia will never forgive me, if Brett gets arrested, and I didn't do anything to prevent it."

"So? Are we continuing our investigation?"

"I'll continue, but you shouldn't feel any pressure. Don't forget, I've had training."

"I remember, and I know you'd be a wonderful cop today if you broadened your search for jobs."

"I'm content in Lutz. It's close to Celia, and I'm available to help Brett with the coffee shop. There's also an amazing woman who's caught my attention. She's a flower farmer. Maybe you know who I'm talking about."

My face warmed. "Oh, I know her, and she is most definitely interested in getting to know you better."

"That's very good news." His hands shifted to my shoulders. He inched closer to me.

Butterflies assaulted my stomach.

"Hi, guys. What are you doing here?"

The moment was broken. I turned to see who had the nerve to interrupt my near kiss with Jake Hunter. It was Elijah Barnes. I took a calming breath. "Hi, Elijah. We're here for a walk."

"Cool. Cool. Cool." He lifted a wide-mouth insulated stainless steel drink bottle to his lips, and soon he crunched ice.

Jake dropped his hands from my shoulders. "What do you have planned today, Elijah?"

"I heard the high school was holding tennis practice here for the girls. I decided to swing by and try to get some action shots."

"For Shelby?" I was curious about his feelings for the teen. He was obviously older than the girl, but if they were in their thirties, it wouldn't be a noticeable age difference.

He shook his head. "I'm here to take pictures of all the girls, not just Shelby. She lost her phone yesterday, and I haven't heard from her."

My pulse skittered. "Do you two usually communicate? Phone calls? Texts?"

Elijah's eyes widened. "I'm twenty-two, and she's seventeen. Almost eighteen. The age difference isn't appropriate, so don't accuse me of anything."

The fact that he'd emphasized she'd soon have a birthday spoke volumes. He knew he was too old for her now.

Jake held out a hand. "Hey, we're not accusing you of bad behavior."

"Good. I've gotten to know Shelby mostly through her uncle. He had her do a lot of modeling for him. The sad thing is, he didn't pay her extra for the modeling. He took advantage of her and Ms. Penn." His pleasant expression morphed into a frown.

I said, "Elijah, forgive me if I offended you. It wasn't on purpose. I'm just trying to figure things out. Did you ask Wayne Johns, if I could see the pictures you took yesterday?"

"I asked, but he didn't give me an answer."

"Then I can look through them?"

He hesitated. "As long as you don't tell Mr. Johns or anybody. I don't see how it can hurt, but I need to get to tennis practice now."

I looked at Jake. "What do you say?"

"In regards to attending the practice? I'll tag along."

I didn't have my sketch pad, but I could take notes on my phone. This opportunity was too good to miss. With a little luck, we'd see Shelby and Elijah in action. Miranda was probably involved in details related to her brother's death, but it couldn't hurt to hope we'd get to observe her, too.

Chapter Twenty-Two

Jake and I watched the high school girls run drills and practice their serves. They seemed to get along, and I didn't hear a cross word between the high school tennis players.

Elijah was on the court, snapping pictures of each player. He appeared to have a system, working his way from one end of the courts to the other. He'd left his backpack and water bottle on the front row of bleachers.

At last, the coach called for the team to gather around him, and Elijah joined us in the bleachers. He scanned through the pictures on his camera. "Here's where I began taking pictures yesterday morning at the farmers market." He handed the camera to me. "If you don't mind, please put the strap around your neck. I can't afford for you to accidentally drop my camera."

"Sure." I did as he requested and started with the first picture.

Jake scooted closer to me, and we looked at them together. Jake said, "Elijah, you've got some real talent."

"Thanks." He replied to Jake, but his eyes were on the court.

Elijah had begun Saturday by taking pictures of men erecting tents as the sun was rising. One by one, the pictures took us through vendors arriving and arranging their products. Expressions of happiness on shoppers were caught. I slowed at the photos of me organizing my booth. "Elijah, can I purchase the pictures you took of me and my booth?"

"Absolutely. Let's see what Mr. Johns selects, and you can buy the rest."

"Thanks. They'll look great on social media, and Abby is going to start a website for me this summer."

"Who's Abby?"

"My daughter." I returned to looking at the pictures. One was of Houston and a young woman with long, curly hair and tattoos on one arm. "Elijah, who's this?"

He looked over my shoulder. "Oh, she's the woman who sells that jewelry we talked about."

"Do you know her name?"

"It's something like Truth." He reached for his water bottle. "I don't remember for sure."

The tennis team left the courts, and Shelby joined us. "Hi, Elijah."

"Hey there."

I was torn between watching the interaction between the two of them and looking at more photos. "Hi, Shelby. How was practice?"

"It was fine." She turned her attention from me to Elijah. "Can I use your phone to call Mom? I need her to pick me up."

I said, "If your mom agrees, I can give you a ride. Do you mind if I finish looking at these pictures first?"

"Sure. Thanks." She sat beside Elijah. "I can't believe I lost my phone."

"I'd for sure be lost without mine. Hey, Ms. Justice asked me about the jewelry lady Houston was friends with. Do you remember her name?"

"I can't believe you forgot. It's Verity Candor." Shelby laughed. "It's gotta be made up."

I tapped the name in the app on my phone for notes. "Maybe her parents had a sense of humor."

"Maybe. She's all about truth and honesty. Love, peace, and blah, blah, blah. She claims that the jewelry she sells is only made by Texans. Every piece has healing properties. Some jewelry helps with arthritis—"

Jake said, "I've actually heard of that."

Shelby removed her thick dark hair from the ponytail holder and ran her fingers through it. "What about warding off colds, depression, and insomnia? I'm surprised she didn't have necklaces to ward off vampires like in the scary movies."

"It doesn't sound like you think much of Verity Candor. Was she dating

Houston?"

"I think they were more like business partners than lovers." Her mouth dropped open. "Sorry. I didn't mean to be disrespectful. It's even worse now that he's gone."

Jake said, "I'm a big believer in telling it like it is."

I turned my focus back to Elijah's camera and clicked through more photos. "Here's one of your mom, Shelby." Miranda was walking to the BBQ Hut food truck.

The teen glanced at the picture. "Oh, she must've been cleaning the tables for the patrons."

I looked closer. Yes, she wore gloves, but there was no spray bottle of cleaner and no rags. I knew for a fact there had been cleaning supplies in the truck, because I'd used them myself when we returned it to the restaurant. Maybe at an event like the farmers market, it was enough to move the trash off the tables. No, that didn't seem right. Wayne Johns took pride in being organized. He probably had a system for keeping the food area tidy. That would explain why Miranda didn't have cleaning supplies with her.

Dag gum it. I'd keep looking for clues and hopefully help solve the murder.

Chapter Twenty-Three

I asked Jake to drive Ms. Daisy, and I sat in the middle of the seat between him and Shelby. The console adjusted so the three of us could ride together in front.

Jake said, "Where to?"

"Momma said she's at the church making plans with Pastor Chisholm for the service. Do you mind to drop me off there?"

"Not a problem." He pulled out of the park.

"When did you lose your phone?"

"It's embarrassing. I'm not some dolt who goes around losing valuable things. Uncle Houston took it away from me. He said it distracted me from my work at the restaurant. I was going to get it back if I agreed to another modeling job for his Good Life drink."

"I had a sip of his drink yesterday."

Shelby giggled. "It's horrid, isn't it? I didn't like being part of his health drink business. It felt like I was lying to people for him. If you drink this, you'll be young and healthy. See what I mean? I'm a teenager who plays tennis and stays busy. I don't drink Good Life."

Jake stopped at a red light. "Did your uncle say anything about running a barbecue restaurant for years, knowing it's delicious but not necessarily healthy? Then, he creates this health drink. The two don't mesh to me."

I agreed with Jake. Either you were into healthy eating, or you weren't. Although to be fair, I enjoyed my cheat days.

Shelby leaned against the door. "I can't argue with your logic, but I never would have said such a thing to Uncle Houston."

I looked at her. "Do you know why he started the drink? Was he having health issues? I've been at the restaurant the last two nights for supper and didn't notice a new healthy eating section on the menu."

"If you ask me, Uncle Houston was only interested in making money. He knew it didn't taste the best. I think it's why he threatened to sue your friend at Anytime Coffee Shop."

"How do you know he didn't like the taste?"

Shelby giggled again. "I watched him spit it out. He called someone and started yelling that he needed to change the ingredients or create a different formula to improve the taste."

Jake pulled into the church parking lot and stopped near the door. "I thought Houston created the drink."

"Yeah, that's what he claimed. It's a lie. Momma could probably tell you more, but she's not very happy with Ms. Emma right now."

My shoulders sank. "I'm sorry for upsetting her, but what if Leigh isn't guilty? The killer could be the person in the healthy drink business with Houston. It's important to catch the real murderer."

"Honestly, it could be a lot of people. I hope it's not Aunt Leigh, though. My cousins would be devastated. They've lost their dad, and it will be awful if their mom is arrested." She opened the door and stepped out with her tennis bag. "Thanks for the ride."

"You're welcome." I waved and watched her enter the church.

Jake said, "Let's go talk to Brett. It's possible he knows who Houston's business partner is."

"Knowing Houston, it's only an employee. It seems like he got pleasure from bossing people around and taking advantage of them."

"You make a very good point." He drove to the bed and breakfast. "Celia's in town and staying here. I offered to let her stay with me, but she's in town for Brett. It seems like she doesn't want me to cramp her style."

"But you still approve of their relationship?"

"Yeah. My best friend and my sister. I trust Brett to be a model boyfriend to Celia."

"And maybe a good husband one day?"

"Whoa, let's not get ahead of ourselves." He parked. "To be honest, though, I couldn't imagine a better husband for my little sister."

"I agree." Jake was much closer to his sister than my brother was to me. It was partly my fault. As a single mother, I'd spent years focused on making enough money for us to survive. My spare time had been devoted to my daughter. Something told me that even when Celia got married, Jake would be active in her life.

We walked to the front door. Celia had already opened it and was waiting for us. "Brett called and asked for us to meet him at the coffee shop. Why don't we walk?"

"Hey, sis. I'm always up for a walk."

It wouldn't take long to reach Anytime Coffee Shop. Along the way, we passed the police station.

Miranda was walking up the steps to the station's front door.

I elbowed Jake but stepped toward Houston's sister. "Hey, Miranda. Did you see Shelby? Is she okay?"

Miranda did a double take. "She's fine. Thanks for bringing her to the church. My sister took her home. I've got to go." She walked into the police station.

I turned back to Jake. "Did you hear that?" With his partial hearing loss, I wasn't sure how much he could hear.

"Yep. Don't jump to conclusions. She might be going in to ask for an update on the case."

"Or Matt may have called her in for questioning."

"I don't know. She and Shelby were questioned yesterday."

"True, but what if Matt has more questions for her?"

"It's possible." We reached the square and continued walking.

Celia said, "Don't tell me you two are seriously on the case of Houston Turner's murder."

I lifted my hands in surrender. "Would you be more supportive if you knew we want to make sure Brett isn't accused by the police?"

She twirled a strand of hair around her finger. "I guess so. Is that why we're getting together?"

Jake opened the glass door. "You bet it is. I can't have a brokenhearted sister, if he's arrested. Let's get ahead of the police."

Celia hugged her brother. "Thanks for always having my back."

"It's what big brothers are for."

Jake always wanted the best for Celia, and he protected her. If Houston had acted the same way toward his sister and niece, would he have been alive today?

Protective brother. Nope.

Protective uncle. Nope.

What if Miranda and Shelby were innocent? Was their safety behind the motive? Had someone murdered Houston to protect his family?

Chapter Twenty-Four

Brett had delicious smoothies prepared when we arrived at Anytime Coffee Shop. At a square table, he had four small glasses setting at each place with a plate of crackers in the middle. "Welcome, and please have a seat." He pulled out a chair for Celia, and she kissed his cheek before sitting down.

Jake winked at me. "What have we got here?"

"These are four attempts at an açai blueberry smoothie. I'd like to hear which one you all like the best. I also have a bowl of crackers. Please eat one between trying each drink. You'll also see a paper to vote. I'd prefer you write down your thoughts first, and then we can discuss."

Celia gave a little whoop. "A smoothie tasting will be so much better than talking about murder."

I was excited to be part of his experiment and sat between Jake and Celia at the square table. "If Houston had done something like this, Good Life might have tasted better."

Brett shook his finger. "He was promoting it as a health product. Feel better, lower your cholesterol, lose weight, you know the spiel."

Celia said, "Wouldn't he need to prove his claims to the government to do that?"

"It might depend on his marketing campaign. How did they word his product?"

"I don't rightly know." I smiled at Brett. "Oh, we learned Houston was working with someone to develop the formula. Even he didn't like how it tasted."

Jake crossed his arms. "Man, it's probably the reason he came after you to stop making smoothies. Yours taste good, and his don't."

"Everybody, stop. If I make a couple of calls to find out who Houston was working with, will y'all please try the smoothies while they are nice and cold?"

Celia lifted a glass. "Oh, sweetie. Of course, we'll start the taste testing."

"Thank you. I'll be in my office, making some inquiries."

I took a drink of the first option on my right. Brett had placed a sticky note on each glass with a number. I recorded the number and my opinions.

Jake crunched on a cracker. "I gotta get the taste of peppermint gum out of my mouth. I feel kinda bad for Brett, like we stole his joy in the process."

Celia shook a finger at her brother. "We all need to make it up to him."

Brett appeared behind the coffee counter. "Hey, no talking until you've finished all of them."

I raised my hands. "Sorry, my friend. If it makes you feel better, we were talking about you, not the drinks. We're sorry for not being more serious. Truly sorry."

"It's all good, but please. Drink up." He disappeared into his office.

I made eye contact with the others, but none of us spoke a word. We tasted the smoothies, wrote down our thoughts, and ate crackers.

When he finished, Jake walked to the office, leaving me alone with his sister. "Celia, how are you doing?"

Her eyes glowed. "I'm happy to be back in Lutz."

"With Brett?"

"Yeah, and Jake too. I only wish it wasn't because of Houston's death. Brett is stressed to the hilt."

"I figured that out when he got bent out of shape over our questions."

"Yeah." She reached for the first glass in front of her and drained it. "These are all good. Honestly, smoothies are healthy options compared to other drinks, but they don't promise health benefits. I don't see how Houston could've sued Brett. If it wasn't for that threat, I doubt Brett would be a person of interest."

I leaned forward. "You're exactly right. Do you suppose the killer is smart enough to have talked Houston into making the threat?"

"What do you mean?" She shifted closer to me, and dark hair spilled over her shoulders.

"If Houston and Brett were at odds, it would have thrown the spotlight off of the real killer." I met her gaze. "So, it seems to me like Houston probably knew his killer."

Jake returned and sat next to me. "It could be why his body was found in a field of clover, and nobody heard a commotion."

"Unless he was drugged, and he couldn't call out for help."

Celia gasped. "You think someone drugged Houston?"

Jake frowned. "Emma, stop."

"Um, well—"

"Drugged? Is it official? Has the coroner done the autopsy? " Brett plopped down in the empty chair at our table.

"Officially, I don't know anything." Sweat broke out along my hairline.

Jake said, "Celia, Chief Young asked Emma for information on poisons, but he never said Houston was poisoned. As far as we know, the police are still waiting on the report."

I nodded. "In fact, Matt told us it'd be a week or two before he had any lab results. It could've been a severed spine for all we know."

Brett dropped his head into his hands. "If they find poison in his body, it'll make it easier to blame me."

"Why?" Celia's voice wobbled.

"Oh, baby. Don't you get it? Houston came here and bought a cup of coffee early yesterday before he went to the farmers market. The cops might think I put poison in it."

Celia smacked her hands on the table. "No. Let's not lose sight of the fact that smoothies have been around forever, and lots of people sell them. You were not a threat to Houston. Not to his business and most certainly not to his life. Now, let's discuss our favorite blueberry açai smoothie."

"I liked the fourth one best because it wasn't too sweet or too tart." I smiled at Celia, who was twelve years younger than me. She was twenty-six, but she carried an air of innocence about her. Maybe because she'd made good decisions in her life, or maybe because she had an older brother to look out for her best interests. Although Jake and Brett had been out of the country as Marines. I really didn't know that much about their military career, except Brett had PTSD serious enough to need a service dog. Jake sometimes jumped at sudden noises, and he had slight hearing loss from his time overseas. One day, I needed to ask more.

Celia said, "That was my favorite also."

Brett's phone dinged, and he looked at it. "Oh, this is my contact. Let's see if he knows who was working with Houston."

I began to add notes to my phone after Brett walked away, to take the call. Too bad I hadn't learned a lot. At least not yet. Maybe the phone call would reveal another potential person of interest.

Chapter Twenty-Five

Brett returned to our table at Anytime Coffee Shop. "The dude's name is Anthony Daniels. He's from Dallas. He was a chemist for an agriculture company. According to my friend, he met Houston at a convention. Houston and Miranda were running the food truck. Houston cooked ribs and chicken on a portable grill and a smoker. My buddy said the food was amazing."

"Focus." Jake motioned with his finger to speed up the story.

"You're right. Anyway, Anthony wanted to know the secret of the amazing ribs, and the two struck up a conversation. I guess one thing led to another, and Houston asked him to create a formula for Good Life. You know what gets me about this?"

I typed notes on my phone like crazy. Brett's tone had grown angry. "What gets you?"

"Houston acted like he created the formula all by himself. It shows what a liar he was. And a manipulator. He—"

Jake cleared his throat. "Calm down, man. He can't hurt you again."

Brett leapt to his feet so fast that his chair hit the ground. "If I'm arrested, Houston will have won. Even though he's dead, he'll still win."

Celia stood and gripped his hands. "You don't mean that."

He slumped. "You're right. What is wrong with me? He's dead, and I'm alive. I've got good friends and a beautiful woman who I love."

"Aw, I love you too. You're innocent, and we'll do whatever it takes to prove it." She wrapped her arms around him.

For the second time, Jake cleared his throat. "We all agree the fourth smoothie is the best. Emma and I should shove off. You know, er, give you two some alone time."

I stuffed the phone into my pocket. "Jake's right. See y'all later."

We walked outside, and Jake took a deep breath. "We need to investigate Anthony Daniels."

"Yoo-hoo!" A lilting voice caught our attention.

I spotted the Nelle sisters. Ruby, Gabby, and Rosalita waved to us from where they sat on a bench. The town of Lutz had various benches around town for when we were inundated with shoppers. People often flooded to our little town for antique fairs and whatnot. I waved back. "Let's go say hi."

We walked to them and hugged each one. Ms. Ruby wore red, her favorite color. Ms. Gaby's hair was in a bun, revealing dangling gold earrings. Ms. Rosalita was probably the most practical of the sisters, and she was as beautiful as her siblings. The sisters were in their eighties and active.

Ms. Rosalita said, "I imagine you two must be investigating Houston Turner's murder. It wasn't as much of a shock as Willow Moore's death, but it's still sad."

"Yes, ma'am, it's always sad to lose someone."

Jake squatted in front of the woman, placing him at eye level with them. "We are looking into the murder. Do you three have any tips for us?"

"We had just arrived at the farmers market yesterday about the time they found the body. What could we possibly know?" Ms. Ruby fluffed her loose gray hair.

Ms. Rosalita said, "You know Houston tried to get me to buy his drink. He knew I'm not in the best of health. He claimed Good Life would be like sipping from the fountain of youth for me. I didn't believe him, of course. And I'm on a fixed income and must be careful handling my money."

Ms. Gaby nodded. "He approached me, too. I told him I was healthy as could be for a woman my age. Sixty-five it is."

"Not a soul believes that whopper. You're eight-three, and we all know it." Ms. Rosalita shook her head.

Ms. Ruby focused on Jake. "I may as well confess. He tried to convince me to buy it too, but I know a shyster when I see one. Although, it's not polite to speak ill of the dead. For that, I apologize."

Shame on Houston for trying to con the sisters. "He approached each one of you individually?"

"Yes," they replied in unison.

I rarely saw the sisters alone. How had Houston managed that feat? "None of you tried it?"

"No. I've lived a good life, oh dear, no pun intended, but when the good Lord takes me, I'll be ready." Ms. Rosalita tapped her chest with crooked fingers.

I smiled at her. "Good one. Did any of you ever feel intimidated or threatened by Houston?"

Ms. Rosalita shook her head. "No, but he was a bully. Ask anybody."

Ms. Gaby said, "He wasn't nice to his family. It just makes sense that if he'd bullied his family, he'd try his best to intimidate three female senior citizens."

I patted her hand. "Are you all still considering a move to the retirement community?"

Ms. Ruby sat straighter, with a sparkle in her eyes. "Oh, dear, it's working out beautifully. That nice Daniel Moore heard we wanted to move, and he made us an offer on our house. It was more than fair and too good to pass up. And The Village at Lutz has three apartments for us. We'll be close together, but we'll also have some privacy."

I laughed at the thought of them wanting privacy. The three of them seemed to do everything together. Daniel Moore had been Willow Moore's father-in-law, and he had said more than once he'd like to move to Lutz to support his family. "That's great news."

Jake said, "If you need help with the move, give me a shout."

Ms. Ruby focused on Jake. "We'll be sure to do that, Jake. Thank you."

I tapped Jake's shoulder. "We probably should go."

He straightened. "You're right. Ladies, I hope you have a pleasant afternoon."

Ms. Gaby stood and motioned for me to follow her.

"Is everything okay, Ms. Gaby?"

"You didn't ask who we thought murdered Houston."

"For the love of daffodils, you're right. Who do you think did it?"

"I'd look at the ex-wife. She's a dental hygienist, but I heard money is tight with two sons. And you must know, Houston is behind on his child support payments. It's not smart to come between a momma and her kids." She watched a car drive by. "Leigh Turner should most definitely be on your list of suspects."

Chapter Twenty-Six

Various shades of pink dahlias made me smile. I'd recently purchased an antique vase at a local auction, and the flowers filled it quite nicely.

Jake sat at my French harvest table in the breakfast room. My airplane bungalow had a mix of cozy rooms and upstairs bedrooms. The open concept of the kitchen and breakfast area was where I often found myself.

After putting the finishing touches on the arrangement, I looked at Jake. "Do you want me to take these to the bed and breakfast while you continue digging to learn more about the chemist who worked on Good Life with Houston?"

"Nah, I'll go with you. Are we walking?" He closed the laptop.

"It's still nice out."

"That answers my question."

Cowboy appeared at my side and whined.

I knelt and rubbed his head. "Not this time, boy. Pets aren't allowed in the bed and breakfast."

"You're doing great with him."

Cowboy walked to his crate, and I gave him a treat. "You sound surprised."

"Don't forget you're the one who had doubts in the beginning. In fact, I had even wondered if you'd pawn him off on me."

I laughed and picked up the vase. "It crossed my mind. If you weren't living in the apartment over Paige's store, I probably would've tried. Did you learn anything about Anthony Davis?"

"That's a professional basketball player." Jake opened the front door for me and locked it behind us. "The scientist in cahoots with Houston is Anthony Daniels."

"Right." We walked up Main Street toward the town square.

"Anthony has a chemistry degree, but he's also into bodybuilding. He's lean and muscular."

"More muscular than you?" I eyed Jake's biceps.

He laughed. "Oh, yeah. He could compete in weightlifting. I wouldn't want to get sideways with him, especially in a dark alley."

"I'm intrigued. In my mind, scientists spend time in labs, wearing white coats and eye protection. They are always working on their inventions and never take time for athletics or stuff like that."

"In this case, you'd be wrong. I was curious how he went from working for an agriculture company to creating Good Life." We rounded the square and turned toward the B and B. "Anthony is fifty-nine, and he has a much younger wife. They met at a triathlon. She writes healthy cookbooks and was handing out samples. They struck up a friendship. It led to romance, then marriage."

"Besides being smart and strong, it sounds like Anthony's superpower is meeting people at conventions. Isn't that how he met Houston?"

"According to Brett's source, it sure is how they met." Jake turned his gaze toward the police station.

It saddened me to know how much Jake wanted to be a cop, yet Matt still hadn't offered him a position on the force. "I'm curious how Houston and Anthony went from talking about barbecue sauce to creating Good Life."

Jake glanced at me. "Maybe Anthony has the gift of gab, and Houston was a big talker. I can see how it might happen."

"We believe Houston and Anthony had an argument the night before the murder. I wonder if the business was in trouble. Suppose Houston believed a tastier drink would improve their sales."

"It could be why Houston threatened Brett. People aren't going to spend money on a bad-tasting drink, no matter how healthy it is." He touched my elbow, and we walked along the sidewalk leading to the door of the Heart of Texas Bed and Breakfast.

I pushed the doorbell.

Jake said, "How about I take you out to dinner after this?"

"I'd like that, and we don't even need to discuss the murder."

His eyes grew wide. "What in the world will we discuss then?"

Zig Meier opened the door. "Come in, come in. Emma, look at your pretty flowers. Did Faith order them?"

I stepped past the tall Black man who was even taller than Jake. "Hi, Zig. I wanted to surprise you."

"That's mighty nice of you. Faith is in the kitchen up to her elbows, preparing an overnight oatmeal muffin recipe. It's delicious, but it's time-consuming. Go on back."

I walked to the kitchen, leaving the men behind, discussing baseball.

Faith looked up. "Hi, Emma.

"Thought you might could use more flowers."

She quirked an eyebrow at me and lowered her voice. "I appreciate it, but something tells me you're here to quiz me on Houston's family."

I put the flowers on a table and stepped next to Faith, who was measuring out sugar. "Do you know anything?"

Before she could answer, Seth Turner entered the homey kitchen, carrying a sports drink. "Ms. Faith, can I get a snack? We're supposed to go out for an early dinner, but Mom's on the phone with her attorney. Who knows when we'll leave? I'm starved."

"What would you like? Something healthy or fun?"

He grinned. "Both?"

I laughed. "Spoken like a teenager. Hi, Seth. I'm Emma Justice. You might remember my daughter, Abby."

He shook my hand. "Yes, ma'am. She was always so smart."

"Thanks. She still is, and she started college in January. I don't know where she gets it from, but I'm proud of her." I paused a moment to change the tone of our conversation. "I knew your dad, and I'm so sorry for your loss."

He scuffed his toe on the floor. "Thanks. I know my dad didn't get along with everyone—"

I stopped him. "But he's your dad, and you loved him. You're allowed to grieve the loss, and you should."

Faith washed her hands. "I've got homemade granola bars and plenty of fruit." She pulled a big bowl of apples, bananas, and grapes from the counter and placed it before him. Then, she retrieved a container of granola bars from the pantry.

"Perfect. Your husband let me work out in the garage. He's got a good setup." Seth took two granola bars and fruit. "I hope to be a starter on the high school football team."

Faith handed him a plate and pointed to the counter. "Have a seat."

I said, "Seth, did you drink Good Life?"

He shook his head. "I didn't like the taste, but Ryan, my older brother, drank it. At least, he pretended to drink the stuff. He always wanted to stay on Dad's good side. Ryan learned to tell people what they wanted to hear from my father. Not me, though. I tell the truth, whether it gets me in trouble or not."

Poor kid. "I find it's best to be honest."

He peeled the banana. "Yeah, it can be uncomfortable, but it saves grief in the long run. Know what I mean?"

"I sure do. Seth, forgive me if this is insensitive, but who do you believe killed your dad?"

His face reddened. "It wasn't my mom. I don't care what Aunt Miranda says. I don't know who did it, but I hope they catch the dude before my family is ripped apart by accusations."

"I believe you." At least, I accepted he was convinced of his mother's innocence.

"Thanks, Ms. Emma."

Faith turned and frowned at me.

"Um, I better scoot. Seth, if there's anything I can do for your family, please let me know."

"Yes, ma'am." He bit into the banana.

I turned on my toe. "Bye, Faith."

Chapter Twenty-Seven

Jake drove with one hand on his SUV's steering wheel, and headed in the direction of the barbecue restaurant.

"I've never eaten barbecue so many days in a row. I think tonight I'll just order a salad."

"We can go somewhere else." Jake slowed and glanced in my direction.

"No, this is the best place to find a clue." Uh oh. "Wait, I promised not to discuss the murder at dinner."

Jake laughed. "I can't imagine us not discussing Houston's death. Once the killer is caught, we'll talk about other things. For instance, tomorrow, I'm working for Coop Henderson on a kitchen remodel."

"You sound excited."

"Yeah, I am." He pulled into the restaurant's parking lot. "I need to be more than a barista, spinning my wheels while hoping Chief Young will hire me. Plus, I enjoy construction work. What do you have planned for tomorrow?"

"I'm going to call Elijah Barnes about updating my website. New pictures and that kind of thing."

"I thought Abby was going to work on it this summer."

I stopped reaching for the door handle. "You're right. I can still ask for photos for social media. He can take pictures of my garden areas, and I can choose some that he doesn't sell to Wayne Johns for promoting the farmers market."

Jake reached for my hand. "I'd feel safer if you don't meet with him alone."

"As in my backyard? You prefer a public place to get together?"

"Exactly. We don't know much about the guy. If he believes Shelby or

Miranda killed Houston, and if he thinks you're investigating the case, he might try to harm you in order to protect them." He ran his thumb over the back of my hand. "The kid is sweet on Shelby."

Chills shot up my spine. Was it from Jake's touch or his warning about Elijah? "Okay, I'll only speak to him in a public place or on the phone."

His cowlick fell forward, and he winked. "Thanks, Sunshine."

I exited the 4 Runner and joined Jake on the sidewalk. How had the big flirt, otherwise known as Jake Hunter, wormed his way into my heart?

"Hi, Emma." Elijah Barnes stood at the front of the BBQ Hut. "Can I get a picture of you two? Shelby's mom wants to get the word out they are open for business despite Houston's death."

"Sure." I removed the band holding my hair back, and I fluffed my hair in hopes I wouldn't look so disheveled.

Jake slid his arm around my shoulders, and I leaned my head toward his.

Elijah snapped a few pictures. "Thanks. To be clear, you're okay with me posting these on social media?"

"Yeah. It'll be even better if you can mention I own Emma's Flower Farm."

He tapped on his phone. "No problem."

"Did Wayne Johns pick the photos he wants from yesterday?"

"Sure did. I'll be in touch tomorrow to show you the ones you can use."

Jake said, "Would tomorrow evening work? We could meet you, say, around six?"

Elijah's eyes widened, and he turned to me. "Six o'clock?"

"Is that okay?" I didn't want to miss my opportunity. If six didn't work, I'd agree to another time.

"Let me check my schedule." He looked at his phone. "I'm free then. At your house?"

"Yes, I thought it might be nice to include pictures of my flowers growing in their beds."

"Cool. Cool. Cool. See you then."

Jake and I entered the restaurant and sat at a table for two. I said, "That was easy enough with Elijah. Thanks for jumping in."

"No problem. I want you to be safe."

Shelby came to our table with menus and handed them to us. "I'm surprised to see you two so soon. Tonight's special is barbecue nachos. What can I get you to drink?"

We placed our drink orders, and Shelby hurried back to the kitchen.

A white paper was taped on the inside of the menu. It listed features and new items. I looked at Jake. "Miranda didn't waste time changing the menu."

Jake leaned forward. "It looks like she's enjoying her freedom from Houston's control."

"One more motive to go on her file." I needed to study the list of people and see who had the strongest reason to murder Houston. "Jake, do you think one strong motive is enough reason to commit murder, or do you think lots of little motives add up and lead to murder?"

He rubbed his chin for a moment before answering. "It could be either way, I guess. You know how some people stuff down their anger until one day they explode? It could be that Houston continually aggravated someone until they couldn't take any more of his abuse. Maybe they lost control and acted in anger."

"Then I better keep my ears open for more motives."

"And keep your eyes open for danger."

I squeezed his hand. "Touché."

Chapter Twenty-Eight

I had weeded my gardens early Monday morning before the heat got to me. Living in Texas, I'd grown somewhat used to sweltering days. However, I'd spent years working in an air-conditioned pharmacy. Long days working outside in my gardens required keeping hydrated, wearing hats, and finding the best times to work without having a heat stroke.

According to my flower farmer research, it was time to plant more zinnias in one of the empty raised beds. By rotating flowers and studying their life cycles, I'd be able to sell flowers throughout the year. Zinnias were said to be a hit with most people because of their wide variety of colors and general cheeriness.

Cowboy barked from inside the house, and I walked to the door and let him out. Instead of exiting, he spun in a circle and took a few steps deeper into the kitchen.

"What's wrong, boy? Are you thirsty?" I slipped off my gardening shoes and gloves before following him into the house.

The doorbell rang.

"Oh, is that why you got my attention?" I walked to the front of the bungalow and opened the door.

Miranda Penn stood there with a frown as big as Texas. She wore a black blouse and black slacks. "I came to apologize."

Cowboy stood beside me, providing some protection, but I wasn't comfortable inviting a person of interest for Houston's murder into my home. I motioned to the small rockers on my porch. "Okay. I'm dirty from working in the flowers. Why don't we have a seat out here and chat?"

Her expression didn't change, but she plopped down on the wood rocker farthest away from me.

I snagged a leash, attached it to Cowboy's collar, and sat in the empty black rocker. My lovable puppy sat at attention by my feet. "Thanks for coming by, Miranda."

"Shelby and I appreciate the ride you gave her, and she insists you're not out to get me."

"I'm not accusing anyone of murder, but a friend did ask me to help prove her innocence. It's the only reason I've asked any questions."

"Your friend is a woman?" Miranda crossed her long legs.

"Yes, but I'd rather not throw her name around."

"Trust me, I don't want the cops looking at me either. I assumed you were helping Brett Tirabassi."

"He's definitely a good friend, and I know he didn't kill your brother." I debated the wisdom of my next question but forged ahead anyway. "The last few days, it seems like Houston was at odds with lots of people. You, Shelby, Brett, Leigh, Eddy Hayes—"

"You know about Eddy getting fired?"

"It's a small town, and I was at BBQ Hut on Friday night. Houston even flipped out on Coop Henderson about trying to leave without paying his bill."

Miranda rocked in her chair. "To be fair, I'm not sure Coop told his waitress he was going to get his wallet."

"But Coop's an honest and decent guy. He wouldn't stiff you for his meal."

"You're right. Houston was off-kilter Friday night. More irritable than usual, if you know what I mean."

I patted Cowboy's side, and he lay near my feet. "Shelby said that Houston wasn't happy with the taste of Good Life. Until recently, I was under the impression your brother created the drink by himself. Now I know he was in business with Anthony Daniels."

"It's true. Sales were down, and Houston blamed everyone but himself." Miranda crossed her arms and looked toward the street.

"Why do you think he wasn't selling as much?"

"It was expensive, and it tasted horrible. Some woman convinced Houston to run the business as a multi-level marketing plan. Many businesses use this kind of model to sell makeup, cleaning products, and other stuff. Trust me, I heard all about it. Houston believed the woman and changed the way he ran the business so he'd earn income from recruiting others to sell Good Life. It didn't help."

"I wonder why."

"I'll give my brother credit for believing the drink improved a person's health. At first, the people who applied to sell the drinks were excited. Time wore on, and they lost their enthusiasm. One of those people may have killed my brother."

Probably because of the sour taste. "What happened?"

"Before long, the new members, or employees, or whatever you call them, quit believing in the product. Then these same people badmouthed Good Life, and Houston started losing his mind. He'd invested big time into the company, and he needed people to buy Good Life."

"Do you think Anthony Daniels could've killed Houston?"

"Maybe." Her shoulders slumped. "I barely know Anthony. We met once, and I heard Houston's side of a few phone conversations between him and Anthony."

"Miranda, who do you think murdered your brother?"

"I won't tell the police, but I think Leigh did it. I'm just not sure how she accomplished the act." Her calm reply made it easier to accept her opinion. "I never saw her at the market Saturday morning, but she may have worn a disguise."

"Okay. That's possible."

"There's another reason I stopped by today." She quit rocking and met my gaze.

"What is it?"

"Good Life wasn't making my brother's life good, and he died in debt. I was wondering if I could buy flowers from you for his celebration of life. My family and I can arrange them, but I can't afford the florist."

"Of course, you can buy flowers from me. What would you like?"

She pulled a folded piece of paper from her pocket. "I'd like to use these flowers if you have them. At this point, I can't be too picky."

I glanced at the list. "Except for the Mexican sunflowers, I should be able to make this happen. When do you want them?"

"I'll send Shelby over tonight when she gets off work. Will that give you time?"

"Absolutely."

Miranda stood. "Thank you, Emma."

"You're welcome. Tell Shelby not to rush tonight. I'll keep the flowers cool until she gets here."

Miranda walked away slowly, as if dreading where she needed to go next.

I led my dog inside and made a quick note to see if I could find out who invested in Houston's business. I also wanted to talk to Paula, so I gave her a call.

"Hey, Emma. Have you caught the killer yet?"

"No, but I'm glad I caught you."

"I keep my phone on my desk for emergencies. If I hang up quickly, you'll know the principal is walking by. What's on your mind?"

"Didn't you say you invested your money in Houston's company so you could sell Good Life? Or am I mistaken? Did you only buy enough for your own personal use?"

"It costs five thousand dollars for the privilege to sell the stuff, and there's no way I could afford it. Promising to give my money back if it didn't work was the only reason, I agreed to give it a try. I never should have bought so much, but there was a discount, and I believed in Houston."

"Do you know anyone who may have invested?"

"No. Lutz is a small town, and you know yourself that most of us aren't high-income people. I imagine Houston must've found investors in Austin or Dallas."

"Good point. Maybe he met them at conventions." It was how he met Anthony Daniels. "Have the police contacted you yet?"

"No, and I keep looking over my shoulder, expecting to see Chief Young.

CHAPTER TWENTY-EIGHT

Hey, is our book club meeting tonight?"

Oh, man. I'd forgotten all about book club. "I've been so focused on Houston's murder, and the meeting slipped my mind. I need to cancel." A local group of women met every Monday night at my house to visit and discuss a book.

Paula said, "I'll handle the announcement, and you focus on solving the murder."

"Thanks. I'll keep you updated."

Chapter Twenty-Nine

By five o'clock, I'd finished weeding and planting new starts in my garden. I'd also cut flowers for Miranda to use for Houston's memorial service. After a quick shower and changing into fresh clothes, I entered my home office and opened my laptop. It was time to discover who may have invested in Houston's business. Cowboy snoozed at my feet.

I began my search by using the name of Houston's business. Not surprisingly, Anthony Daniels had plenty of posts promoting the health drink. He'd gone so far as to claim it helped him reach his magnificent physique.

With my mouse, I tapped a box to become friends with Anthony and even sent him a private message with a request to chat about Good Life.

There were more posts. Some were negative, but others were positive.

One comment caught my eye.

A woman posted, "There's nothing good about Good Life. In fact, it ruined my life." Her name was Riley Bliss. I reached out and asked her to contact me.

Cowboy barked, then the doorbell rang. I looked at my dog. "I have no idea how you do that, but good job." He raced to the door with a happy bark. Again, I had no clue how he suspected he'd be happy with our visitor.

I opened the door. "Hi, Jake."

Cowboy leaped out at Jake with his tail wagging.

"Sunshine, how's it going?" He winked at me and bent over to greet my dog.

"I've learned more today, but who knows if they are legit clues or red herrings?" I stepped back. "Come in."

Jake moseyed to the kitchen. He wore a solid blue T-shirt, khaki shorts, and Hari Mari flip-flops. He eased himself onto a barstool, bracing himself with his arms.

"Are you hurt?"

"I tweaked my back when some knucklehead let go of his end of the kitchen countertop. We were trying to save it to be recycled."

I opened the freezer and reached for an ice pack. "Try this."

"Thanks." He held it against his lower back. "Tell me what you learned today."

I launched into the details of Miranda's visit and my conversation with Paula.

Cowboy barked, and then the doorbell rang.

"That must be Elijah. Would you be more comfortable if we sat in the gathering room?"

"Naw. It'll be easier to work at your table." He stood. "I'll take Cowboy out back then meet you in here."

"Thanks." I took a deep breath and went to answer the door.

Elijah stood at the door with a backpack I'd often seen him carry. It wasn't a special photographer's bag. It looked like a typical school backpack. We chatted about the warm weather on the way to the breakfast room.

"Have a seat. Would you like something to drink?"

"I'm good." He pointed to his insulated water bottle, then sat at the head of the table and opened his bag. "I loaded all of the pictures on this jump drive, but do you want me to take pictures of your garden first?"

"That sounds like a good idea. I can point out what's growing in raised beds—"

"Emma, I find it's better if you let me take pictures first. When you look over them, you can tell me if I missed something you want to include." He gave me a crooked smile. "It's just my process."

"Oh, sure. I'll stay here and look at your photos on the jump drive instead of watching over your shoulder."

"Cool. Cool. Cool."

"Oh yeah, Jake Hunter is in the yard with my dog. If you're not comfortable around dogs, send Jake in with Cowboy."

"Well-behaved dogs don't bother me." He left me alone in the breakfast room, so I plugged the drive into my laptop and got comfortable.

Jake returned with Cowboy and filled the dog's water bowl. "The kid suggested I come inside. He was nice about it, but still. What's going on?"

"He's an artist and doesn't want me interfering with his process. It looks like Cowboy was also interfering with his artistic process. Or was it you?" I shot him a smile.

"Very funny."

"Have a seat. I'm going through Elijah's pictures from Saturday morning at the farmers market."

Jake picked up the ice pack and sat in the chair next to me. He smelled clean and outdoorsy.

I took my time with every picture in case Houston was in the background. "There he is with Paula." I made note of the exact photo.

"Has Elijah shared these with Chief Young?"

"I don't know." I continued tapping the button to click through the pictures. "Oh, that looks like Houston and the lady with the long curly hair. I feel like it's the same lady that Elijah identified as Verity Candor. You know, the jewelry lady."

Jake leaned closer. "Can you enlarge it?"

I hit the edit button and made the picture bigger. "It's getting fuzzy."

"Yeah, but it's not terrible." Jake used his phone's camera app to make a copy of the photo. "Let's study the vendor list tonight in case it's not the jewelry lady."

I added this image number to the previous one on my sketch pad. As we scrolled, I continued adding to the list of photos I wanted to buy from Elijah. We reached the end, and I looked at Jake. "I thought there would've been more to choose from."

Jake shrugged. "It's possible Wayne Johns wanted all the others."

Elijah walked into the kitchen. "I got some great shots. I'll edit these and get back to you before the week is over."

Cowboy circled Elijah, then went to his crate.

"You mean I can't see them tonight?"

"No, ma'am. Give me a few days, and they'll look better. Trust me."

Something in his tone made me not want to trust him, but I didn't know why.

Jake nudged me and pointed to the second line on my list. I said, "Elijah, can you confirm who is in one of these pictures? Hold on just a second."

He moved closer and sat in the empty chair by me.

I found the image of Houston and the woman with the long curly hair. I turned the screen so Elijah could view it.

He nodded. "That's the jewelry gal. Verity Candor."

Cowboy barked and raced to the front door.

The doorbell rang.

Jake said, "I'll get it."

I met Elijah's gaze. "This is the girl you and Shelby were telling me about."

Shelby appeared. "What girl?"

Chapter Thirty

Elijah leapt from his chair at the harvest table in my breakfast room. "Shelby, hi. What are you doing here?"

"Hi, Elijah. I came to pick up some flowers. What girl are y'all talking about?"

Jake edged around Shelby. "We were asking Elijah about Verity Candor."

"Oh, yeah." Her eyebrows rose and lowered in a quick motion. "I don't trust her. She's the one who talked Uncle Houston into running his business as a pyramid scheme. I overheard them arguing over it more than once. He didn't think pyramid schemes work, and I looked it up. They aren't legal, and I told him that later. He worked me hard and wasn't always fair, but he was my uncle. I didn't want him to go to prison."

"I've been hearing about her suggestion. How did Houston reply to you about the illegality of her model?"

"He told me to mind my own business."

"That wasn't nice." I stood. "Would you like something to drink, or maybe a snack?"

The teen laughed. "A snack would be great. You'd think working at a restaurant would give me lots of opportunities to eat, but we've been crazy busy the last few days."

I peered in the refrigerator, wishing I'd considered the food options before opening my big mouth. "On the lighter side, I've got veggies and dill dip. Or I can fix an almond butter and jelly sandwich. Cheese and crackers? Bowl of cereal?"

"A sandwich would be amazing."

Jake opened a cabinet. "I'll fix something to drink. Is Dr. Pepper okay with y'all?"

They both agreed to the Texas soft drink.

Cowboy barked.

Shelby rubbed his head. "I can take him outside."

"I'll go with you." Elijah moved to the back door and held it open for them.

I pulled items from the refrigerator. "It's obvious Elijah cares about her, but he's aware the age difference isn't appropriate."

"Yet. There's a ten-year age difference between Brett and Celia. If Elijah loves Shelby, he'll be able to wait."

"Make sure they don't see me." I popped into my secret pantry and grabbed a bag of chips and a box of wheat crackers. After shutting the door, I opened the potato chips. "It won't remain a secret, if people are around when I go into my pantry. Have you had supper?"

"No, I was actually going to offer to order Chinese food."

My stomach lurched. "I could go for veggie fried rice and sesame noodles. As soon as they leave, let's do it."

"Sounds like a plan." Jake reached for the cheese and began slicing it. "Your appetizers should tide us over."

"Let's hope so." I stirred the almond butter and spread it on a slice of multigrain bread.

By the time Shelby and Elijah rejoined us, we had veggies, dip, chips, cheese, crackers, and a sandwich waiting.

Elijah asked me to refill his water bottle with ice and water, so I did.

Shelby sat on one side of the table, and Elijah sat beside her. Jake and I took the seats across from them. "This looks amazing."

I said, "If you need to take it home to be with your mom, I'll understand."

"No, ma'am. Momma has a support team around her nonstop. I need this break from all the drama. It's nice to take a deep breath and not feel like I'm being judged."

Jake reached for a cracker. "Why would anyone judge you?"

Shelby added chips to her plate, ignoring the carrot and celery sticks. "I think plenty of people wonder if I murdered my uncle. Then there are others who believe my mother did it. The rumors are brutal, and I can't take much more."

Elijah gripped his stainless steel bottle so tight his knuckles whitened. "That's crazy talk. No way would you harm Houston, or anyone else. How can they even consider it?"

"Maybe because I had the most to gain from his passing. Now that he's gone, I can focus on tennis and my grades instead of modeling and being a waitress." The teenager stared at her plate without blinking. "It sounds terrible, but they're right. I probably gained the most by his death. Still, I wish he was alive."

"It's ridiculous to imagine you'd hurt your uncle. To consider you'd kill him is absurd." Elijah took a drink and soon crunched his ice so loudly I was amazed he didn't break a tooth.

I said, "Let's consider Verity Candor again. Where do you suppose I can find her?"

Elijah turned his moss-green eyes my way. "You should start at the Lutz Drive Up RV Campgrounds. If she's not there, she's traveling. I'd almost guarantee she'll be back next weekend for the antique and vintage market."

The four-day event was popular with tourists, and it always brought a boom in sales to local business owners. "I plan to go Thursday and look for creative pieces to be used as flower vases." My business goal was to only sell arrangements at the farmers market. The rest of the time, I wanted to sell cut flowers.

"If you don't find Verity before Thursday, keep your eyes open there."

"Okay, it sounds like a good idea."

Shelby finished her sandwich and drank the Dr. Pepper. "Thanks for this, but I better head home."

I hopped up. "Let me get the flowers your mother ordered."

"Yes, ma'am." She followed me to the garage, where I kept a refrigerator for my business.

"Your mother apologized to me. She said you were responsible for her change of heart, and I thank you for that."

"We'll see how long her softened heart lasts, but it can't be good for her health to be so angry."

I removed the flowers and handed containers with dahlias and zinnias to the teen. "You're right. I'll help you get these to your car."

"Thanks."

We crossed paths with Elijah. "Emma, I'll be in touch with the photos of your gardens. Shelby, see you later." He left us with a wave.

Shelby and I secured the flowers in her car, and she drove away.

Jake met me in the driveway. "It turns out the Chinese restaurant is closed on Mondays. Now, the way I see it, we can place an order at Amalfi's, drive to the campgrounds and look for Verity, and manage to pick up our food while it's still hot."

"Pizza and salad?"

"Yep. Veggie on your side and meat on mine."

"Perfect." I squeezed his hand. "Thanks for understanding."

He laughed. "Hey now, I want to check out the RV campgrounds too. Let's bounce."

Chapter Thirty-One

The sign at the front of Lutz Drive Up RV Campgrounds announced there were no vacancies. Jake drove us around anyway. Many spots were occupied, but there were a few empty sites. There were public bathrooms with showers, a game room, and a laundry facility. Outside the buildings were play areas for children and pickleball courts. The grounds appeared clean and well kept.

"If I was a camping kind of person, this is where I'd like to stay. I wonder why the sign said they were full?"

"I imagine some vendors might reserve spots for the entire week to have close access during the Lutz Antique and Vintage Market, even if they don't stay the entire week. It's probably worth the price compared to driving back and forth from another place farther away." He continued his slow journey through the campground. "We're looking for a large van with living quarters in it, correct?"

"Yeah. I guess she could even be running an errand or something."

"Good point. What do you say we go pick up our dinner?"

"There's no sign of Verity, and I'm starved."

"That sounds like a yes to me." Jake followed the exit signs, and soon we were on the way to the Italian restaurant.

I searched the Internet on my phone for Verity Candor. "Listen to this. Verity sells jewelry made by Texans, and each piece has healing properties."

"Good. You've confirmed what we thought we knew." Jake turned down the country music playing. "It seems plausible that she'd only sell jewelry created in Texas, or that'd she only sell jewelry with the power to heal. But when you combine them—"

"Timeout. Do you mean she's marketing to a customer base that wants Texas-made jewelry that heals?"

He nodded. "Exactly. It seems like a very small niche. How many customers focus on both?"

"I see what you mean. You know, the people coming to the antique market this upcoming weekend will probably be looking for specific items, bargains, or they're open to options. How will Verity fit in? It seems more like she should be a vendor at a jewelry expo. Is she trying to run her own pyramid scheme without getting caught? I mean, that's the idea she pushed to Houston. Maybe all the moving around keeps her off the grid."

"That's an interesting theory." Jake pulled up next to the restaurant. "Be right back."

I was curious about the prices of Verity's products. I returned to her website. Whoa. Nothing was cheap. There were testimonials claiming the jewelry was well-made and beautiful. On the page highlighting health benefits, there were more testimonials. It amazed me that so many people were willing to give reviews. Unless they were fake. I searched for one of the men claiming the pros of buying Verity's jewelry who supposedly lived in Waco. Sure enough, I found someone with the same name living in Waco. Axel Roberts. I broadened my search to see if the man posted much on social media.

Bingo, there he was on a platform discussing sports. I found a way to reach out to Axel and sent him a message. I opened my sketch pad and made myself a note to check for a reply.

The driver's door opened, and my heart gave a slight lurch.

Jake handed me the brown paper bag and a pizza box. "Your place or mine?"

"Let's go back to my bungalow in case we want to review our notes on Houston's murder." On the short drive to my place, I told Jake about Axel Roberts and Verity's website. "The name of her business is Precious and True Stones."

"When she picks a theme, she sticks with it. True. Verity. Candor.

Anybody who uses that many words to make themselves sound trustworthy, must surely be hiding something." He parked in my driveway behind Ms. Daisy.

"Aren't you just so smart? That's a great point." Jake never ceased to impress me. I gave him a break and didn't discuss the murder investigation the rest of the night.

It was a nice surprise to find out besides wanting justice for all, we had other things in common. We enjoyed reading, watching action movies, and listening to country music from the nineties. He even left with a cozy mystery by an author he hadn't heard of.

After he departed, I texted Sophie. **Can we prepare something to take to Miranda Penn and her family tomorrow?**

Sophie sent a quick reply. **Yes. Meet me at the bakery. Early.**

Early for my best friend was like four o'clock in the morning. I'd set my alarm, but I made no promises.

Chapter Thirty-Two

I made it to Sophie's Bakery a little after four on Tuesday morning. Cowboy had been groggy, but I'd made him go outside to do his business in case it took me a long time to prepare food for Miranda's family. It was still dark, and there was a slight chill in the morning air. I tapped on the front glass door, and Sophie let me in.

"Good morning. I'm impressed you're here this early." She gave me a quick hug.

I lifted an insulated container. "I even brought hot tea sweetened with honey."

"Lovely. Let me get some mugs." She walked behind the counter and into the kitchen. "Would you like a piece of leftover butter kuchen?"

"Yes, please." It didn't matter to me if it was a day or two old; it'd still be delicious.

I poured the tea into white mugs, and Sophie placed slices of the kuchen on plates. We sat in her tiny office and ate.

Sophie finished first and wadded up her paper napkin. "What do you have in mind for Miranda's family?"

"Visitation is this afternoon. I thought about taking sandwiches to them for lunch, and they can even take whatever's left to the church to snack on if they get hungry later."

Sophie licked her fork. "I like that. We should include cookies."

"Of course." I took another sip of my tea.

Sophie went to a shelf and pulled a clean hairnet out of a box. "You'll need to wear this while you help prepare the food."

"And I'll wear gloves." I'd worked in the bakery with Sophie before, and I knew the rules. "I'll also help pay for the supplies."

"I appreciate it." Sophie's bakery had ups and downs like any other small business, and she was savvy enough to accept my offer.

I worked on preparing a variety of sandwiches, then wrapped and placed them in the refrigerator. Next, I made a batch of chocolate chip cookies while Sophie prepared morning pastries for her customers. I told her as much as I knew about Houston's murder, and while the cookies baked, I checked my messages.

"Oh, Axel Roberts replied to me." I read his response twice.

"Oh, the guy on the jewelry blog? What did he say?"

"You've been paying attention. Nice. Verity promised Axel the gold bracelet with amethyst would help him sleep better, which would, in turn, give him more energy. Oh, and there was a matching necklace to improve his chances."

"More sleep does translate into more energy." Sophie turned on the water and began washing the mixing bowls.

"Lavender might have been a better option, but oh well. He goes on to say, the bracelet and necklace he bought were not made in Texas like Verity had told him. He found markings to prove they were made in China. He has no problem with things being made in China, but he didn't appreciate being lied to. Then, the real kicker is the testimony she put on her website. He didn't give her a glowing review. In fact, he didn't give any kind of review. Axel believes that she stole his picture from another site. He attached his cell number and assured me he'd be glad to discuss the matter in more detail."

Sophie laughed. "It sounds like he went into quite a bit of detail already."

"Yeah. If there's more, it must really be good."

"Or bad. You need to tell the police."

"Speaking of police, I thought you and Matt might start dating." I found a clean towel and dried some of the bowls.

"We have a connection. Maybe call it a little zing when we're together, but he's married to his job. There's no room in his life for romance. You are lucky to have found Jake."

My heart leapt. "Our relationship is just beginning, and we mostly talk about murder. We'll see how it goes."

"I've seen how he looks at you. Don't push him away, Emma."

She made a very good point. Since my husband had died, I hadn't allowed myself to open my heart to a man. It didn't help that Bo had been a secret drug abuser. At least he'd kept it a secret from me. We'd been in the process of getting divorced when he died. The two best things to come from my relationship with Bo Justice were Abby and money from his life insurance policy to help pay for Abby's college.

"I hear you, and I'll try to do better." Meeting Jake had been a surprise. In the beginning, I'd thought he was a big flirt. Then I figured out it was to keep himself from getting involved in a romantic relationship. We'd learned to respect each other. While solving my first murder, Jake had been the person who helped me time after time. Jake was a man of integrity, and we'd become friends.

Somehow, our feelings grew deeper. I really did need to put more effort into our relationship if we were going to date. I needed to figure out how to accomplish that, while juggling my business, and solving Houston's murder.

Chapter Thirty-Three

Tara Thompson arrived at Sophie's Bakery to work, which allowed Sophie to go with me to take the food to Miranda's house.

The large tray of sandwiches wobbled in my arms as I rang the doorbell of the modest ranch house. "Thanks so much for coming with me. Miranda apologized yesterday, but having you here as a buffer will probably help."

"Buffer. I've been called a lot of things, but I don't remember 'buffer' being one." Her straight hair was pulled back in a ponytail, and she wore her blue work shirt, jeans, and an apron advertising the bakery.

"Sorry, but you know what I mean."

The door swooshed open. Miranda's head jerked back. "I didn't order anything."

I smiled. "This is from me, and Sophie helped. To be honest, I helped Sophie. She's the professional. It just seemed like you should have something easy to eat before the visitation. I've got sandwiches, chips, cookies, and veggie strips."

"Oh, thanks. Well, you should come in. I was going to order a pizza, but this will be so much better." She pointed to the kitchen, and I walked into the cramped space. On the counter were the flowers she'd ordered from me, lying scattered.

Sophie bumped into me. "Oh, would you like us to put this on your table or in the refrigerator?"

"The table. Houston's sons are visiting with Shelby, and those boys are always hungry."

Sophie laid her food containers on the table, then took the tray of sandwiches from me.

I didn't know where Leigh was, but it made me happy to know Miranda had opened her home to Seth and Ryan. "Would you like some help with the flowers?"

"Yes, please. I needed to save money and thought I could do it myself. It's not as easy as it looks. I probably should've used the florist."

"Next time, you can use Yarrow's Floral Shop. You've already got these, though, so let me help out. Just don't spread the word, because I'm a flower farmer. Not a florist. I'll do this as a favor, because we're friends."

"I understand. I watched a video online and bought the right supplies to make a standing spray from Shelby and me. It looked so easy on the video, but I can't make them look right." Her hands shook.

"Eat something, and I'll handle this."

"Thank you, Emma. I may have misjudged you."

"Don't worry about it. The past few days have been stressful. I'll work on this as quickly as possible so you can take it to the visitation."

"Thank you so much. Houston donated his body to science. I think it'll be used at a medical university, which means there'll be no casket or burial. I really want nice flowers for the memorial service and today's visitation." She turned to the food and filled her plate to overflowing.

Miranda's house was small but efficient and neat. There weren't a lot of knickknacks, but she had a few houseplants. Silver Pothos, an African violet, an aloe plant, and a foxglove plant were spread throughout the living areas. The aloe plant probably came in handy for a cook.

The attractive curtains at each window appeared to be homemade. The home reflected Miranda's practical personality.

As I worked on the flower arrangement, other people came into the small but comfortable house and filled plates. Sophie poured soft drinks into glasses and kept things moving along.

A shriek silenced everyone in the house. One of the aunts pulled Miranda into the kitchen. "I can't believe that boy is here. It's not appropriate."

I stood at the kitchen counter, and my hands stilled over the flowers.

Miranda shushed her. "He's paying his respects."

I was dying to get a look at the inappropriate boy. It couldn't be one of Houston's sons because they'd been here when I arrived.

The sister said, "He should pay his respects at the church. Not here."

Miranda threw up her hands. "Maybe he's scheduled to work later today. What if this is the only time he could come? He did work for Houston, and it makes sense to me for him to come here. Don't forget, this is my house."

"Sister, you better open your eyes to reality. He's here for Shelby's sake. The boy is smitten with her, but he's too old. You need to put a stop to their relationship before something bad happens."

My hands shook. Elijah. It couldn't be anyone else.

Miranda's face turned red. "That's foolish talk. Yes, he knows Shelby, but it's work-related. He's an up-and-coming photographer, and there's nothing to worry about. He's like a big brother who wants to protect her."

"No, he's bad news." The sister shook a finger at Miranda. "We must present a united front at the visitation, but Shelby needs to keep her distance from the photographer. It's our duty to protect her. Not his."

Miranda pressed her lips together and nodded. Not another word was uttered. The two left the kitchen, and I finished the flower arrangement.

It shocked me to see Miranda back down from her sister, but she'd been bullied by Houston for years. How could she appear so strong but let her family tell her what to do?

Sophie entered the kitchen with dirty paper plates. "Where's the garbage can?"

"There's a bag by the back door." I hung my arrangement on a metal easel, then stepped back. It would suffice. "Did Elijah hear Miranda's sister?"

"I'm not sure if he did, but Houston's sons heard. They went and stood on each side of Shelby. Elijah spoke to all three of them until Miranda appeared. She took Elijah by the arm and talked to him alone. That's when I came in here."

My heart skipped a beat. "You need to get back out there, so you can tell me what's happening."

"You are so bossy." Sophie smiled and walked back to the main room.

Before his death, I hadn't realized how big Houston's family was. I'd imagined Miranda was his only sibling, but relatives had come crawling out of the woodwork for his memorial service. Why hadn't they been part of their brother's life? Did they live far away from Lutz, or was it something personal? If he treated other family members like he had treated Miranda and Shelby, I had to wonder if they were grieving. Or were they relieved by his passing?

Houston and Miranda didn't always get along, but they worked together. It could make a difference in their relationship. What about the rest of the family? Did any of them have a motive for Houston's murder?

Chapter Thirty-Four

As the crowd in Miranda's house thinned, Sophie and I boxed up leftovers for the family to take to the visitation. They left in a flurry, and peace descended on the little house. Sophie and I remained, and we cleaned the kitchen. I made sure we were alone in Miranda's house by looking for signs of life. When I was confident all the visitors had left, I sighed.

"Are you snooping?" Sophie lifted an eyebrow.

"No, even I won't take advantage of a woman who has gone to her brother's visitation. She trusted me enough to leave the house, and I won't dishonor her. But what happened with Elijah?"

Sophie started the dishwasher. "Sorry, but there's nothing to report. Miranda and Elijah talked, she gave him a quick hug, and he left."

"Did he interact again with Shelby?"

"They made eye contact, and he waved to her on his way out." She removed her ponytail holder. "There was a chill in the room until he was good and gone."

I wiped down the kitchen counter. "He cares about her, and in my opinion, he plans to wait until she's old enough to date."

"You make it sound like a love song from the seventies. Is he on your list of suspects?" Sophie was a fan of American music. When she lived in Germany, she'd taken English, but she believed listening to our music had helped her American language skills to be more natural.

"Yeah, but I don't have a convincing motive for him. Houston paid him to photograph models, mostly Shelby."

"I think it was only Shelby. I never saw another model, and I watch ads from local businesses." Sophie leaned against the linoleum countertop.

"Why?"

"To get ideas on how to market the bakery better. I make notes on advertisements I like, and I even record what not to do." She crossed her arms. "To be a success, I need good products and good customer relationships. Those aren't my problems. Marketing is my challenge. I need to get strangers in the door." She reached for her water bottle and took a drink.

"You must be doing better if you can hire Tara Thompson and Katie Paxson."

"Katie mostly works special events or helps when I get big orders." She straightened. "But you're right. Business is better these days, and I need to get back to the bakery."

"Thanks for helping with this." I'd already paid Sophie for the food. She'd given it to me at cost, and I appreciated her generosity. "Are you going to the visitation?"

"Yes, and I also plan to attend the memorial service."

We locked the house and left. Soon, I was home, changing into appropriate clothes for the somber event. Cowboy enjoyed the backyard until I had to leave for the church.

My phone vibrated with a text message from Jake. **I got off work early. Do you want to go to the visitation together?**

It'd be so much easier to attend with Jake. **Yes.**

I'll pick you up in five.

A funeral visitation wasn't a date, but I double-checked my appearance. Jake appeared in his 4 Runner, and I met him in the driveway. "Thanks for the ride."

He opened the door for me. "Anytime."

It only took a few minutes to get to the church, park, and enter the sanctuary. There was no sign of Elijah, giving me hope there'd be no new drama this afternoon. Shelby stood between her mom and Houston's sons. We walked through the line of the family, conveying our condolences. Once again, I pondered all the individuals related to Houston. How had I never met most of them?

I studied the other people sitting and standing around in small groups. Leigh Turner wasn't in sight, but she'd remained in Lutz after the murder. "Jake, why do you think Leigh didn't leave town?"

He stopped and looked over his shoulder. "I'd say she stuck around to be a support system for her kids."

"I would've done the same thing in her position."

Jake pulled his phone out of the pocket of his black slacks. "It's Celia."

"Let's hurry outside so you can hear better." I did my best to match Jake's long-legged stride.

He pushed to door open and waited for me. "Celia, what's up?"

We stood under a shade tree, and I watched the locals come and go. Houston may not have gotten along with everyone, but the citizens of Lutz had come out to support the family. No doubt more would be attending the celebration of life.

Jake ended the call. "Celia got a job working at Paige's Turn Bookstore."

"But she's a librarian."

"Correction, she is a librarian in love with a barista in Lutz. She quit her job and is using her paid time off days to serve as her four-week notice."

"I'm surprised they allowed her to do that."

"Me, too. Celia says she shared some ideas with Paige on how to grow the business."

"Paige rented you the apartment to help her business survive. I hope Celia doesn't regret giving up a secure job by taking a chance on Paige."

"She won't. Celia wants to start story time for children of different ages. She also thinks having monthly events featuring published authors will bring in business. She has lots of fresh ideas."

"Good. The bookshop is so cute, and I hope it works out for both of them."

Jake nodded. "Me too. Anyway, Paige wants to drive to Waco to get more clothes. Plus, she wants to meet with a real estate agent to sell her condo. I don't like the idea of her driving back here alone tonight. Some of the roads go through farmland without much traffic. So, I'm going with her."

"There's a man in Waco who might shed some light on Verity. I need to learn more about Precious and True Stones jewelry and the owner. If he'll talk to me, I can drive Celia. Maybe we can squeeze in a short visit with Abby."

"I appreciate your offer, but that's a whole heap to squeeze into one day."

My face grew warm. "Oh, Jake. I just barged into your day. I'm so sorry. You go with your sister, and I can drive separately."

"No apology necessary. I'll get to spend lots of time with Celia now that she's moving to Lutz. I'll see what she thinks about you two going without me."

"I'll call Axel on the way, but if your sister doesn't want me to join you, I can drive on my own." It turned out to be a quick conversation. Axel quickly agreed to meet me at a local coffee shop when I got to town.

Jake had another brief conversation with his sister. He pulled into my driveway, and we looked at each other. "Celia wants me to come along just in case she has something heavy for me to carry. That's code for her, but she most definitely has something heavy for me to lift. So, it'll be the three of us."

"That sounds like fun, and I can get to know your sister better on the drive. Do you mind dropping me off at the coffee shop near campus for my meeting with Axel?"

"It's a public place and should be safe. How soon can you be ready to leave?"

"I need to take Cowboy out; oh dear, how long do you think we'll be gone?"

"We won't be back until late."

"Maybe Sophie can take care of Cowboy."

"If not, we'll ask Brett. Why don't I pick up Celia and swing back for you? It'll give you time to prepare."

"Sounds good." I hopped out of the SUV and hurried inside. Besides taking care of my puppy, there was something I needed to get for Axel.

Chapter Thirty-Five

Two hours later, Jake pulled into the coffee shop's parking lot. Sophie had agreed to take care of my puppy, joking it'd cure her desire for a dog of her own. If it wasn't for her crazy baker hours, she'd have a dog of her own.

I climbed out of the backseat. "Wish me luck."

Celia lowered her window. "It's going to take me a while to pack some things. Will you be okay?"

"Yes. Take your time. My daughter is going to meet me here later, so we'll visit until you return."

Jake said, "Be careful. Celia's place is only a couple of blocks away. Give me a shout if you run into trouble."

"Don't worry. I'll let you know." I waved and walked into the coffee shop. There were students studying, people talking, and others sitting alone.

Sitting at a table by a window was my baby girl. My heart leapt at the sight of her, and tears sprang to my eyes. Oh, how I'd missed Abby. I took a step in her direction, but she shook her head, like she used to do in middle school when she was afraid I'd embarrass her.

My phone vibrated with a text message. **Mom, don't act like you know me. I want to watch and make sure you're safe with the man you're meeting.**

I sent back a heart emoji.

"Are you Emma Justice?" A man wearing a T-shirt advertising a fitness gym, athletic shorts, and Asics stopped in front of me.

"Yes. Axle?"

"Yes. I don't have a lot of time, and you need to hear my story."

"Let me order you a drink."

"Thanks. The cold brew of the day works, and I'll grab a table for us. Inside or outside?"

"Inside." If Abby had gone to the trouble to spy on us, I wouldn't make it harder by going outside. I placed our orders and joined him at a table for two. My back was to Abby. "I appreciate you taking the time to meet with me. Do you mind if I take notes?"

"Go for it." Axel removed his horn-rimmed glasses and rubbed the bridge of his nose.

I opened my sketch pad and turned to the next clean page. "Tell me about your relationship with Verity Candor."

A barista appeared carrying an iced coffee and a hot green tea. "Emma?"

"Yes. I'm sorry I didn't hear you call my name."

"It happens." She placed the drinks on our table, and my focus returned to the man across from me. He was in good shape, nice looking, with green eyes and short dark hair.

Axel said, "I met Verity at a health and fitness Expo in Austin. She was hawking her jewelry, promising health benefits, and claiming Texas artists had created all the pieces. I already told you my bracelet was made in China, and that was only the first of many lies."

"Yes, you did. First, she fibbed about the origin of the bracelet and necklace. Did they help you sleep?"

"Not even a little bit. When I reached out to her and asked about a refund, she gave me tips for better sleep."

"So, no refund?"

"Nope. The jewelry was pricey. But I thought my purchase would help small local businesses, and I believed it'd help me sleep better. I misjudged the situation on multiple levels. I feel like a fool for believing her."

"You shouldn't feel that way. Plus, if we work together, maybe we can stop her from ripping off other people. Let's start with her testimonials. How do you think she got your picture?"

"I'm not on social media much. From what I can tell, she cropped it out of a post of me with an ex-girlfriend."

"That's rotten." I reached for my large teal bag. "I brought you something. It's fresh lavender, and it should help you sleep. Just put these stalks under your pillow or on your bedside table." I handed him stalks of lavender wrapped in tissue paper.

"Oh, thanks." He lay the gift in the middle of the table and took a drink of coffee.

"What else can you tell me?"

He shrugged. "Verity works out of her van, and she also sleeps in it. That part seems legit."

"I stopped by the Lutz Drive Up RV Campgrounds, but she wasn't around."

"You should try again. Somebody needs to stop her from scamming other innocent people."

"The Lutz Antique and Vintage Market begins Thursday, so I'll go back in the next few days." I reached for my tea. "To be clear, my main goal isn't to bring Verity down for the scam. I'm trying to solve a murder. Do you believe she could resort to murder if she became desperate?"

"Like, could she have committed it herself?" He crossed his arms and looked at the ceiling.

"Exactly." I held my breath, waiting for his answer.

"She's conniving. She's a schemer. Is she a cold-blooded killer?" He shrugged. "I don't rightly know, but if she did, she'd be sneaky."

"How's that?"

"I can't imagine she'd face the victim when she murdered him. Like she wouldn't shoot or stab Houston. She'd use a car bomb or use poison or something."

"Whoa, that's interesting. What else do I need to know before meeting her later this week?"

He reached into his backpack and pulled out a forest green accordion-style folder with an elastic band closure to keep the papers safe. "Here's the research I did on Verity. She's lived in Texas the last few years, but if she's a native Texan, she went by a different name. I don't see any proof that she's been married, which would allow for a different name. Some of the jewelry sold is made by people in our great state. It's like she gives you just enough to make you think she's legit. Know what I mean?"

"I can see how she'd mix jewelry from China with pieces from Texas. But what about health benefits?"

"Copper bracelets supposedly help with arthritis. So again, some pieces are helpful. Others are fake. The pieces I bought don't work." He glanced at his watch. "You've got my phone number if you have more questions later." He pointed at the folder. "Read that information. I believe you'll find it enlightening."

"Should I just copy the pages so you have a set in your possession too?"

"Already done, and it's secure. I mailed the only other copy to my attorney to open in case of my demise."

"Thanks for trusting me with this information." I clutched the expandable packet in my hands. He must be nervous, if he believed there was something so sensitive it'd get him killed. "I'll be extremely careful."

"If I didn't trust you, I wouldn't have given it to you. While I'm anxious, it's not worth dying over. If I could only get a good night of sleep, I might not be as uptight."

"Try the lavender and see if you don't notice a difference. If it helps, you can use fresh or dried stalks. You can buy essential lavender oil and rub it on the soles of your feet or your temples before bed. Some people find it helpful."

"It's worth a shot. Thanks for the coffee and the lavender. Good luck." He walked away with his backpack on his shoulder and carrying his drink.

As much as I wanted to deep-dive into his research, I wanted to visit with my daughter more. Any information Axle had given me could wait, but I'd keep alert to signs of danger.

Chapter Thirty-Six

Abby hugged me and then sat in the empty chair. "Mom, who was that guy? He looks kinda familiar."

"Axel Roberts." I sipped my hot tea. "I really don't know much about him."

"What did he give you? Sophie says you're working on another murder case." She frowned.

"Sophie has a big mouth, but it's true." My daughter and my best friend had ganged up on me at different times in the past for my own good. At least, that was what they always claimed, and they were probably right. "Paula Jones, you know the lady who works in the high school office?"

"Of course, I know Ms. Jones. What does she have to do with you putting yourself in danger?"

I squeezed my daughter's hand. "She's afraid the police will arrest her for the murder. Then there's also Brett Tirabassi from the coffee shop. They both asked for my help in solving the murder."

"Mom, I've only been gone for three months. Not three decades. I know these people."

"Right. Anyway, Brett and Paula have motives, and both are concerned they could be arrested." I told her just enough to satisfy her curiosity.

"Okay, but why you?"

"I'm honestly not sure they believe Chief Young can solve a murder case, which is crazy because—" Could he solve a murder? He was good and nice, but if I hadn't helped with Willow Moore's murder, would he have caught the killer?

"Because what?"

"It's silly. Matt wouldn't be police chief if he couldn't solve a murder. Let's talk about you. Are you feeling good about your exams?"

"Yeah, pretty good. I'll be happy to come home, though. Do you have a job for me?"

"Oh, boy. I sure do. Elijah Barnes has taken pictures, and I need you to use them on my website."

"I know Elijah. He's a little creepy. How'd you decide to use him for your photographer?"

"Creepy? Explain, please."

Abby leaned closer. "We used to joke about how it took him longer to take pictures of the girls' teams than it did the boys. Then there were events, and he'd be there taking pictures. He stuck to the shadows, snapping away. Oh yeah, he was always crunching ice."

"Isn't that part of what makes him so good at capturing candid shots? People are more relaxed and natural if they don't realize a photographer is around. Plus, there's nothing wrong with crunching ice."

She threw up her hands. "True about the ice, but Mom, you should be careful around him."

Sirens wailed in the distance.

My phone vibrated. "It's Jake. Do you have time for dinner with us? He mentioned a Greek restaurant."

"It sounds good. I'll drive, and we can meet them there."

The wailing sirens grew louder. I texted Jake, and we gathered our belongings.

A firetruck followed by an ambulance appeared and stopped at a nearby intersection. Police cars came from the opposite direction.

"Oh, no. I hope everyone is okay. I know CPR, do you think we should go over there?" I felt like I should help.

Abby studied the scene. "It looks like they have it under control. I don't want to gawk."

"You're right." We got in her car and left.

"The wreck will probably slow us down, so you might warn your new friend." She pulled onto the road. "Can you see anything?"

"There's only one vehicle, and it looks like they were T-boned on the driver's side. It's a little car."

"Ouch." Abby gripped the steering wheel. "Accidents like that make me want to drive Ms. Daisy instead of a car."

"We can trade this in on something bigger this summer."

A policewoman stopped our lane to allow a tow truck to pass by.

Two firemen helped the driver of the little economy car get out of the passenger side.

I gasped. "That's Axel Roberts. We should stop."

"No, ma'am. He's got plenty of help, and we'd only be in the way."

One fireman handed him the backpack he'd had with him earlier. "The least I can do is text him. Don't you find it odd that there's no sign of another vehicle?"

The policewoman waved for our lane to move.

Abby followed the traffic. "Hey, you're right. I don't see any other damaged cars."

I snatched my phone and took pictures as we drove past the accident.

"Mother, what are you doing?"

I laughed at her tone. "It can't hurt. We don't know for sure this was an accident. There could be evidence, a spectator, or a witness. If the police believe it's an accident, they might not look for clues."

Abby glanced at me. "Are you insinuating the man you just met with was intentionally T-boned?"

"Maybe."

"Why?"

My mind raced. Why indeed?

Chapter Thirty-Seven

I texted Axel but didn't get a reply before we met Jake and Celia at the Greek restaurant. We placed our orders and sat at a table in front of the restaurant. Abby was shaken about the accident. She downed her Dr. Pepper, then went for a refill.

Jake leaned toward me. "Is she okay?"

"I think so. At least she will be."

"It's easy to understand she's shook. She was watching you with a strange man. When the guy leaves, he's in a wreck. Notice I didn't say accident?"

"Hey, it occurred to me it might have been intentional, too."

Celia poked Jake's arm. "Shh. She's coming back."

High on the wall, in the corner of the restaurant, the local news came on. Abby returned to her seat with a full glass.

Celia pointed at the TV. "Look, there's a news crew at the accident you saw."

The reporter said that the police were looking for the driver of a minivan, and she gave the tag number.

Good. At least they considered the wreck to be worth an investigation.

Scenes of the crime were shown, then the station cut to the anchor, who promised updates as they became available.

Abby latched onto Jake's arm. "Can you talk my mom out of investigating Mr. Turner's murder? Did she tell you that man at the coffee shop gave her a folder of information before his wreck?"

Jake's gaze cut to mine. "Really?"

I nodded. "It's notes on Verity Candor and her jewelry business. I've got the file in my bag."

"See what I mean?" Abby's voice screeched. "Sorry, but this is freaking me out."

Jake patted Abby's hand, still clenching his arm. "I hear ya, but do you really believe the papers are connected to the wreck?"

"Maybe." She pulled her hand away and crossed her arms.

I said, "Very few people knew Axel and I were going to meet."

Abby glared at me. "Maybe someone was following him. Or you."

Jake whistled. "You are a lot like your mom. I guarantee nobody followed us. I've had experience watching for people tailing me, and I know what to look for."

I focused on Abby. "Why would anyone follow Axel?"

"You tell me, Mom. You're the amateur sleuth." Abby's face flushed. "Sorry for being rude."

I smiled. Sometimes, I scared myself, but I wouldn't admit the truth to my daughter. "Axel met me to share information about Verity. What if she found out and followed him? Suppose she saw him hand the information to me. It was in a folder, but what if she knew it contained evidence that could get her in trouble? Maybe it was the same folder of information she'd given him about the jewelry. So, she tried to kill him with her vehicle? Her big van is large enough to live in and carry her business supplies."

"The news said a minivan hit Axel. It probably wasn't a van big enough to live in." Abby placed both hands on the table. "What if the jewelry lady rented a minivan so she wouldn't be a suspect?"

I considered her words. "If that's what happened, it'd mean—"

"She's coming after you next."

Celia gasped. "Emma, I agree with Abby. Quit your investigation."

Jake grimaced. "Ladies, let's not get carried away. We're making a lot of wild assumptions. Abby, you need to relax. I'll help your mom and do my best to keep her safe."

Her nostrils flared. "You can't watch her day and night. Even if you two lived together, you wouldn't be able to constantly protect her."

My face grew warm. "Abby, that's enough. I won't take unnecessary risks, and I'm surrounded by good friends. I'll be okay."

A waitress approached our table with a tray of salads and gyros.

Jake said, "I think it's time to call a truce and eat."

I met my daughter's gaze, and she nodded. After hugging, we dug into our food and discussed food, flowers, and coffee.

Before the day ended, I planned to read through the paperwork Axel had given me. I'd even give him another call to check on his condition after the wreck.

"Mom, the reporter is back on."

We all turned to the TV.

The jaunty reporter, with black hair pulled into a ponytail, faced the camera with a serious expression. "This just in. The police have caught the driver of the hit-and-run incident that we reported on earlier. It was a woman trying to get to the hospital with her husband. She told police he was having a seizure, and she never saw the other car. She was aware she'd hit another vehicle but decided it was more important to get her husband to the hospital than to check on the other driver. Stay tuned for more updates as we receive them."

I patted Abby's shoulder. "That should make you feel better. Axel wasn't targeted. His wreck was an accident."

She nodded. "It does make me feel less anxious, but you still need to be careful."

"Okay." I agreed if for no other reason than I didn't enjoy getting lectured by my seventeen-year-old daughter.

Chapter Thirty-Eight

On the drive back to Lutz, Celia slept in the backseat. I used my ultralight LED flashlight and tried to read the paperwork.

Jake yawned. "I know it's not much farther, but I may need to stop for coffee."

I turned off the light and put the papers in my bag. "Why don't we talk about something? And I'd be happy to drive, if you're too tired. You've probably had a long day."

"It has been a long day. I enjoy working with Coop and flipping houses, but something you said a long time ago has stuck with me." He ran a hand over his face.

"What was it?"

"You said that sometimes a homeowner only needs a fix-it man."

"Right. Like when you helped me set up my security system last month, I imagine lots more people would install security systems if they had help."

"You're right. Take the Nelle sisters. They may have a few minor home repairs before moving to the retirement community. Who's going to help them?"

"Exactly. You'd be doing a service to the community and getting paid for it." I couldn't help but notice the circles under his eyes. "You can also set your own schedule, but can you make enough money to live on?"

He rubbed his chin. "Paige doesn't charge a whole lot for the apartment I'm renting. I've already paid for the first few months, because of her financial woes. Plus, I'm a saver. If the beginning months of starting a fix-it man business are lean, it'll be okay."

"We have that in common. I wouldn't have been able to start Emma's Flower Farm if I hadn't scrimped and saved." Not only had I saved money, but I'd learned every possible thing about growing flowers in Texas. The owner of the pharmacy where I'd worked had given me advice on starting a business. "Even Paige has gotten creative to make her bookstore survive by renting the upstairs apartment out to you."

"Yep. I'm willing to make sacrifices to succeed. I guess it's time to decide what I want to be when I grow up." He chuckled. "More than likely, working for the police department isn't going to happen. I can work for Coop a couple of days a week, then do my handyman gig the rest of the time."

"Oh, that sounds like a good plan." We breezed past a sign indicating we were close to Lutz. "Do you still need to stop?"

"Nah, I can make it from here." He rotated his shoulders while keeping one hand on the steering wheel.

"Jake, how far would you go to protect your business? I mean, after you start it?"

He glanced at me. "Why don't we turn the question on you? How far would you go to protect Emma's Flower Farm?"

"That's fair. We installed the security cameras around the house and the spike strips on the fence. Although, that was as much for my protection as it was to guard my flowers."

"What about when your yard was ransacked?"

Many flowers had been beyond saving. Some of the dahlias and zinnias had survived thanks to the work we'd done to save them. "If it hadn't been for the community—"

"Led by the Nelle sisters."

"True." I pictured their sweet faces. "I might have given up and gone back to work as a pharmacy tech."

He reached for my hand. "It was obvious to everyone that you were down in the dumps, but given time, I believe you would've rallied. Determination and survival are woven into your soul."

The warmth of his fingers around mine comforted me. "Survival, for sure. There's nothing I wouldn't do for my daughter. Er, in a good way. I didn't spoil her, and Abby didn't always have as much as her peers, but we got by. Take Ms. Daisy, for instance."

"Tell me about your truck." His tone was warm and happy.

"I'd been looking for a truck in good shape and dependable. This may sound silly, but I even prayed about it. One day, an older friend told me he needed to sell his truck. He was one of my customers at the pharmacy, and we had become friends. The moment he mentioned selling his truck, my body broke out in cold chills. He was the sweetest thing when his wife had cancer, and we bonded." I swallowed hard at the memories of his loving care for his spouse. "She died, and his daughter wanted him to move to Galveston. So, he agreed. When I told him I was interested, he gave me a great deal on the truck."

"Nice. Stories like that make me want to stay in Lutz. The people here are amazing. You know, I'm going to talk to the Nelles. If I can convince them to let me take on a project for free, maybe they'll spread the word to others about my new business."

"For our little town, that's a sound marketing plan." It was also nice of Jake to help the women who were on a limited income.

"Why'd you ask how far I'd go to protect my business? Is that something to consider when making a business plan?"

"No."

"Let me guess, you're back to Houston's murder."

I squeezed his warm hand for a moment, then I angled myself in the seat and faced him. "Houston had two businesses that I'm aware of. The restaurant seemed to be doing well. Good Life was struggling. How far did Houston go to protect Good Life? Was it related to his murder?"

"Maybe. What about Verity Candor? How exactly were she and Houston connected? Was he a threat to Precious and True Stones? If he was, how far would she go to protect her business?"

"Good question."

Celia sat up in the backseat and held her pillow in her lap. "Sorry about falling asleep. How close are we?"

"I'm almost to Emma's house."

I glanced back. "Where are you staying until you get your own place?"

"I'm going to live with Jake until I can find affordable housing."

Jake's apartment only had one bed. It was small, but Jake had said he didn't need much at the time he agreed to rent the place. "If it gets cramped there, you're welcome to stay with me."

"Thanks, Emma. I may take you up on your kind offer."

"Hey, now. There's nothing wrong with my place."

Celia laughed. "It's perfect for a single man, or a single woman. It'll be fun to see how it works for adult siblings."

"My offer can be your backup plan, if you need one." In business and in life, I'd learned it was good to have a contingency strategy for survival.

Survival. I grew serious. Someone had murdered Houston. It'd help me to zone in on the killer, if I could just figure out the motive.

Chapter Thirty-Nine

When I walked into my house, Cowboy was snoozing in his crate. Sophie had left a note detailing the evening with my dog. According to her, they'd had a lot of fun. I sent her a thank-you text, fixed a cup of chamomile tea, and set the security system.

The coziness of my airplane bungalow suited me. The large yard was the first thing that had attracted me when I bought the place years earlier. It hadn't taken long for the cute little house to become my home and refuge. In my upstairs bedroom, I settled in the comfortable blue chair and propped my feet on the matching ottoman. With my sketch pad, Axel's notes, and my tea cup on a little table beside me, it was time to get down to business. I opened the folder and began reading Axel's research.

At thirty-four years old, Verity Candor was older than I'd expected. She traveled the state in her van and appeared at antique fairs and other big events. It was interesting to note she even sold merchandise at local farmers markets all over Texas, and not just in Lutz.

She claimed some of the stones in her jewelry protected bodies by providing balance and power. In bold writing, Axel added 'sleep aids.'

I decided to text Axel one more time despite the late hour. **Are you okay?**

My attention drifted back to his notes. Verity had made some of the simple pieces of jewelry. The next page revealed research proving it didn't all come from Texas.

My phone rang, and Axel's name appeared. I swiped the screen. "How are you?"

"I've been better, but my car was totaled." Defeat sounded in his voice.

"I've gotta leave this area."

"The main thing is you're alive."

"Yeah, but did you hear the news?"

"The last thing I saw was the cops figured out it was a lady driving her husband to the hospital."

He groaned. "Call me paranoid, but I'm not sure the cops caught the correct driver."

"Why?"

"My head's a little fuzzy, but I could've sworn the driver of the van was a man. The woman interviewed on the late news did not look anything like I remembered the driver. I hope sharing my research with you doesn't put your life in danger. Be careful, Emma."

My hands shook. "I'm reading your file now. How is it possible this information put you in danger?"

"I'll tell you how." His tone grew agitated. "It's possible Verity is behind the accident that really wasn't an accident."

"Whoa. That would mean she hired someone to drive another vehicle and put you out of commission by causing a wreck." I couldn't even utter the word murder. "Is she that conniving?"

"I don't know. Maybe she's a cutthroat business owner. It's even conceivable she has investors, and they are coming after me."

I sighed. "Axel, it's also likely that today's event was an accident. What about the woman the police questioned? Was her van damaged? She said she didn't remember hitting you, but if her van was in a wreck, it seems like it must be her. Did the woman you saw on the news have manly features or short hair?"

"I wasn't wearing my glasses when the news came on, and the cops haven't shown me her photo. I suppose it's possible you're right."

"Until you see the woman's picture or watch the news with your glasses, it's best to be cautious. Do you have a safe place to stay until we can figure out what's going on?"

"I'm not going to tell you where I'm heading, but it's far, far away. Emma, you need to be careful. I sure hope giving you the file of information won't cause you harm."

"By the way, is the folder the exact same one Verity gave you?"

"Um, what are you getting at? It was some of her jewelry propaganda along with my research notes."

"Yeah, but if she'd been in the coffee shop today, would she have recognized the folder?"

"No. The papers I gave you are either extra pamphlets or copies. When she gave me information on her jewelry, it came in a thin manila folder with pictures of jewelry on it. That's with the information I mailed to my attorney."

"Is there any possibility you have a photo of Verity?"

There was a pause. "No, but she has dark hair. Kinda curly. Her height was probably average. The most distinguishing feature is her green eyes."

"What about moles or anything?"

"None that are visible. One of her arms is covered in tattoos, and the other doesn't have any." He yawned. "Sorry."

"I'll let you go. Thanks for talking to me. If you remember anything else, please let me know."

"Will do, but I may buy a burner phone."

"No problem. I answer almost all calls because of my business."

"Okay, but I'm serious that you need to be careful."

"You too, Axel." I disconnected and moved from the chair to my comfy bed. When I finished reading the case notes, I searched social media sites using my phone.

Verity's posts showed pictures of jewelry. There were none of her as an individual. Why? Was she concealing her identity? Was it possible Elijah had any good photos of Verity? Maybe he'd already posted some.

I switched to Lutz Farmers Market and hit paydirt. There was an image of a woman with dark wavy hair, holding up a necklace for a customer with an arm covered in tattoos. I saved the photo to my phone.

I went back to Verity's page and sent her a direct message asking if I could meet with her. I studied her posts. She made statements, indicating her jewelry potentially had positive health benefits. There were never any definitive promises made by her to customers. She was a sly one. Less chance of being sued if she didn't make a guarantee.

My phone flashed. There was a reply from Verity, asking if I could meet her at the empty farmers market parking lot at six the next morning. It seemed like a perfect opportunity to get myself attacked.

I texted Jake. **Would you like to meet with Verity and me at six tomorrow morning?**

My phone rang, and I smiled. "Is this a yes?"

"You realize it's after midnight?"

"Oops. Never mind, I can meet her by myself. If I disappear, you'll know who to question first."

Jake growled. "After all the promises I made your daughter, there's no way I'll let you go alone. Tell you the truth, I would want to go with you even if I hadn't promised Abby to watch your back. Where is this going to happen?"

"The farmers market."

"Oh, man." There was a rustling of covers. "Same place Houston was murdered. I'm glad you called. I'll pick you up, and I may have Brett stake it out from a distance, in case we run into trouble."

"Thanks, Jake." I set my alarm and placed my phone on the charging station. If Jake and Brett were going to be around, I'd leave my baseball bat at home. I turned out the light and slept fitfully.

Chapter Forty

At five-thirty Wednesday morning, the alarm on my phone startled me awake. My dry, scratchy eyes and weak muscles confirmed I hadn't gotten much sleep. Oh well, it was a good opportunity to question a person of interest. By the time Jake arrived at the house, I was presentable, and Cowboy had been cared for. I opened the door with a yawn. "Good morning."

"Morning, Sunshine." He handed me an insulated mug. "It's an elderflower latte we're experimenting with."

"Sounds interesting." I locked the door and held up my keys. "In case she knows what I drive, it seems like we should arrive in Ms. Daisy. If a strange vehicle pulls up, she might take off."

"All right then. We'll drive your truck."

I sipped the specialty drink. "This is good."

"Thanks."

It didn't take long to reach the large parking lot that converted into Lutz Farmers Market most Saturdays. I parked and looked around. "Should we get out?"

"Let's wait until we see either her or the van. After your new friend was T-boned, there's no good reason for us to stand around like easy targets."

"Good point." I tried to appear relaxed, but my heart raced. We sat sipping our drinks as if we weren't about to meet a potential murderer.

Headlights swept across the empty parking lot, and the van stopped near us. Verity exited the modified van. I placed my drink in the cup holder. "Wish me luck."

"Not so fast, Sunshine. You're not meeting her alone. I'm going with you."

We hopped out and joined Verity in front of my truck.

"Who's this? Your bodyguard?" The woman's green eyes sparkled. "Just kidding. I'm Verity Candor."

I stuck out my hand. "Emma Justice, and this is Jake Hunter."

If the eyes hadn't given her away, the tattooed arm was a good indication I was speaking to Verity. She shook my hand, then shifted her gaze to Jake.

"I'm her boyfriend. Nice to meet you." He winked at me.

My belly did a little flip. We had agreed to date but hadn't labeled it yet. To be fair, we weren't dating anyone else, so yeah, Jake was my boyfriend. "Thanks for meeting us."

"Why did you want to see me?" She wore an athletic tank top and super short shorts.

"Were you and Houston Turner friends, or maybe business partners?"

"I gave him some suggestions on running his health drink company. We had some fun together, but we were not partners." She wrapped her hair into a ponytail.

Jake said, "What kind of suggestions?"

Verity narrowed her eyes. "Why do you care?"

He spread his feet out and stuck his hands in the pockets of his faded jeans. "I'm considering opening my own business. Your tips might help."

"As long as you don't plan to sell jewelry, I don't mind giving a few suggestions." Her gaze bounced between Jake and me. "You're the flower lady who always gets one of the best spots at the farmers market."

I inhaled deeply. Getting defensive wouldn't be a smart move. "Yes, I'm a flower farmer. I think most vendors prefer the same spot every week so customers can easily find them. Mr. Johns had an opening and offered it to me. I just got lucky it's near the front."

"That's some good luck." She crossed her tattooed arm over the arm with no markings. "Why don't you give your boyfriend business tips?"

Jake said, "I need to hear from different successful business people, not just Emma. So, will you help a guy out?"

She shook her head. "I don't buy your story, and I sure didn't get up before the sun rose for this, whatever this is."

"Wait, we really would like to hear what you know about Houston's death."

"Why do you think I know anything? We were friends, nothing more."

"Yes, and I'm sorry for your loss. Did he share any fears or concerns? Like was somebody giving him a hard time?"

"Are you an undercover cop?"

Jake laughed. "Not by a long shot. In fact, the cops have asked Emma to stop butting into their investigation."

"Hmm. Well, if the cops are against you, Emma, then I'm on your side."

I didn't feel great about her motivation, but yay if it led to a clue. "Thanks. So, any thoughts?"

Verity uncrossed her arms and jogged in place. "I suggested to Houston that running Good Life as an MLM—"

"I'm sorry, but what's that?"

"A multilevel marketing company. If he could have gotten others to sell his product, he'd make more money. I also told him he needed to make it taste better. He confessed another man had helped him with the drink. Then you know what he did? He asked me to invest in his company, but I told him to ask me when it tasted better."

"That was gutsy. How'd he respond?"

"At first, he was angry, but he understood." She stopped jogging in place, propped one foot on the front bumper of my truck, and stretched.

"You're really limber."

Jake walked away from the woman who didn't hesitate to display her fit body.

"The turquoise bracelets I sell help my flexibility." She pointed to her wrist. Sure enough, there was a silver bracelet with dark turquoise stones.

I looked closer. "Do those things really work?"

"Yeah. I'm going to have a dealer booth at the vintage market this weekend. You should stop by, and I'll show you the turquoise jewelry. Everything I sell is beautiful, but there's also a purpose for each piece. Plus, I support Texas artisans." She looked me over, head to toe. "I guess you're approaching forty. It's not too late to invest in healthy jewelry. It can help with joint pain and flexibility."

I was only thirty-eight. Forty was two years away, but I'd play along. "I'll be sure to look for your booth."

"Great. Now, if you and your boyfriend are finished, I need to go for my morning run before traffic gets bad."

It wasn't even seven o'clock, and traffic was never too bad in our little town. Was there another reason for her hurry to leave? "Thanks for your time."

After Verity ran to the sidewalk, Jake joined me. "If those bracelets could make me that limber, I might become a believer."

I elbowed him in the ribs. "I'm still doubtful, but who knows? It could be legit."

"Aw now, don't get soft on me. We know she's lying about where the jewelry is made. The entire business could be a wicked scheme to part people from their money."

"Thanks for the reality check. What did we learn this morning?" I leaned my back against the truck and faced Jake.

"Let's suppose some of her comments were truthful. Verity and Houston were friends but not partners. They discussed business, and she wouldn't invest in Good Life until the taste improved."

I sighed. "Yep, and that gives Houston more of a motive to kill Verity than vice versa."

"Don't write Verity Candor off yet. My hunch is everything from her name to her business is phony. We just need to dig harder."

"Speaking of dig, I should get to work on my garden."

Jake glanced at his watch. "I'm working for Coop on a kitchen remodel this morning. This afternoon, I may visit the Nelles."

"It sounds like it's time for us to get busy. Thanks for coming with me, Jake."

"Anything for you, Sunshine." He tweaked my nose.

As much as I would have enjoyed hanging out with Jake this morning, I needed to pluck out weeds, transplant some baby plants to raised beds, and tend the herb garden. All the while, the clues to Houston's murder would steep in my mind.

Chapter Forty-One

By late morning, I'd finished working in my gardens. I refilled my insulated water bottle and let Cowboy in the house. He paused to lap up water from his bowl before getting comfortable in his crate. Cowboy always drank water when he came inside. Was that normal? I had a water bowl on the patio, and he drank from it, too.

Was my dog drinking a normal amount of water? Was he sick, or was the Texas heat the cause of his thirst? I made a note to ask Dr. Erb. The veterinarian would be able to answer my questions. Cowboy had a checkup scheduled for next week. Until then, I'd keep both water bowls full.

I wandered back outside to work on my business plan.

The land behind my fenced-in yard was untapped potential, at this point. It was part of my one-day-in-the-future expansion plan. I walked through the area with my sketch pad, pencil, and my insulated water bottle. Sweat poured down my back, and it was only April. I gulped the cold water before glancing around.

There were neglected strawberry plants waiting to be picked. With a little care, the peach trees could produce a bountiful crop. If I chose to sell either one of these products, it'd take time away from the flowers. The fruit shouldn't go to waste, though.

Whoa. Sophie could probably use the strawberries, and maybe Miranda could, too. Even though she specialized in barbecue, strawberry shortcake or fresh strawberry pie might make for nice desserts. I'd be willing to help pick the berries, but I couldn't do it by myself.

I'd studied hoop houses. They were a new way for urban farmers to grow flowers during the winter without building a big greenhouse. If Jake became a handyman for hire, I might ask for his help in either building a hoop house or a greenhouse.

Hoop houses would allow me to stay busy all year long, and it could help my flower farm's income flow. I sketched how I imagined four hoop houses would fit on the back of my property. It didn't seem too expensive to create the hoop houses. The fence would need to be adjusted to enclose this half-acre of yard, and that would be the expensive part. It might be good to do more research before proceeding because I needed to have a good return on investment before taking on an expansion.

Return on investment.

Had Houston made a profit on Good Life before he died? Did he pay Shelby for modeling? What was his return on investment for marketing the health drink?

Verity had been discussing the benefit of making his company a multilevel marketing business. Had he investigated the potential of MLMs?

What about Verity? Did she have others selling jewelry for her?

I moved to a shady spot and drank more water. How was Axel Roberts? Had his accident really been an accident? I sent him a quick text to inquire about his health. I wanted to make sure no symptoms had appeared later.

Houston may have been poisoned. The early afternoon heat convinced me it was a good time to research fast-acting poisons.

Maybe Cowboy really was just thirsty because of the heat. Next time we came outside, I'd add ice cubes to his water bowl.

After a cool shower and eating a sandwich for lunch, I settled into my office and opened my favorite search engine.

Cyanide topped the list of poisons. Not surprising. It was used in many of the mysteries I read, and it was popular in movies. Arsenic, atropine, and strychnine were also listed as popular poisons. Digoxin. Yeah, that was a prescription medication for the heart. I tried to remember who filled prescriptions for it at the pharmacy when I'd worked there as a tech. HIPPA laws wouldn't allow me to share the information, but I couldn't help what I knew.

Cowboy barked, and the doorbell rang.

I met the dog in the gathering room and rubbed his head. "You amaze me. How do you know people are here before the bell rings?"

The bell rang again, and I moved to answer it.

Paula Jones stood there, wringing her hands. Instead of her hair being neatly styled, it frizzed around her face. "Emma, let me in."

"Of course." I held the door wide, and she swooped inside.

Cowboy barked a greeting.

She gave him what appeared to be an absentminded pat, then collapsed on the couch. "Do you know where I've been? I'll tell you where. At the police station. This morning, Chief Young sent an officer over before I left for work. At least Officer Koch allowed me to call the school. He was always a good student. I left a message and told them I felt sick. It wasn't a lie, either. After I heard the chief wanted to discuss the murder with me, I felt sick. Literally. And I don't use that word lightly."

"Paula, take a breath. Do you need something to drink or eat?"

She nodded. "Is it too much trouble to ask for coffee? I think it'd comfort me."

Tea was my thing, but I did have a coffee maker. "Come back to the kitchen."

Cowboy walked at Paula's side. She said, "It's too much to ask you to fix me coffee. Water will be fine."

"Don't be silly. Have a seat." I pointed to the table and chairs in my breakfast room. "I've got cookies from Sophie's Bakery, or I can fix you an almond butter sandwich."

"Sophie's cookies sound divine."

It didn't take long to brew coffee, and I took a flowery mug of java to Paula along with a plate of chocolate chip cookies. After I gave her cream and sugar, I sat beside her at the harvest table. "Chief Young didn't arrest you. So, that's good news. Did you learn anything from him?"

"Are you kidding? I kept thinking I going to be arrested. Who would I hire for an attorney if they didn't let me go?" She added cream and a generous spoonful of sugar to her coffee, then stirred. "I know this isn't good for my diet, or my health in general, but I'm craving sugar."

"This isn't a normal day, and there's no judgment from me. Besides, I offered it to you." I took a cookie for myself and nibbled on it, giving Paula time to collect herself.

She downed two cookies and the first cup of coffee.

I took her mug and refilled it before sitting back down. "Did Chief Young say why they questioned you today? Is there more to it than your argument with Houston Saturday morning?"

"He quizzed me on my purchases of Good Life. They've found all of Houston's customers, which means they found me. Not that I was keeping it a secret. It was the reason we argued." Paula doctored her coffee again, same as before. "The chief also asked about my personal relationship with Houston. I told him that we'd only hung out together long enough for him to snooker me into buying his disgusting drink. The one date wasn't even a real date."

Uh, oh. "Were there questions along the line about jilted lover? Jealous ex-girlfriend? Anything like that to add to your motive?"

Her face reddened. "Well, yes. I wasn't jealous of anyone. Just mad."

"Mad about what?"

"That he tricked me by playing on my heartstrings. I blame myself for being the kind of dummy who'd fall for his sweet talk."

I patted Paula's hand. "Don't blame yourself. You've got a big heart and believe in people being honest. He took advantage of you."

"Do you think everyone in town knows the police are questioning me?"

"I really don't know, but you're innocent. Anyone who knows you won't believe you're a killer. What do you think about Elijah Barnes?" Abby's opinion about the young man concerned me.

"He's the photographer, and he's always friendly to me. The school ran a background check on him before they allowed him to take pictures of any of the school teams or other groups. If there'd been even one red flag, the principal wouldn't have let him come onto campus."

Her words made me feel better. "That's good to know."

Paula dunked a cookie in her coffee and took a bite. "Yum. These are so delicious. After this experience, I'm swearing off dating. You know my history with Nick Jones."

A shiver zipped up my spine. "Yeah."

"Chief Young does too. He even asked me how much I'd learned about pesticides and poisons while I was married to Nick."

"It makes sense." Did she suspect Matt's poison theory?

"It does?"

"Well, yeah. Nick's an exterminator. It'd be convenient if your ex-husband had a motive to murder Houston."

"Definitely. Two birds with one stone as far as getting them both out of my life."

My pulse leapt. "Don't say that again. Next thing you know, the cops will accuse you of killing Houston and framing Nick."

Paula's face grew splotchy. "Yikes. I didn't think about it that way. But as much time as the chief spent questioning me on the topic, I believe Houston was poisoned." Matt only had himself to blame for Paula's hunch. "Is there any chance Nick was jealous of your relationship with Houston? Could he be the killer?"

"Ha. There was nothing to be jealous of. Houston and I did not have a romantic relationship. If we had, Nick wouldn't have been jealous. He moved on years ago."

"I'm missing something." An elusive thought flitted around like a dragonfly. Back and forth. Up and down. What was vying for my attention? The thought hovered, then broke through. "The rumors about Nick. He may have poisoned his first wife."

Paula's mouth dropped open. "You're right. Do you think Chief Young knows how Rhonda Johns died?"

"I'm sure he knows." At least it seemed to be a well-known story circulating through town for years.

The momentary excitement in her expression fell flat. "Nick doesn't have a good motive."

"I reckon you're right. If there was no ax to grind, there'd be no motive for Nick to commit the murder. Shoot." It didn't look good for Paula. On

Saturday morning, she'd spent time with Houston. They argued. They were supposed to have been friends, and Paula could possibly have knowledge of poisons. "Do you know much about the chemicals Nick uses?"

Paula sipped her coffee and avoided eye contact. "I've never told this to anyone. Can you keep a secret?"

Gulp. "You can trust me. I never told anybody about your pregnancy."

"Right. I do trust you, Emma. There were very few people who knew I was pregnant. I couldn't risk Nick learning. He would've fought me for custody just for spite. He abused me, and there's no doubt in my mind that he would have been an abusive father." She pressed her hand against her mouth and closed her eyes for a moment. "I didn't answer your question. When we were married, I did read some of Nick's books on rodent killers."

"Why?" My pulse pounded in my temple.

"I was desperate to get away from him. It had reached the point where I thought it was kill or be killed."

My hope ebbed away. "You must have been desperate to resort to reading about rodent poisons."

"Yes, but it all worked out with nobody dying."

"Did you ever consider killing Houston?" I sure hoped this was a better answer than the previous reply.

"It was a totally different situation. I'm a strong woman now. Yes, I fell for his spiel, but I could walk away from Houston anytime."

"That makes a big difference. Don't tell anyone else what you just shared with me."

"This would be a really good time to take a vacation." She stood and headed for the front door.

"Wait. If you leave town now, it'll make you look more guilty. Stay here and hold your head high. You're innocent."

She gave me a long hug. "Of course. What would I do without you?"

I couldn't answer because, with the way things were looking, it'd be easy for the police to finger Paula as the killer. With her knowledge of pesticides and her history of hiding her daughter, it wasn't hard to see how the police could come up with enough circumstantial evidence to arrest Paula. Although, I might have been the only local person who knew about her daughter. That was about the only thing I could see in her favor at the moment.

Life would be easier on my friend, if I could solve the mystery of Houston's murder before she was arrested.

Chapter Forty-Two

Sophie picked me up for Houston Turner's funeral service. No, not a funeral, but a celebration of life, because he'd donated his body to science. It didn't take long to reach the church, and we found seats near the back of the sanctuary.

I'd never had a bad encounter with the Houston, but it could've been because I kept a polite distance. There were plenty of stories circulating around Lutz to realize there were two sides to the man.

Some people thought he was the salt of the earth. He'd been known to help people out when they faced hard times. I wondered about the timeline of his life. When he was younger, had Houston been kind and helpful? If so, what had changed him?

Leigh Turner, Houston's ex, and her sons walked in. Heads turned, and Leigh lifted her chin. She wore a black dress, black pumps, and a minimum of jewelry. I caught a glimpse of white in her fisted hand. It appeared to be a wadded tissue.

Ryan and Seth ushered their mother into a pew behind Shelby, Miranda, and Houston's other sisters. They sat on each side of Leigh like bodyguards. It couldn't be easy for Leigh to attend this service. She'd loved the man once, and he was the father of her children.

Shelby glanced back and squeezed her cousins' hands. There was a brief conversation, and then Leigh patted her niece's shoulder.

Sophie elbowed me and motioned for me to scoot over.

Jake smiled at me but sat beside Sophie.

My best friend whispered, "This is silly. You should sit by Jake."

"It's all good."

Country gospel music ended, and the pastor took his place at the podium.

I only heard about half of the short eulogy. Instead, my attention was fixated on the people attending the service. Family and friends filled the room. The Nelle sisters sat near some of the church's older adults. Nothing suspicious there.

Chief Matt Young and Officer Steve Koch sat opposite of us, and both faced forward.

Many of the local businesses had closed so the owners and employees could attend the funeral. For the love of daffodils. It was a celebration of life ceremony. Why couldn't I keep it straight? The sanctuary was packed, but I didn't see Verity Candor. She didn't seem like a person who put much thought into death, so I wasn't too surprised.

At the end of the service, the family filed out behind Miranda. They appeared stoic, and there were no blotchy faces. That is until Leigh walked out. Her nose was red, and mascara was smeared under her eyes.

We waited our turn to leave, and then Jake followed us to Sophie's Prius. "Are you ladies attending the burial?"

I shook my head. "No burial. Remember, he donated his body to science. I'm heading home."

"That's right. I'm not sure I ever knew anybody who donated their entire body to science, but it's a nice thing to do."

"This is true." Sophie shrugged. "I'll drop Emma off, then return to the bakery."

"Okay. I'm heading back to work as well. See y'all round." Jake winked at me.

My face grew warm. "Bye."

Once we were heading back to my place in Sophie's car, I glanced at her. "You're aware I have no idea how to be a good girlfriend. I don't know what to do or say. Maybe—"

"Shush. It's not as if you failed at a lot of relationships. Your husband died, then you focused on raising Abby. Plus, you started Emma's Flower Farm. This is a good time to focus on Jake. I've noticed most long-lasting relationships begin with the couple being good friends. Take your time, and enjoy the relationship." She pulled into my driveway.

"Hmm. I see your point." I opened the car door. "Whatcha doing tonight?"

"The mayor is hosting breakfast for a tour company tomorrow, and I'm in charge of baked goods. Brett is providing coffee, teas, and juices. The mayor hopes it'll boost tourism. So, I'm experimenting with a new recipe."

"Have fun, and thanks for the ride." It didn't take me long to head inside and change clothes. I'd promised Sophie and Brett I'd grow herbs, and this seemed like a good time to expand my offerings.

A couple hours later, I sat on the grass with my back against one of my raised garden beds. It was full of mignon dahlias. The airy flowers were colorful and would compliment most other flowers for bouquets or floral arrangements.

Cowboy nudged me.

"Hey there. Where's a weed when you need one?" Weeding helped me work off stress, and Paula had left me plenty stressed. "I guess I did too good of a job working out here this morning."

"Arf." His tail wagged.

"Let me check your water bowl." I rose and walked to the patio. Sure enough, the bowl was empty. I filled it with cool tap water, and my golden retriever lapped it up. I refilled it, and this time, he showed modest interest.

I dragged a patio chair to the shade and plopped down.

Paula had to be innocent even though she had motive.

I believed Elijah was innocent, but Abby didn't feel great about him. I'd only met him a few days ago, so it seemed as if I should trust her gut instinct. I gave her a call.

"Mom, are you okay?" She sounded breathless.

"Yeah, honey. I'm fine. Do you have a minute?"

"Sure. I'm finishing my run. When I get back to the dorm, I plan to clean up and meet a study group for my economics final. If I'm going to be a business major, I need to figure it out. What's up?"

"Tell me more about Elijah Barnes." Abby had taken extra classes and graduated early. If she hadn't been mature for her age, I wouldn't have let her go to college so soon.

"It's not like we're friends, but I've seen him around school. He's older, and we never had classes together. I know you said photographers stay in the background sometimes to get candid shots, but it seemed like Elijah was fixated on Houston Turner's niece."

"Shelby Penn. What do you think about her?"

"I always felt sorry for her. It seemed like her uncle worked her to death, but she never had much money. A lot of times, she'd ask friends for rides because her mom was working, and she couldn't afford to buy a car. Not even a clunker. Wouldn't you think Mr. Turner would've given her something to drive if he wanted her to work for him? Between the restaurant, modeling, tennis, and school, it's hard to imagine when she slept."

"Do you think she could've killed her uncle?"

"Physically? Not a chance."

"How about if he died from being poisoned?"

My daughter paused before answering. "She takes a lot of science classes, so she's smart enough to figure it out."

"But?"

"It'd be hard for me to imagine her doing it. Listen Mom, I'm back at the dorm. Can we talk later?"

"You answered all my questions. Good luck figuring out econ."

"Thanks. Be careful."

"You, too. I love you."

"Love you too, Mom." The call ended.

It was time to move. Get some answers. Or at least get one answer. I needed to make every day count in general, in business, in relationships, and in trying to solve the murder.

I focused on Elijah. Did he have an alibi for Saturday morning at the time Houston was murdered? Was it possible Elijah slipped poison into Houston's drink, or had he even somehow applied poison to his body? If Elijah committed the murder, what was his motive? Protect Shelby? Or was there bad blood between Elijah and Houston unrelated to Shelby?

Okay, I had more than one question. Alibi was the most pressing. Had

Elijah come into direct contact with Houston the morning he was murdered?

Chapter Forty-Three

The high school would've dismissed classes by the time I'd cleaned up, but there might be athletic activities taking place. I drove to the high school. Shelby was probably still with her family after the service, but my goal was to find Elijah.

I pulled onto the high school campus. Sure enough, there were cars parked near the baseball field and the tennis courts.

According to Abby, Elijah was more interested in taking photos of girls, so I walked to the tennis courts. My steps faltered at the sight of Shelby playing doubles on the second court. Her partner was a girl I recognized, but her name escaped me. On the far side of the bleachers, Miranda sat with Elijah.

Whoa. I had wrongly assumed they would have skipped the match. They must have come straight from the service.

Well, all right. If they could focus on tennis, I could resume my investigation. Maybe I'd get some answers.

I headed toward Miranda and Elijah but paused as Shelby prepared to serve. Tennis fans were quieter than volleyball crowds, and I didn't want to do the wrong thing. After the point, I bustled over to my target. I whispered, "How's she doing?"

Miranda did a double take. "They're ahead, but it's a close match. Why are you here, Emma?"

"Honestly, I'm surprised to see you here. Don't you need time to grieve with your family?"

"I've grieved enough. It's time to focus on Shelby's future. Houston worked us hard for his benefit. From now on, I want my daughter to live a more balanced life. School and sports will come before work. And if she doesn't want to work at BBQ Hut, that's fine. So, tell me why you're here." She drummed her fingers on the bleacher space between us.

Elijah stared at the tennis courts and ignored me.

"Um, I just miss Abby and thought it might be fun to see some of her friends play tennis." Shelby's double partner's name popped into my head. "Savannah Larkin is a friend of Abby's. Do she and Shelby always play doubles together?"

"Yes. They call themselves the S and S Doubles Team. Shelby and Savannah, get it?"

"Clever."

"Shh." Elijah glared at us, then turned his attention back to the match and chomped on ice from his insulated cup.

Shelby aced the other team, and the girls switched sides of the court.

"Sorry." I smiled. "Elijah, how are you doing?"

"I'm good." He avoided eye contact.

"Can I ask you a quick question about Saturday?"

His shoulders slumped. "Here we go again."

Miranda said, "I've got to get to the restaurant. Emma, is there any chance you can give Shelby a ride after the match?"

"Sure, but please make sure she knows you approved." I didn't mind one little bit, but why hadn't she asked another tennis parent? Didn't she know them well enough to ask? The volleyball parents were a tight group, and I could've asked any of them for a favor.

"Thanks. I'll make certain that she knows." With sure feet, she climbed down the bleachers and hollered to her daughter. "Mrs. Justice will give you a ride."

"Okay." She wiped her face with a towel, then jogged to her position on the other side of the court.

I scooted closer to Elijah but not too close. "So, did you interact with Houston on Saturday morning?"

"Yes. We spoke. It was more like he told me what he wanted me to do."

"And that was what?"

"Take pictures of the BBQ Hut food truck, and if I saw anyone drinking Good Life, he wanted me to take their pictures. It felt kinda eerie, knowing he might use the photos to advertise his drink. As in without their permission."

"You're right. That is a little creepy. Had he done that before?"

"Once that I'm aware of."

Interesting. Verity had used Axel's picture with a false narrative to promote her jewelry. Had the two collaborated on that method of advertising? "Do you have an alibi for the time of Houston's death?"

"It depends on what time he died."

Oh, he'd gotten me. "Let's go about this another way. Were you alone much that morning?"

Shelby and Savannah lost the game, and it was Savannah's turn to serve.

"Well, yeah. I was alone some of the time, but I was always out in the open. If you're going to get candid photos of people, you must be with the people. It's not like I was hiding. Somebody probably saw me, but I can't tell you who."

Good point about being around people. "How about Miranda and Shelby? Do you think they have alibis?"

"As far as I know, they were at the market to work. Ms. Penn was handling the food truck, while Shelby manned Houston's tent for Good Life."

"I don't suppose you noticed, if one of them stepped away for a period of time?"

"Not a long period of time, but I wasn't sitting around the food court, watching to see if Ms. Penn left. Neither was I spying on Shelby."

The crowd clapped and cheered as the home team girls won the game. The four teens went to the benches to hydrate before changing sides of the court. None of them had a Good Life bottle, and that wasn't really surprising.

"But one of them left? For a short period of time?"

"I saw Ms. Penn carry a drink, and I figured it was for Shelby or a customer. She put a sign on the service counter, saying she'd be back in five minutes."

I mulled over the information. Miranda had taken a drink to someone, and Elijah had noticed. More than once, Jake had brought a drink to me during the farmers market. There was nothing suspicious about Miranda delivering a drink to a friend or family member.

Shelby had worked the booth for Good Life. I couldn't let myself think too long about Shelby being the killer. Then there was Elijah. He didn't have a tight alibi, and he'd given me the information on Miranda. Was he a reliable source? Or was he trying to shift the focus from him to Houston's sister?

He stood and clapped. "They won."

I joined him in clapping for the doubles team. He didn't seem like a creep to me. No, he was a man in love and couldn't do anything about it. Yet. "Elijah, did Houston guess how you feel about Shelby?"

His face blanched. "I take pictures for a living. Yes, Shelby and I became friends. Nothing else."

"Your willingness to wait is admirable. Miranda and Shelby seem to care about you. When the time is right, I'm sure Miranda will approve of you dating her daughter."

"I've got to go." He avoided looking at me.

And just like that, Elijah took off with his insulated cup and my hopes of continuing the conversation.

I'd promised to give Shelby a ride home, and I sat back down to wait. I observed Shelby. Except for her hair being shorter than most of the high school girls, she appeared to be a normal teenager. Her dark hair grazed her shoulders, and the teen was beautiful enough to be a model, for more than her uncle. She talked to her friends, then came to sit with me.

"Thanks, Ms. Emma. I'm supposed to wait until all the matches are finished, but if you're in a hurry, Coach will understand."

"It's okay. I'm not in a hurry." It wasn't because I wanted to pump Shelby for answers, but I felt sorry for the girl.

"Great. I've missed so much tennis this spring, and it's fun to cheer for my friends."

We waited until all matches had been played before we made a move to leave.

Once we were in the truck, I looked at Shelby. "Where to?"

"My house, please. I need to shower before showing up to serve at the restaurant." She laughed. "Hopefully, they'll leave better tips if I don't smell sweaty."

I started in the direction of her house. "How will you get to work?"

"Probably walk, because Uncle Houston took away my phone, and I still don't know where it is. I don't have a car because my uncle promised to sell me one, but he just changed the terms of our deal last week. He wanted me to work six more months to pay it off."

That didn't sound fair. "How'd that make you feel?"

"I wasn't happy. It's a 2010 Camry and in good shape. I was so excited because we recently reached the number of hours he insisted needed to be worked. Trust me, I kept meticulous records, so he couldn't accuse me of miscalculating. Anyhow, he decided the car was worth more than he originally thought. Momma works so much, and I frequently have to catch rides with friends. It's much easier when I have a phone and can call or text."

"You don't hitchhike, do you?"

"Never. Momma would kill me. When I had a phone, it wasn't so terrible, but Uncle Houston confiscated it Saturday. We don't have a house phone, so there's no way to ask a friend to give me a lift."

"I can give you a ride. I'll even text my friends and ask them to meet me for dinner there."

"Oh, Ms. Emma, you just made my day. I'll hurry." She pulled a lanyard from her backpack.

"What's that pink thing?"

"It's a personal alarm. You just pull this thingy out, and an alarm blares and lights flash."

"I probably should get one of those for Abby."

"Definitely. They're not too expensive." She leapt out of the truck. "Why don't you come inside?"

Looking for a clue hadn't been my motive, but why not go in? "Thanks."

Soon, I sat on the couch and texted Jake. **Can you meet at BBQ Hut again? In a few minutes?**

I walked around the living room and studied family pictures hanging on the walls. Houston was in a few, and his sisters always stood on each side like one big happy family. If I ruled Miranda out, I might need to investigate the other sisters.

Leaves on Miranda's Silver Pothos plant drooped. I tapped the soil and found it dry, so I carried it to the kitchen sink and added water. I placed it out of direct sunlight and on a side table with good daylight.

My phone vibrated, and I looked at it. Jake's name appeared on my screen. **I'm coming with Brett and Celia.**

Yay. Maybe we could discuss Houston's murder.

"I'm ready, Ms. Emma. Thanks again."

"No problem."

After we were in the truck, it seemed like a good time to ask a question or two. "Shelby, where do you want to go to college?"

"Wherever I get the best scholarships is where I want to go. Hopefully, it won't be too far from Lutz."

"Abby is struggling in economics. Do you feel like the high school is preparing you well for the next step in your education?"

"I think so. Momma says people often change their career choice after they start college."

"She's right. What do you think you'd like to do for a career?"

"I had hoped to try to be a professional tennis player, but Uncle Houston crushed that dream." She slumped in the passenger seat.

"How?" I slowed the truck in hopes she'd continue to answer my questions.

"By modeling. It took up a lot of time, and he wanted me to promote Good Life on social media. He thought other teens would buy it if I promoted it." She shook her head. "My friends who did try it got mad because it tasted so bad. I paid all of them back. My best friends understood I was pressured to work for Uncle Houston."

"And the others?" I pulled into the restaurant's parking lot.

"You could say I learned who my real friends are."

"I'm sorry they are treating you like that."

"Thanks. So, tennis isn't a realistic plan. I think I'd like to be a nurse. That's why I'm taking as many science classes as I can."

I stopped by the door. "It sounds like a solid plan. You're smart, and you'll make a terrific nurse."

Her eyes lit up. "Thanks, and thanks again for the ride."

Chapter Forty-Four

While waiting for Jake and the others to arrive at BBQ Hut, Police Chief Matt Young appeared at my table. He pointed to the other side of the booth. "May I?"

"Sure. How's the investigation going?" I did my best to act normal.

He settled into the seat and then crossed his arms. "Despite my warning, it's come to my attention that you're nosing around. In fact, one of my officers spotted your truck at Miranda Penn's house earlier. They followed you and Shelby here, and that's when I decided to pay you a visit."

"Oh, Matt. First off, Miranda asked me to give Shelby a ride after tennis. I'm sorry to upset you." I didn't want to get Paula in more trouble by trying to solve the mystery. Matt knew we were friends. "I can't seem to keep myself completely out of your investigation. I mean, Lutz is a small town."

"I'm aware that people like to spill their guts to you." One side of his mouth quirked up. "You may as well tell me what you've learned."

"I feel like a garden wind spinner. One minute, it's like I'm close to the answer, and then something else seems more likely. There's really not much to tell you, at least nothing solid. Did you learn anything else about how Houston died? Was it poison for real?"

He scratched his head. "This isn't to be shared with everyone in town, but yes. Houston Turner was poisoned. It appears to be arsenic."

I met his gaze. This was probably not going to go well for Paula. "Arsenic is found in the soil, some pesticides, bad water in poor countries, and where else?"

He leaned forward and rested his arms on the wooden table. "The coroner reported some indications that it's more of a long-term poisoning."

"Why? And how?" That would surely rule out Paula.

"Houston's hands were calloused. Hair loss was also noted. These signs are consistent with long-term arsenic poisoning. The coroner will examine hair follicles and study Houston's corpse a little longer for clarification on the timeline."

"Nothing he drank Saturday morning was poisoned?" That meant Brett was off the hook.

"I'm not saying that."

My pulse accelerated. "Are you implying that he was poisoned two ways? Do you think two people tried to murder Houston?"

"Hold up. I'm not saying that either."

I stared at the police chief. "Okay. Let's review. There are signs of long-term poisoning. At first, we believed Houston had been poisoned on Saturday through his drinks or food. It seems as if you're trying to decide which method is correct."

"Or if both are correct. We're working on it, but please—"

I raised my hand to stop him. "Don't tell everyone. Got it. We need to find ways to poison Houston for a long time. I'll study arsenic more and try to find out how easily it's administered. For it to be long-term, Houston would need to be in contact with his killer on a daily basis."

"Or near daily."

"Arsenic doesn't have a taste, making it easy to hide in food or drinks." My brain whirred. "Have you looked at his house? Did he have coffee grounds that could've been tampered with? Flour? Sugar? I guess any food could have been laced with arsenic."

Matt wrote in his trusty little notebook. "Good idea. What else?"

"Shelby told me that Houston had taken away her cell phone. Any chance you've come across it?"

"We found a phone, but we haven't figured out the password. I thought Houston might have multiple phones." He tapped his pen on the table. "Although I should have been suspicious because the phone case is decorated with colorful hearts."

"I think Houston had a solid black protective phone case." I looked around the restaurant's dining room. "Shelby's working tonight. You can ask her what her phone looks like; then maybe she can get it back. I mean, you know, if it's her cell."

Matt stood and surveyed the restaurant. He waved at Shelby, who was handing out drinks to a large group. She signaled she'd soon come over.

Matt settled back into his seat. "Do you have any more leads?"

It'd been a long day, and nothing else came to mind. At least there weren't any solid clues worth sharing. I shook my head. "Helping with Willow Moore's murder may have been a fluke. It's doubtful I can do it again."

Shelby appeared. "Can I take your orders?"

Matt said, "I understand your phone is missing. It just so happens that we found a phone under Houston's body."

The teenager's head jerked back like she'd been punched.

"Shelby, are you okay?" Her paleness concerned me.

"Yes, ma'am." She placed the fingertips of her right hand on the table as if to steady herself. "What does the phone look like, Chief Young?"

"It has a purple background, er maybe it's blue. Whatever. There are also hears of different colors."

Her shoulders slumped. "Yes, sir. Mine is blue. It's kinda cute, and it's handy when I drop my phone."

"Would you mind telling me your security code? If it opens, I'd like to examine it."

I gasped. Shelby was a teenager. Was his request appropriate without a parent or attorney present? "Matt—"

"Stay out of this conversation, Emma."

Shelby's eyes darted from the police chief to me and back to Matt. "No disrespect, Chief Young, but, um, maybe I should ask my mother."

Matt frowned. "All right. You might mention to her that I can get a subpoena, if necessary."

"Yes, sir." Shelby darted to the kitchen and practically plowed down another server.

"Matt, you should be ashamed. You have teenagers."

"The difference is my kids aren't murder suspects."

Chapter Forty-Five

Matt's words had been like a punch in the gut. I'd been the one to mention Shelby's phone. When he had questioned her at the table, she probably thought I was the worst person in the world.

"Matt, I'm so disappointed in you." My heart hurt for Shelby. Even if she'd killed her uncle, she must have been beside herself. Desperate even.

"My job isn't to be everyone's friend. I am here to solve crimes."

A shadow fell over the table. Jake, Brett, and Celia appeared.

Jake slid in beside me. "What's going on?"

Matt motioned for the others to step aside. "If you'll excuse me, I have a potential suspect to question."

I snagged his wrist before he slid out. "Houston took her phone away as a control tactic. She's just a kid."

"Teens don't like to be disciplined. She wouldn't be the first teenager to commit murder." He glared at me before sliding out of the booth and walking away.

Jake took my cold hand in his while the other two settled in across from us. "What was that all about?"

I inhaled deeply, trying not to cry. "I don't need to tell y'all this is highly confidential."

Celia shot me a sympathetic smile. "You can trust us."

I began the story with the tennis match and chauffeuring Shelby around. "Her phone has been missing since Saturday, and there was an unidentified phone under Houston's body. I opened my big mouth and asked Matt if it could be Shelby's phone. Turns out it is. Matt asked for the password, and he wanted to examine her phone. Thank goodness she said she wanted to talk to her mom first. Of course, he can request a subpoena, but it just seemed wrong to witness him pressure Shelby."

Jake cleared his throat. "Especially if the girl's mother wasn't around."

Brett said, "Hold up. Shelby's heading our way."

Her face was still pale, but she stopped at our table and handed out menus. "Tonight's special is beef brisket, barbecue beans, slaw, Brunswick stew, and peach cobbler for dessert. May I take your drink orders?"

I was last to order. "Unsweet tea. Shelby, I'm so sorry about how Chief Young treated you. It was smart to tell him you needed to talk to your mom."

She pressed her lips together, nodded, and walked away.

Celia said, "That poor girl. Do you think she's guilty of murdering her uncle?"

"Let's hope not. He was a brute, but nobody should be murdered."

Jake squeezed my hand and then slid his menu to the middle of the table. "Do you know the exact cause of murder yet?"

"He was poisoned, but Brett, you may be in luck. They aren't sure if it's been going on for a while."

"Say what?"

"Long-term poisoning. That's when somebody slips the victim a little bit of poison each day. I'm sure you've seen true crime shows where this has happened. The victim doesn't understand why she's so sick. Doctors can't figure it out. She goes to the hospital and gets better because her husband isn't poisoning her while she's not at home."

Brett tilted his head. "Why do you keep talking like a woman was poisoned?"

"Oh, sorry. I'm just remembering the story of a woman in California who was poisoned by her husband. You get what I'm saying, though. Right?"

"Yeah." He leaned forward. "Then I should be in the clear. There's no way they can look at me. I rarely ever saw Houston. Well, except for the days right before he died."

I didn't want to give my friend false hope. "Not so fast. Matt plans to inspect Houston's house and see if poison was mixed with other food or coffee or tea or something."

"Meaning it's possible I'm behind the poisoning." Brett shook his head. "I can't seem to catch a break on this investigation."

Celia rubbed his back. "We're all on your side, and you're innocent. The truth will set you free."

"I hope you're right." Brett's gaze met Celia's brown eyes.

Brett and Celia were a beautiful couple. He was a blue-eyed African American, and she was a brown-eyed, brown hair, fair-complected woman.

Jake said, "We've been in worse situations than this. Keep the faith. You're gonna make it through this battle."

Shelby returned with our drinks, and her expression was pinched, like it would be easier to climb Guadalupe Peak than to smile. We all ordered the special, and she hustled away.

Jake inserted a straw into his Dr. Pepper. "What kind of poison?"

Before I could answer, our food appeared. Another teen passed around the plates and promised our server would soon check on us.

Jake said, "You were going to tell us about the poison."

"Arsenic." I studied my food and drink. There was no way to tell if you were being poisoned with a chemical that was odorless and tasteless until you developed symptoms. "It'd be good to know if the poisoning happened over time, or was it administered Saturday morning? Could the signs it occurred over time just be coincidental? For instance, callouses. Jake, you're probably getting callouses from working with Coop. It doesn't mean you've been poisoned with arsenic."

"True." Jake took a drink, then set his plastic glass on the table. "Let's consider another option. What if it happened both ways?"

"Matt suggested that possibility." I squeezed the slice of lemon into my tea.

Brett said, "I see where you're going. Someone was trying to slowly poison Houston and hoping authorities would think he died of natural causes. Then, on Saturday, either he pushed another person to the brink of committing murder, or the original person was forced to speed up the process."

Matt walked toward our table.

I kicked Brett under the table. "Shh, Matt's coming back."

The police chief pointed to our side of the booth, and we scooted closer to the wall so Matt could sit with us. "My ears have been burning. I'm not completely heartless, and I had a nice discussion with Miranda and Shelby. They gave me the passcode and agreed to let me examine the phone if I'd return it to Shelby at the earliest possible time."

Nice? I wondered if Shelby would agree. The teen didn't seem too happy, but I could be pleasant. "How can we help you, Matt?"

"I'm working the case, but if you hear anything you think is important, give me a holler."

Jake said, "Do you want to join us for supper?"

"Thanks, but I better shove off. I had planned to eat with my staff, but time's a-wasting if I'm gonna solve Houston's murder. Y'all have a good evening." He moseyed away.

Shelby appeared and refilled our glasses. Our attention shifted back to dinner. At least, we all pretended to focus on the food. Houston's mysterious death hovered over us.

Chapter Forty-Six

Jake rode home with me, and we took Cowboy for a walk. My golden retriever had already taken care of business in the yard, so we moved along at a pretty good clip up the sidewalk to the town square.

A group of ladies exited Yoga House, laughing. They walked past us and knocked me into Jake.

Cowboy barked.

"Sorry, Jake." I regained my footing.

"You can bump into me anytime." He rubbed my back.

"Did you see the Nelle sisters today?"

"Yes. They are planning to move soon. They told me all about the Village—"

"The Lutz Village Retirement Community."

"Yes. So, each lady will have their own individual apartment. The place has homes, apartments, and assisted living. Daniel Moore officially bought their place, and he may hire me to make a few minor renovations. Back to the sisters, they have changes they'd like me to make to their apartments."

"Let me guess." I paused while Cowboy sniffed a mailbox. "Ruby probably wants you to design her dream closet. She loves her clothes."

"Yeah. Good call. What else?"

"I don't know for sure, but I doubt they have a big budget."

"True. Those women are special to me. It's almost like I've got three grandmothers. I'm going to give them a discount on the items I order. I won't charge them for my work, though. But I will ask them to recommend me to their friends. Ms. Rosalita wants a nice bookshelf, and she'd like a sitting area for her Bible study ladies."

"What about Ms. Gaby?" I tugged on the leash, and we walked toward the B and B.

"She's quieter and didn't ask for much. I'm going to think up something special for her."

"That's so nice of you. I'm glad you'll be able to help them."

"Me, too."

"So, are you up to discussing the murder?"

"I figured we would. Do you believe Houston was poisoned both ways?"

"Maybe. It's too bad we can't explore Houston's house." I paused for Cowboy to sniff a speed limit sign. After a few sniffs, he began sniffing bushes.

Jake rocked back on his heels. "If you could get in there, what would you look for?"

"The poison or anything that might give us a clue to his killer. It's possible that there isn't a clue in his house. What if he saw his killer every day? And what if that person slowly slipped arsenic into his body? Who did he frequently see? Was it a love interest? Business partner? What about a family member? I never knew he had so many relatives until he died."

"There are quite a few opinionated women in his family tree."

I laughed. "You can say that again. Who had the most to gain by his death?"

Jake stuffed his hands into the pockets of his faded jeans. "Shelby Penn."

I sighed. "Yeah, I agree."

"Are you discussing my niece?" Leigh Turner interrupted our not-so-private conversation.

Cowboy lurched toward us, ignoring the bushes.

I gasped. "Oh, Leigh. I didn't see you coming."

Faith Meier walked beside Leigh. "Hi, guys. It's a nice evening for a walk."

Jake nodded. "Ladies. Good to see you."

I tightened my grip on Cowboy's leash. "Hi, Faith. Leigh, I'm friends with Miranda and Shelby. I also got along with Houston. His death has affected a lot of people, including Shelby."

"Faith told me you helped solve Willow Moore's murder. Are you two having a casual conversation, or are you trying to solve Houston's murder, too?" No beating around the bush for Leigh. Her eyebrows dipped in, but she didn't look mad. Maybe she preferred for us to catch the killer, so she'd be free of suspicion.

"Right now, it's a casual conversation. Who do you think killed your ex-husband?"

"Houston was ruthless and a cheat. He ripped off people in business deals, and I think it was someone like that. Although, he was also unfaithful in personal relationships."

My thoughts went to the man who created the formula for Good Life, Anthony Daniels. There was also Verity Candor to consider.

Faith said, "We need to move along. We're heading to Amalfi's for drinks and dinner. We don't want to be late for our reservation."

"Goodnight, y'all." I had questions for Faith, but they could wait. We headed in the opposite direction, with Cowboy walking close to my side. Once we were well out of earshot, I glanced at Jake. "It's a good thing we weren't saying anything worse."

He chuckled. "What's worse than saying we believe Shelby had the most to gain from Houston's death?"

"That's it. She had the most to gain, as far as we know. We've got to determine who had a stronger motive."

"To be fair, just because a suspect has a stronger motive, it doesn't mean they are the killer."

"Good point. It sounds like we need determine who our next suspect is." I gazed at the setting sun. The colossal pale blue sky was streaked with orange, reds, and yellows. "Let's try to deep dive into Verity Candor's background and life."

"Don't forget the scientist. I'd like to find the contract between him and Houston." He stuffed his hands in his pockets. "I haven't told you much about my past relationships. I think I told you about Susie Rawlings. We were engaged. When I was in Afghanistan, she took up with my best friend. No need to go into the gory details, but it's one thing to get dumped. Susie betrayed me, and that made it worse. I like to think I'm a level-headed guy, but what if I wasn't? If we run out of suspects, we should look at Houston's romantic relationships."

Poor Jake. "You're better off without Susie, and as sorry as I am about your situation, I'm so glad you're part of my life."

"Appreciate that, Sunshine."

We stopped at the corner to cross the street. It was a designated crosswalk, but trucks and vans didn't stop.

Jake put his hands on his hips. "This is ridiculous. Where is all the traffic coming from?"

"I bet they're vendors for the festival this weekend. Tomorrow is Thursday, and people can begin setting up their booths. It officially opens tomorrow night. Some will begin selling items in the afternoon, even if the vendors only sell to each other before the gates open."

A white conversion van stopped for us, and we crossed the street.

"Emma, you know who we're forgetting? Eddie Hayes."

"The cook Houston fired? But Miranda hired him back."

"It doesn't mean he didn't have a burr under his saddle when it came to his relationship with Houston. Anxiety and embarrassment may have surfaced when he got fired. I imagine Miranda didn't hire Eddie back until after the murder."

"Yeah, I bet you're right."

"I'm going to walk you home, then head to the restaurant to question Eddie."

"I can go with you."

Jake rubbed his jaw. "This is a time we should divvy up responsibilities. If it's not too late, I'll come back over so we can compare notes."

"You better come back, because I won't get a lick of sleep until I know what you find out."

"Deal."

After Jake dropped me off, Cowboy drank his water and settled into his crate.

My first job was to text Faith. I asked to arrange a meeting.

Her reply came through. **I can meet tomorrow. Any time after**

breakfast.

Great. Thanks. I'll be in touch.

With our get-together arranged, I needed to learn more about Shelby. If she had the most to gain, did she poison her uncle? She'd admitted she took science classes. Paula had told me that Shelby arranged for the school to provide an organic chemistry class. Was it because she wanted to become a nurse? Or had she been planning to poison her uncle? It'd be easier to poison him than shooting or stabbing the man. Plus, she was around him all the time.

Wait a second. Was I wrong? It might have been easy for her to poison him for years, but she was only seventeen. And she seemed so nice and excited about her future.

Shelby feared her uncle. She even allowed him to take her phone away when she worked at his Good Life booth at the farmers market. Most teens would've rebelled. Shelby was different. Had she been more afraid for her own safety or her mother's well-being? Either way, it was hard to imagine her coming up with enough gumption to poison her uncle over a long time period. Desperate times and all that, though.

Did somebody else have more to gain from Houston's death?

As far as the murder went, I knew the when, how, where, and with what. Saturday. Poison. Farmers market. Arsenic.

I just needed to determine who did it, and that was always the hardest part.

Chapter Forty-Seven

I fell asleep on the couch in my gathering room, making my to-do list. My phone woke me up, and I swiped the screen. "Hello." I yawned.

"Emma, it's Jake. Sorry if I woke you, but you said to tell you how my conversation went with Eddie Hayes."

"Yes. I'm glad you called." A glance at my watch showed it was almost midnight.

"You sound tired. Would you rather discuss it tomorrow?"

I reached for my notes and clicked my pen. "It's almost tomorrow, and I can't wait to hear what you learned."

"According to Eddie, Houston fired him for stealing beer and cash. Eddie admits they had an altercation, but he didn't steal anything, and he didn't kill Houston. He pointed the finger at Coop."

I gasped. "Your Coop? The man you flip houses with?"

"The same one. Do you remember Coop ran out to his truck to get his wallet to pay for dinner last Friday?"

"Of course." A vision of Jake's boss flashed through my mind. Coop was of average height and had wavy dark hair. The man usually had a smile for everyone.

"Houston accused him of trying to rip him off, and they allegedly had words. Again, this is according to Eddie. He believes Coop offed Houston."

"For being accused of not paying his bill? Surely, that's not a strong enough motive. What do you think?"

"No way on earth. Coop doesn't have a temper, but he won't be pushed around. If there was an altercation, it was in the heat of the moment. I don't believe Coop would commit a premeditated murder, and poisoning a person takes planning."

"And your thoughts about Eddie? Did he steal money and beer? Would his motive be revenge for getting fired? Or was he mad that Houston was going to stop his ability to get free beer and cash?"

"Slow down there, Sunshine. Eddie claims he's innocent of the theft. Also, he has an alibi for Saturday morning."

"Shoot." I twirled my ponytail. "Who, or what, is his alibi? Is it reliable?"

"There's a local farmer. Let me check my notes." He whistled a country tune. "Here it is. Blaze Davis. Eddie was cooking for Blaze's tent at the farmers market. Blaze doesn't have a food truck, but he sells meat for people to take home. So, he was giving out samples, and Eddie was grilling. There's nothing like the smell of meat on the grill to draw a crowd."

"Hunh. Makes it hard for a flower farmer to compete." I added this information to my notes. Blaze had high blood pressure and prediabetes, but I couldn't discuss it with Jake, because of HIPPA laws. Still, I knew it from my days working at the pharmacy. Blaze was a good guy and only a few years older than me. "Eddie's innocent. We don't believe Shelby murdered her uncle, even though she'll benefit from not living under his controlling ways. That leaves Leigh Turner, Miranda Penn, Elijah Barnes, and Paula Jones."

"Don't forget the jewelry lady, Verity Candor. I thought we weren't considering Paula. She's the one who asked you to solve the case." Jake's voice was rumbly, like he was tired.

"You're right. She did." I yawned.

"But?"

"Jake, is it possible that Paula did it? I mean, she was married to Nick Jones, and she admitted to reading some of his information on poisons."

"But she's your friend. Is a lack of sleep making you loopy?" His tone held amusement.

"Possibly, and you're right."

"Hold up. I'm not saying you're wrong. Let's discuss it tomorrow when we're more rested. What do you have planned for tomorrow regarding the murder?"

"Hmm. I'll work on the flowers early, then head over to the vintage market. Verity Candor will be there, and I might get lucky and find Miranda with her food truck. At some point, I want to talk to Faith. She agreed to meet with me. It was so awkward when we ran into her and Leigh Turner. I want to make sure we're good. What about you?"

"I'm working with Coop for a couple of hours; then I may draw up a design for Ms. Ruby's closet. She's a woman who knows what she wants, and I'll present the plan before I buy the shelving."

Cowboy exited his crate with a growl.

Goosebumps popped up on my arms.

Ruff. Ruff. His deep growl returned.

"Jake, something's spooking Cowboy. Let me call you back." I headed toward the secret pantry and reached for my baseball bat. I gripped it in one hand and shut the door.

Chapter Forty-Eight

"Emma, don't hang up. I'm heading your way." Jake's tone was urgent. I didn't want to waste time arguing, but something was outside. I needed to protect my property. "The problem is in the backyard. I'm turning on the floodlights."

Cowboy continued barking.

"Don't disconnect. I'm in my SUV. Two minutes out."

"Thanks." I flipped on the switches for all outdoor lighting and peered into the yard. "Shh, Cowboy. Hush now."

He didn't stop woofing.

I moved to him and stroked his side. "Quiet."

His ferocious barking ceased, but he whined. Despite being a puppy, his desire to protect me was strong.

"Good boy." I glanced outside and looked for a clue as to what had upset my golden retriever. A clay flowerpot wobbled, then crashed onto the patio.

Meow. A gray cat limped across the concrete.

"Oh, no. Stay here, Cowboy." He moved. "No. Stay."

The doorbell rang. "Emma, it's Jake."

I hurried to let him inside, but my dog beat me to the entry. I opened the door. "It's only a cat. At least, I think that's all it is. I'm sorry you wasted time coming here."

"No problem. I was driving back from talking to Eddie." He locked the door behind him. "We won't just assume it's a cat. There could also be a thug. Before I take off, let's confirm what's going on outside."

Jake must have been exhausted, but he wouldn't leave me if there was even the slightest possibility of danger. I appreciated him and his desire to protect people. I walked through the gathering room, past the dining table, and into the kitchen. I pointed out the back. Cowboy stuck close to my side, and Jake brought up the rear. I tapped the window. "See the flower pot? It fell over; then a cat crossed the patio."

"Can we put your dog in his crate? Then we can look for the cat."

"Let's hope I don't hurt his feelings. If it wasn't for Cowboy, I wouldn't know about the cat." I pulled his favorite treat from a box and held it in front of my golden retriever. "Go to your crate."

His tail wagged, and he entered with no resistance.

I tossed the dog bone treat to him and closed the door. "I guess he's not worried about the threat any longer."

"Can't say I blame him. He alerted you, I arrived, and now the pup can relax. His work is done. As for me, I won't leave until we're positive the yard is clear."

His words confirmed my belief in his hero qualities. I reached for my baseball bat and opened the door to the backyard. "The cat went this way."

Jake reached for my arm. "What's our goal? Rescue the cat or check for an intruder?"

My hand tightened on the bat. "Intruder is first priority, but once I saw the cat, it seemed like I was overreacting."

"Hmph. It wouldn't be the first time a creep entered your yard to do you harm."

A memory surfaced from the days when I was trying to solve Willow Moore's murder. "Of course. You're right. Should we circle the yard together?"

He pulled a heavy-duty flashlight from the pocket of his gray cargo shorts. "I'd be happy to lead."

"Considering I only have a bat, go for it."

Jake pushed the button on the light. Despite my flood lights shining on the yard, there were shadows and dark corners.

It didn't take long to assure ourselves that no killer lurked in the shadows, and we made our way back to the patio.

"Here, kitty, kitty." I looked in each direction. "The shed may be a good spot for the cat to hide."

"Don't suppose you have any cat food?"

"No, but I have almond milk."

His eyebrows shot up. "Might be better than nothing. We can set it out, and maybe the cat will come to it."

"Would you mind getting the milk? I'll inspect the shed area for the cat." I passed the Louisville Slugger to him.

"No problem." He entered the house.

"Here, kitty, kitty." What did I know about cats? Probably less than I knew about dogs. Cowboy had been in a back alley when I found him. Our local veterinarian encouraged me to adopt him. It was more like he shamed me into adopting Cowboy. I couldn't desert the poor puppy after I found out there was no family.

Was this cat feral? Or was he a stray? There were stories of people abandoning their animals near the train tracks, but none had ever made it to my place. At least I'd never noticed a stray cat. I probably wouldn't be aware of this cat if Cowboy hadn't barked.

Meow.

I stopped and tried to decide the exact direction of the sound. I circled around without spotting a cat.

Meow.

There. The mound of mulch. I tiptoed to it. Sure enough. In a beam from the floodlights, I saw the gray cat. It almost appeared to be a dusty blue. I knelt. "Hey, kitty. What's wrong?"

The animal met my gaze.

"I won't hurt you. Can you come here?" The cat appeared to wear a collar. "Did you lose your family? Come here, and let me help you."

Meow. She licked her paw.

I scootched closer. With Cowboy simple commands were best. He didn't respond as well to lengthy conversations. "Come."

The feline studied me. Seconds ticked by. The poor cat must have decided to trust me. She limped in my direction, favoring her front right paw. When she stopped, I slowly reached out and picked her up. "That's a good girl. Sorry if you're a boy." With slow movements, I returned to the patio, where Jake stood with a small bowl of milk.

"Impressive."

"I think her paw is injured, and I should contact Dr. Erb."

"It's after midnight." He held the dish toward me and the cat. "It looks like a Russian Blue Cat."

"Are you a cat person?"

He shrugged. "I'm an animal person. Do you have a travel crate for Cowboy? If you'd like me to take the cat off your hands, I'll take him to Doc tomorrow, er, later this morning."

"Thanks, Jake. I'm sure Cowboy will be more content without an injured cat in the house."

The Russian Blue leaned forward and lapped at the milk.

"This is one time it'd be nice to live in a big city; then we could easily buy her some real cat food. Nothing's open in Lutz at this hour."

"You're a small-town girl, and I mean that in the best possible way. You know and love the people of Lutz. So, how about it? I'll take the cat."

"You have to work."

"Coop will understand if I'm running late." He chuckled. "It won't be the first time."

The cat finished lapping the milk and curled back to me. "I don't think she's feral. She has a collar."

Jake stood closer and reached for the collar. "Most of the name has rubbed off. It could begin with the letter D. The area code is four-six-nine. Dallas. Not much to go on."

"Off the top of my head, I can't think who'd have a Dallas area code." If I couldn't find the cat's family, how did I imagine I could help solve another murder?

"A few of my buddies live in Dallas, but if they came to Lutz, they would've looked up Brett. Doubtful, this cat belongs to them. Maybe Doc can identify her. She might have an identifying chip or belong to one of Dr. Erb's clients. What do you say? I'll take her for now."

It was almost like I had more trouble than a farmer had oats, and Jake couldn't keep rescuing me. The cat had appeared on my property, and I had to deal with the animal. "Thanks, but at this rate, I'm going to be the neediest girlfriend in the big ole state of Texas."

"Not likely, plus I'm offering."

Good point. "Okay, thanks. The travel crate is in the garage near the flower refrigerator."

It didn't take long to load the cat, and Jake took off. I headed upstairs to my bedroom and fell asleep without even plugging my phone into the charger.

Chapter Forty-Nine

A few hours later, I deadheaded and weeded a row of zinnias. In the future, I'd like to create unique varieties, but I needed to focus on what I could grow now. Zinnias loved the Texas heat and were drought resistant. I'd already watered them with my drip irrigation system.

Because of the damage to my gardens a few weeks earlier, I hadn't registered to have a booth at the Lutz Antique and Vintage Market. Today was the first day of the event, and it would've been a boost to my profits. Hopefully, by the next big event, I'd be ready. For today, I planned to arrive and question Miranda and Verity.

No word from Jake about the stray cat, and I couldn't help but feel sorry for the critter.

My phone alarm sounded. I finished my task and put the supplies in the shed. Faith had contacted me earlier and requested we meet at a specific time. She was doing a favor for me, and I didn't refuse her timeline.

Where was my dog? "Cowboy, come."

The golden retriever bounded my way from the back of the yard with a happy bark.

"You need water, and it's time for me to clean up. I'm meeting Faith at Anytime Coffee House."

He gave a happy bark as if he understood me.

Less than an hour later, I entered the coffee shop. I'd driven, knowing I'd head to the antique market after this. My friend was seated at a table in the back, and I joined her. "Hey, thanks for meeting me. What would you like to drink? My treat."

She laughed. "I already ordered. Brett told me he knows your favorite drink. Green tea with honey."

"Exactly, and thanks." I sat across from her.

"What do you want to discuss?" Her neutral expression gave me the impression she wasn't angry.

"I felt awkward about last night when we ran into you and Leigh. We never meant to offend either one of you. It was a private conversation, and we shouldn't have discussed the murder on a public street." I placed my cold hands on the wooden table.

A young lady appeared with our drinks along with two breakfast cookies. She placed each drink in front of the right person and set the plate of cookies in the middle. "The cookies are on the house. They are lemon blueberry and came from Sophie's Bakery, so you know they're going to be good."

"Thanks." I placed a napkin in front of me and reached for the food. "Faith, if you're anything like me, you've been awake for hours and working."

"That's right. Usually, I eat a muffin real quick before feeding my guests." She took a sip of her coffee. "To be honest, you caught Leigh and me off guard last night. I try to be a good host to all my guests."

"I remember how good you were to Celia when she struggled over Willow's death."

"Thanks. Leigh is no exception. She is a strong woman, but she seems kinda lost. I've tried to treat her with kindness. It must be hard to lose your ex-husband to murder, especially when you are mad at him. No, more than mad. They were fighting over child support, but I'm sure you're aware of that."

"Yes, it seems to be a well-known fact in Lutz."

"Emma, I barely slept last night. Your conversation with Jake left me unsettled. Do you think Leigh murdered Houston?"

"She wouldn't be the first person to murder her ex, but for now, she's not a strong suspect." If Houston was gradually poisoned for a few weeks, it didn't seem like Leigh could be guilty.

"Why? I thought the spouse was always a primary suspect in murder investigations."

"I'm sorry, Faith. I can't reveal my reasons unless I want to make Chief Young mad. If he was Santa, I'd be on the naughty list. I'm not sure what all you and Leigh heard last night, but Jake and I were thinking about who had the most to gain from Houston's death. It seems like Shelby is the answer, given our limited knowledge."

"That's hard to imagine." Faith shook her head. "I'd hate for it to be a young girl with her whole life ahead of her."

"Me too." I bit into the cookie. Soft, juicy, and tasty. "These are good."

"I agree. Knowing Sophie, there are healthy elements to her breakfast cookies. I can bake muffins, but I don't have healthy options like this." She took another bite. "What are you doing next in your investigation?"

"When we finish here, I'm heading to the Lutz Antique and Vintage Market. I want to ask Miranda some questions."

Her eyes widened. "Can I go with you? Zig's studying for a test, and it'll be easier if I'm not hanging around."

"Sure, you can go with me." Zig had retired from acting, and I thought he just managed his money and helped around the bed-and-breakfast. "What's your hubby studying?"

Faith licked a finger. "He's bored. No, it's more than that. He doesn't feel like his life has purpose. Zig's smart in business and investments, but he wants to help others. So, he's taking online classes to get a degree in law. Then he plans to help people who need a good attorney but can't afford one."

"Super cool." I finished my tea and cookie. "Do you want to ride together?"

"May as well. Parking is probably a nightmare." She dabbed her mouth with the paper napkin. "I already left a tip, so we can boot, scoot, and boogie on out of here."

I laughed and agreed.

The event was on the outskirts of town. Under normal circumstances, it was a short drive, but heavy traffic made it a longer trip. Faith rode shotgun, and I drove Ms. Daisy to the event. "If you don't mind, I want to head to the food trailers first."

"Why don't we stick together?"

"Actually, I've got a mission for you." I explained about Verity Candor and her jewelry. "She knows me, but would you approach her as an unsuspecting customer?"

"Absolutely. I used to run lines with Zig when he was an actor. This time, I'll act. My role is customer looking for nice jewelry. I can act blonder than I pay to be." She pointed to her blond ponytail.

I laughed. "Okay. Text me when you finish, and be careful."

"You should be careful too. Miranda knows who you are."

We parted ways, and I considered what I'd say to Houston's sister. It was mid-morning and the perfect time to question Miranda without holding up her line.

My first questions would pertain to Eddie Hayes.

Chapter Fifty

"Hi, Miranda. Can you talk for a minute?" I gave her my best smile. The woman in the barbecue truck frowned and looked behind me.

"There's no line. If people show up, I'll stand to the side until you can talk."

"You ask more questions than the police." She heaved an exaggerated sigh. "What do you want to know, Emma?"

"Eddie Hayes has an alibi for Saturday morning, so he didn't murder your brother. He thinks Coop Henderson is guilty. What do you think?"

She drummed two fingers on her cheek. "Coop argued with my brother Friday night. It grew quite heated, and they caused a scene. One day this week, Coop came to me and apologized."

"Do you believe he might have murdered Houston?"

"Possibly, but I don't understand why he'd do it. Surely not because of skipping out on paying his bill."

"But Coop didn't skip out. He returned from the parking lot and paid his ticket."

"Believe me, Emma, I heard the story. Coop said that he accidentally left his wallet in the truck and only stepped out to get his money. He should've told his waitress his intentions."

Good point, but we'd had this conversation. "True, but he's a local customer. Was there some other conflict between Coop and Houston?"

Miranda shrugged. "Not that I know about. Customers are coming. Please, leave."

"Thanks, Miranda. You know I'm only trying to save Shelby."

She fisted her hands until her knuckles whitened. Her red fingernails probably dug into her palms. "Save Shelby? What are you talking about? Do the police think she did it?"

I raised my hands. "I don't know, but it seems like Shelby had the most to gain from Houston's death. Why wouldn't they investigate her background?"

"You should be ashamed of yourself, Emma." Miranda's nostrils flared. "She's innocent. My baby didn't murder her uncle. She has too much to live for. My girl is smart and has plans to attend college and make something of herself. There's more to my girl than being a waitress."

"There's nothing wrong with waitressing."

Her nostrils flared. "True, but you know what I mean."

"Don't get upset. I'm on your side, Miranda. I want to help Shelby."

"Sorry." Her hands relaxed. "It scares me to think about my daughter going to prison for a crime she didn't commit."

A man standing behind me cleared his throat.

"Sorry." I smiled at the man, then turned back to Miranda. "I'd feel the same way in your shoes. We can talk later."

Once again, I smiled at the man. "Sorry for taking so long."

"Not a problem." He moved up and ordered.

I found a map of the area and walked around.

My phone vibrated. It was a text from Jake, so I swiped to read it.

Cat is a male with a sprained paw. Confirmed he's a Russian Blue. Doc said he's yours if you want.

I tapped back a reply. **Ha. Ha. Would you ask Coop if he had any problems with Houston before last Friday night?**

His response was quick. **Sure. Sounds like you're a cat owner now.**

Oh, boy. Just what I didn't need. A cat and a puppy.

Faith appeared with her ponytail swinging. "Hey there. Wait until you hear what happened. We need to talk somewhere private."

"There aren't many people at the food court yet. We can buy drinks, and it'll look like we're visiting or waiting on our food."

"Let's do it." Faith's peppy step made it a challenge to match her pace.

I laughed and caught up. "This must be good."

We approached a truck featuring only drinks. I ordered a fruit smoothie, and Faith ordered lavender lemonade. We sat at a shady table, and I sipped the icy, cool drink. "What happened?"

"Verity was talking to an older lady, and I casually looked at a few of her bracelets. When I focused on the other woman, Verity was going on and on about how wearing her Texas-made jewelry would improve the lady's health. The woman had a cane, and Verity claimed she'd be able to walk without any assistance in no time. Well, I couldn't let that slide, and I interrupted the conversation."

The thought of Verity taking advantage of an older adult made me queasy. "What'd you say?"

"I didn't come right out and call her a liar, and I didn't warn the other lady to save her money."

"Well?" I couldn't wait to hear what mild-mannered Faith said.

"I told her the bracelet in my hand had a sticker saying it was made in China. That rattled her. I also asked if she had information on who ran the research showing what jewels helped what physical conditions. I mentioned coming back and buying some of her pieces if I could read over the research materials. I assured her that if she'd only give me the links, I'd pull up the information myself. Then I told her it didn't matter so much to me if the jewelry was made in China or Texas as long as it worked. She reiterated it was all made in our state. I asked again about the sticker on the copper bracelet. By the time we went back and forth a few times, the other lady had left." Faith snickered.

"Good for you."

"Thanks. It just made me so mad to think about the woman wasting money, and she probably doesn't have much money for splurges." Faith's smile dimmed. "There was a hole in her tennis shoes. You could tell they'd once been white, and now they're grayish. It broke my heart."

"That's sad. I'm glad you were there to protect the woman."

"Could be her name is antonym for her personality. Instead of being truthful, she's a big liar."

"Clever. I wonder if Verity could've murdered Houston."

"If you'd seen the fire shooting out of her eyes during our conversation, you'd think it was possible."

"It sounds like I should keep her on my list of suspects." My thoughts drifted to Axel Roberts. "There's a man I met in Waco. He claims Verity is a scam artist. Almost immediately after we talked, he was in a car wreck. The police said it was an accident, but I'm not convinced. The victim believes Verity is dangerous. The timing of his so-called accident is suspicious, and I believe it could've been intentional."

"Is the man alive?"

"Yes, but he's gone into hiding because he fears he's in danger. He gave me a file of information on Verity and her business. Jake believes someone followed Axel to our meeting, because he knows we weren't followed. His days in the Marines taught him how to spot a tail."

"Oh, poor guy." She stirred her straw in the lavender lemonade. "Jake's so nice. And he's very handsome. Are you two dating?"

"Yes. He's my boyfriend." I burst into giggles. "That probably sounds like a schoolgirl reply, but we're dating, and we're exclusive."

"Love should make you feel giddy at any age."

"Giddy. That's a good word." I couldn't stop smiling.

"Has he heard anything about a job from the police department?"

"No, and he's not sure Matt will hire him. There's some weird undercurrent between the men, and I don't understand it. For now, Jake's working construction with Coop Henderson. Jake and I discussed that there are a lot of people who need a dependable fix-it man. He's considering starting his own business."

"Tell him not to give up on investigations. When Zig passes the bar, he might need a private detective sometimes. At least lawyers do on television, but what do I know?"

I sipped my smoothie. "Perry Mason always calls Paul Drake or one of the younger guys later in life. At least in the TV series. Wouldn't it be cool if Zig became the local Perry Mason?"

"Definitely cool. I always thought Della Street was smart and beautiful. Maybe I could be Zig's assistant." She giggled. "Okay, that's enough silliness.

What's our next step?"

"How about walking around the event? I've got a map." I opened up the folded paper. "We can be on the lookout for clues. Also, we should keep an eye on Miranda and Verity."

"There's also an app you can download on your phone for this event."

"Whoa, we're definitely high-tech if there's an app." I searched and downloaded it. "Together or separate? How'd your conversation end with Verity?"

"She provided no research materials or links."

Ugh. I hoped their conversation hadn't put Verity on high alert. "Then we may as well stick together for safety's sake."

"Sounds good to me."

Chapter Fifty-One

Thursday. Was I making this day count? It'd been five days since Houston Turner's murder, but was I any closer to catching the killer?

Faith and I were walking back to my white truck. I didn't feel like my amateur investigation was advancing. Who murdered Houston? I turned to Faith. "Thanks for hanging out with me today."

She stopped and met my gaze with a smile. "It was fun, but I wish we could've learned more."

"Me, too. Is there any chance Zig has secret research tricks?"

"Um, not that I'm aware of. Why?"

"I guess it was wishful thinking to believe attorneys had special devices or programs to investigate people. I want to learn more about Anthony Daniels, the creator of Good Life. There's also a woman who caught my attention. Her name is Riley Bliss. She posted a lot of negative comments about the drink. She went so far as to claim that Good Life ruined her life. It makes me curious, and I'd like to learn more about her."

"Do you think she killed Houston?"

"It's a long shot, but possible. People have murdered for less. We probably only need to watch a few true-crime shows to discover lots of motives for murder." I paused. "I know nothing about Riley Bliss."

"I hate to bother Zig until after he takes his exams, but I may try to research her myself. I'll let you know if I learn anything." Faith gave me an encouraging smile.

"Great. I hate to ask this. Did we come to a decision about Leigh Turner?

Miranda thinks Leigh is behind Houston's death. What do you think?"

"It's a sad story." Faith's smile dimmed. "Leigh never stopped loving Houston, at least the man she fell in love with. Sometimes, she saw glimpses of the man she married, but he changed. She couldn't live with the mean, conniving version of her husband. He was cruel, and when they split, he didn't keep up with child support."

"I heard the child support was a percentage of his monthly income. How could she ever know if he was being fair?"

"I don't know, but he wasn't giving her anything for the boys. She didn't ask for alimony even though she could have, but she expected him to help with their sons. They deserved more than what she alone could provide."

"Kids can be expensive. I only have one child, and it was impossible to afford everything she wanted to do. I think Abby has learned to be selective about where to spend her money, but I could be wrong. It makes sense Leigh would want Houston to help with their sons' expenses."

"He disappointed her right up until the day he died. Leigh's life might've been easier if she'd hated him."

"You're right. That is a sad story. I'll never understand how a person can change so drastically."

"Greed." Faith shook her head. "I think there's a saying about greed stirring up strife. Houston was greedy and stirred the strife pot wherever he went."

"Strife pot? Very interesting." We finished walking to my truck in silence, and I drove Faith to her bed and breakfast before heading home.

Once in my bungalow, I kicked off my shoes and went to my dog. Cowboy greeted me with a slobbery kiss. "Hiya, boy. I don't suppose you'd like a cat around here, would ya?"

His tail wagged, giving me hope, but it was doubtful he even knew what a cat was. Oh well. I'd contact Dr. Erb after a while.

First, I checked social media for responses from Anthony Daniels and Riley Bliss. One thing was for sure, if I solved another murder, I needed to get better organized.

Anthony had replied. He admitted he created the original Good Life, and he gave me his cell number. There was no response from Riley Bliss.

I called Paula.

"Hey, Emma. Have you caught the killer?"

Not even close. "Well, I'm still working on it. I'd like you to try to contact a lady who claims Houston ruined her life with Good Life. I reached out to her on social media with no luck. Houston took advantage of both of you, so maybe she'll open up to you."

"Yes, I'll give it a try. What's her name?"

"Riley Bliss." I shared the information, and we ended the call.

Cowboy barked, and I stood. "Do you want to go outside? I'm getting better at delegating tasks on this case, so I have time to go outside with you."

We exited the house. It was a beautiful day for the vintage show to begin. The sun warmed my face, but I moved to the shade to prevent a burn. From the patio, I watched my golden retriever romp around the backyard. He'd learned to respect my flowers, and he loved the little paths between raised beds.

I relaxed in an Adirondack chair and called Anthony.

"This is Anthony. How can I help?"

"Hi, this is Emma Justice. Do you have time to discuss Good Life and Houston Turner?"

"Oh, yeah. I remember your message about Good Life. I'll be at an event the next few days, so maybe we can chat next week. Hold on." There were muffled voices. "Sorry about that. Say, you know what? I might be in your neck of the woods. Houston registered us for this fair in Lutz. Are you nearby?"

"The Lutz Antique and Vintage Market?" It couldn't be that easy to meet Anthony.

"Yeah, that's the one. Hold on a second." His voice muffled as he spoke to someone in the background. "Emma, you still there?"

"Yes. I was just at the antique and vintage market, but it's no trouble to come back if you have time to talk."

"Absolutely. Feel free to stop by, and we can chat between customers."

"Thanks, Anthony. See you soon." I swiped my phone and enjoyed watching Cowboy play.

Plenty of people took their pets to the sale, and I'd feel safer with Cowboy for support. He was usually well-behaved on our walks about town, and it should be doable.

His travel crate had gone with Jake and the cat, but I'd bought a dog car seat. I'd figure out how it worked and take my retriever with me. "Cowboy, let's go for a ride."

His ears perked up, and he ran to me. Fifteen minutes and a perspiration-soaked shirt later, I had the dog car seat positioned in back to safely take Cowboy with me to the antique market. I returned to the house, changed clothes, and grabbed my cowboy hat. Once my dog was safely harnessed in his seat, we took off to meet the inventor of Good Life.

It took even longer to get there this time. Along the way, I noticed crowds at the local restaurants, and there wasn't an empty parking space on the street. Yay for local business owners. This would be a boost to their earnings.

At last, I reached the event and parked. Instead of using my map, I opened the app on my phone. Finding the Good Life booth was easy, and I planned how to walk there without referring to my phone. Head up and alert to danger was my motto for this venture.

It was probably silly to be paranoid. There were lots of people shopping and milling around. But less than a week ago, Houston had died at the farmers market.

I hopped out of my truck and leashed Cowboy. Soon, we entered the market area and headed for Good Life and Anthony Daniels.

"What are you trying to pull?" A female voice hissed in my ear, and a hand squeezed my arm.

A cold shiver shot up my spine, and my knees wobbled.

Cowboy barked.

I turned and faced an angry Verity Candor. Her furrowed brows and tense jaw alarmed me.

Yikes.

Chapter Fifty-Two

People scooted around Verity and me, but nobody stopped to see if I was okay. Except for Cowboy. My very special best friend.

Grr. Ruff. Ruff.

I didn't tell him to stop, because I was nervous. Maybe more than nervous. Terrified was more like it.

"Shut your dog up." Her fingernails dug into my skin.

"No way. Let go of me, Verity." I tried to wiggle free from her grasp.

Her grip lessened, but she didn't release my arm. "We need to talk."

"What about?" My voice squeaked.

"Your lies."

I yanked my arm free and stepped back. "I haven't lied about anything."

Cowboy lunged. I skidded, but maintained my grip on his leash. Cowboy continued to growl.

Camera-in-hand, Elijah Barnes appeared. "Hi, Emma. What's wrong with your dog?"

"Elijah, it's so good to see you." I wanted to throw my arms around him and burst into tears of relief. Instead, I knelt beside my retriever and rubbed his sides. "Good boy. It's okay now."

"Oh, hey, Verity. I'm scheduled to take photos of your booth this afternoon. Houston already paid me. Are you cool with that?" Elijah's tone was casual, but his brow was marred with confusion, and he rubbed his forehead. "I mean, it's free publicity, you know, if you want it."

"Houston paid you ahead of time? That doesn't sound right."

"It's my new policy. I got stiffed a couple of times and decided not to take photos without getting paid upfront." He shrugged. "Houston knew I wasn't stupid enough to cross him. I've seen him in action, and he usually won a confrontation. Correction, I never saw him lose when there was an argument."

Verity took a deep breath. With her attention on Elijah, she appeared calmer. "Where will the pictures appear?"

"On social media for the event. At least that was the plan before, uh, you know."

Verity crossed her arms. "Oh, yes, we all know what you mean. What a tragedy."

I stood and gave a gentle tug on Cowboy's leash. "If you two will excuse me, I'm meeting someone. Don't want to be late. Good to see you, Elijah."

"See you around." Elijah gave me a lopsided smile.

I took off before hearing what Verity had to say. The Good Life booth was supposed to be set up in the back white tent. I hoped, like everything, that I'd get to meet the scientist who created the drink.

Fans whirled air around without being too strong to blow items off display tables. My steps slowed when I spotted a tan, older man with muscles to rival TV bodybuilders. His black hair was slicked back, and he was speaking to a woman in the booth beside him. From the looks of her table, she was selling healthy cookbooks. There was also a white shelf behind her with cookbooks, potted plants, and a few well-placed colorful dishes. Could the beautiful woman possibly be Mrs. Anthony Daniels?

Man, what I wouldn't give for her thick dark hair, full eyebrows, sparkling brown eyes, and trim physique. Red hair, fair complexion, and freckles weren't much to get excited about. I wasn't ugly, but I wasn't stunning like the woman with the cookbooks.

I approached and waited until someone noticed me.

The woman turned my way. "Hi, I'm Star Daniels. Are you interested in healthy cooking?"

"I cook enough to survive, but thanks for asking. I'm here to meet Anthony Daniels."

Star pointed to the man. "Right here."

We fumbled through the introductions.

Anthony said, "I'm not sure what I can tell you, Ms. Justice."

"Please, just call me Emma." I knew he was more than twenty years older than me, and there was no need to be formal. "A friend of mine has been questioned by the police related to Houston's death. She asked me to help prove she was innocent. Since you two were business partners, can you think of who might be inclined to murder Houston?"

He crossed his bulging arms. "You probably heard we had an argument the day before his death. Houston was complaining about the taste of Good Life. When we went into business together, he was in a sure-fire hurry to start selling the drink. The recipe we're selling could be improved. I told him that we needed to make a couple tweaks to the formula."

"Let me guess. One of the tweaks was the taste."

"Exactly. The interesting fact is I asked Houston to give me more time. I didn't want to use artificial sweeteners or flavoring because we're marketing it as a health drink. Let me rephrase that. We were marketing it as a health drink." Anthony's demeanor didn't match the T-shirt advertising Good Life and his fitness shorts. He'd be more believable to me if he wore a white lab jacket, but I probably watched too much television.

I debated if his tan was real or not. "What kind of a scientist are you, Anthony?"

"I work for an agriculture company." He mentioned the name, and I recognized it. "Development and research. I've worked in that department for years."

"Do they care that you created Good Life and are selling it?"

"Nah. It's not a health drink for animals. I've always been interested in improving my health, even when I was a teen and in college. When I signed a contract to work for the agriculture company, we agreed that I could sell anything I created for humans. Of course, I couldn't research my products while I was at work. So, I converted a room in my house for my own personal lab."

"It sounds like you were smart to think ahead. How was it to work with Houston? Did y'all get along?"

"Mostly. My life philosophy is everything is better, if we can all get along. If things, as in the business and Good Life, went Houston's way, he could be downright congenial. If there was a glitch, you better watch out. I was usually the target of his anger."

"Oh, I'm sorry. That must've been tough."

"Some days were better than others." He shrugged, and a vein in his neck bulged.

"So y'all fought the day before he died."

"Fight might be a strong word."

I moved out of the way of a lady pushing a stroller with twins, and to my surprise, a little boy rode on a platform in back. I smiled at her and ignored the twinge of my biological clock. At thirty-eight years old and with one daughter in college, I wasn't in a good position to even consider having a baby.

Anthony cleared his throat.

"Oh, sorry. They sure were cute." I met his gaze. "Do you have other business partners?"

"No, but some jewelry lady kept giving Houston ideas for different business models. I created the drink. Houston marketed it too soon. No one was more surprised than me when Good Life started being sold. I went along with Houston, though, and helped promote our drink at events. Normally, I get along with people." Warmth shone from his eyes.

"I believe you."

A middle-aged couple walked up to the table and asked about Good Life. Anthony was articulate and nice. He listened to their concerns and answered their questions.

I stood to the side with Cowboy. He was so well-behaved, and I gave him a treat.

After a few minutes, the couple bought two bottles of Good Life and walked to another booth.

I rejoined Anthony. "What else can you tell me?"

"Let's go back to the jewelry lady."

"Absolutely. If it's the person I'm thinking about, her name is Verity

Candor."

He clapped his hands together. "That's exactly right. So, Verity told Houston how we could make more money. Houston listened to her, then told me to change the taste. That's when I started losing my cool. I had told him from the very beginning that we needed to tweak the flavor. I couldn't believe he listened to a stranger over me, his business partner."

"How did he respond to your concerns?"

"You know Houston. He was in denial, and the tension was killing me. Instead of continuing to argue, I told him it'd take some time to improve the taste. Then he died. That's about all I know."

The dark-haired lady touched Anthony's shoulders. "Darling, you're forgetting something, or should I say someone?"

He grimaced. "You're right. Star, this is Emma Justice."

"Nice to officially meet you." I reached out and shook her hand.

Cowboy's tail wagged, giving me confidence. Unlike being in Verity's presence, I was safe with these people.

"You, too. Anthony is a genius, but once in a while, he's forgetful. He and Houston received messages—"

"Threatening messages."

Star gave her husband an adoring smile before turning her gaze back to me. "Yes. There were some people who claimed the drink wasn't improving their health. They also complained that Houston talked them into becoming representatives of Good Life, with a money-back guarantee on their investment if they couldn't sell the product. Anthony felt terrible, but Houston told him not to worry. He knew how to handle the situation. For a while, it got better. But a few people persisted in their complaints."

My blood pressure leapt. "Is there any chance one of these people was Riley Bliss?"

Star's mouth fell open. "How'd you know?"

"I saw her posts on social media claiming Good Life ruined her life."

A young couple approached Anthony's table and picked up a bottle of Good Life.

Anthony said, "I need to help them."

Star motioned for me to follow her behind the display table with a blue tablecloth. Cowboy lay by my feet, and I looked at Star's pretty cookbooks. They were colorful and displayed in an attractive manner. Star said, "Have you spoken to Riley?"

"No. She didn't reply to my attempt to reach out."

"She's very angry, and we don't blame her. Anthony dealt with the science and recipe, while Houston handled the business end of Good Life. My husband is a peaceful man, and his goal has always been to help people improve their health. We don't know how many people Houston misled, but it's heartbreaking to hear about some individuals who invested everything in Good Life."

"Have you heard your husband talk about Verity Candor?"

"Yeah, yeah, yeah." She nodded and pressed her lips together. "That's the jewelry woman. She drives around Texas in a van and goes from one festival to another. She's very pretty and sells jewelry made by Texans."

"She's here, and she threatened me a few minutes ago."

"Oh, no. That's dreadful. Are you all right?"

"Yes. Thankfully, a photographer showed up and started talking to us. While Verity was distracted, I slipped away with Cowboy. Please be careful until the police arrest Houston's killer."

"Sure, and you be careful too."

"What are we being careful about." Anthony's deep voice soothed my nerves.

"Verity Candor." Despite the age difference, I could see why Star was drawn to her husband. The man was smart, kind, handsome, and appeared to love his wife. "What happens to Good Life now?"

"The attorneys will handle the legal matters, but I intend to return to the lab and tweak the recipe. The drink is chock full of antioxidants, vitamins, and other good stuff. People will only tolerate the taste if they see visible results. It wasn't intended to be a diet tool, and that seems to be where so much animosity has been generated. I blame Houston for those foolish promises."

Star touched her husband's arm. "Honey, don't forget people lost money in Houston's pyramid scheme."

He nodded. "You're exactly right."

So many questions raced through my mind. I looked around to make sure there was no sign of Verity. "If the jewelry lady tried to convince Houston to run a pyramid because it's been successful for her, then what she's doing isn't legal."

"I have to agree with you." The muscular man knelt beside Cowboy and ran a hand over his head. "Aren't you a good boy? I've been part of creating dog food and treats. Believe me, they taste better than Good Life."

Cowboy wagged his tail.

"You're good with him. If you're interested in a cat I recently rescued, let me know."

Star shook her head. "Sadly, I'm allergic to cats and most dogs."

"That's too bad. I'm not sure how Cowboy will adjust if I decide to keep the cat, but that's not your problem. Do you think you can convince Riley Bliss to talk to me?"

"I can try." Star gave me a genuine smile.

Great. Now I had two people reaching out to Riley. "If she refuses, would you be comfortable asking if she has an alibi for Saturday morning? If I found her comments online, the police will too. I sometimes share what I learn with our local police chief, Matt Young, and I could pass along her alibi."

"Give me your contact information. It sounds like it'd save her a lot of stress if she shared the information with one of us."

I pulled a business card from my purse and gave it to Star, and she passed her information to me. "If you've ever seen an interrogation room, you'd know how true your words are. Thanks."

Star smiled again. "I'd be happy never to have that experience."

Anthony stood. "Are you safe here, or do you need me to walk you to your car?"

"I'll be okay with my dog at my side. Thanks for your offer, but you're here for business reasons."

We said our goodbyes, and I adjusted the leash to keep Cowboy close at my side. Good thing, too, because just about the time I exited the tent, Verity reappeared.

"Thought you could escape? Think again."

Chapter Fifty-Three

With cold fingers, I held onto Cowboy's leash for dear life. "Verity, I have no quarrel with you."

Cowboy growled.

Verity inched back but didn't leave. "That's where you're wrong. I believe you are in possession of some business files belonging to me."

I squared my shoulders and faced her. "I haven't taken anything from you."

"Maybe not directly, but we both know our mutual friend Axel Roberts gave you information on my business."

My heart raced. "What makes you say that?"

"I happened to be in Waco when you met him."

Should I run away or push for information? Had she been the driver who T-boned Axel? "You just happened to be there?" My voice carried a note of hysteria. "Did you cause his accident?"

"What accident?" She batted her eyelashes.

I reached for my phone. "I'm calling the police."

Her hand darted out.

Cowboy barked and sprang toward her.

Verity scratched my arm with her long fingernails.

I yelped.

My dog bit into Verity's jeans, and he didn't release even though she tried to shake him off.

People stopped and stared.

Anthony appeared. "Oh, there you are, Verity. I thought we were going to discuss a business proposition."

Her eyes grew wide. "Oh, yeah. That's right."

"This is a good time for me, if it's convenient for you. Why don't you meet me at the food court? I'll give you time to put a sign on your booth about taking a break." He turned his back on Verity and looked at me. "Nice dog you got there."

"Thanks." I looked at my dog. "Release."

He released her jeans and whimpered.

Anthony made a motion with his hands for me to leave.

I took off and beelined it to the parking lot. Possibly the biggest thing I'd learned today was that Verity was a threat. Even if she didn't murder Houston, there was something bad going on. I didn't plan to interview her again. In fact, it'd make me happy never to see her again.

How had she known about my meeting with Axel? He seemed to believe a man had been driving the van that hit him. It wouldn't have been hard for Verity to stuff her hair in a ball cap to disguise herself.

It was time to chat with the police chief. There might be something important he needed to know.

After Cowboy and I settled into my truck, I texted Matt. **Do you have time for an update?**

His reply was quick. **Lunch at Sophie's Bakery? Noon. Best I can do. Perfect.**

"Cowboy, there's time to take you home and even cut a few flowers for Sophie." From the truck, I called Jake.

"Sunshine. What's up?" Jake's greeting brought a smile to my face.

"My morning's been busy, but I haven't made it to Dr. Erb's yet. They really want me to adopt the cat?"

"Yes, ma'am. She's been spayed, and her family just disappeared. Her name is Bluebell."

"Hmm, seems appropriate since she's a Russian Blue and lives in Texas. How can her family just disappear?"

"They left unpaid bills and won't reply to the clinic. Dr. Erb believed they skipped town without paying, but now that he's seen their cat, he's worried. I urged him to report it to the police department."

"I hope he takes your advice. Speaking of our police department, I'm meeting Matt for lunch at the bakery. Can you join us?"

"Can you handle the friction?"

I pulled into my driveway. "I wouldn't have invited you if I was worried."

"What time?"

"Twelve o'clock. If you're going to run late, I can order your food."

"Thanks. I'll be cutting it close. If you don't mind, order the daily special for me."

"But you don't know what it is."

"True, but if Sophie makes it, I'll enjoy it."

The man made a valid point. "Did you learn anything from Coop?"

"He argued with Houston, but it was mostly Houston blowing off steam. Last time Coop saw Houston, they were cool."

"When was the last time they saw each other?"

"One step ahead of you. Coop saw Houston at Anytime Coffee early Saturday morning. Coop was waiting on his order, when Houston entered the shop. They chatted about the weather and the farmers market. I confirmed with Brett that the men had seen each other. Brett said they did, and they were cordial. Coop was the first to leave, and that's when Houston got rude with Brett about the smoothies."

"Okay, so they got past the altercation from Friday night. Does Coop have an alibi?"

"For the record, I didn't ask. Lucky for you, he offered the information. Officer Steve Koch wants to convert his garage into a den, and they were together Saturday morning at Steve's house."

"An alibi doesn't get much stronger than being with a policeman. I'm glad we ruled him out. But there's one thing I keep forgetting."

"What's that?" Men were talking in the background.

"Matt hinted that there were physical indications Houston had been poisoned for a period of time."

"Right. You said Houston had callouses and hair loss."

"Hold on a second." I grabbed my bag from the passenger seat and dug out my notebook. I flipped through the pages and found my research on poisons. "There can be other signs from long-term poisoning. It's surprising he didn't have stomach issues."

"Maybe he had health issues that he didn't discuss because he sold a health drink."

"Good point. I wonder if they've studied the hair follicles yet. That can indicate how long he was poisoned."

"Put it on your list to ask Matt."

I shut off the truck and helped Cowboy out of his restraint. "Good idea. I'm home and need to get Cowboy inside. If you're running behind for lunch, I'll place your order. Remind me to update you on Anthony and Star Daniels. Also, Verity."

"And we need to decide about the cat. Maybe you can foster her and see if she and Cowboy get along."

"I'll consider it. See you in a bit." In forty-five minutes, I would need to be in Sophie's Bakery. "Let's go Cowboy. We need to giddyup."

My dog wandered around the backyard while I snipped pink zinnias for Sophie. There'd be a lunch rush at the bakery, so I arranged them in an old milk bottle once we were inside the house.

Cowboy lapped his water and headed for his crate.

"You were such a good boy this morning. My protector deserves a treat." I plucked a dog biscuit from the cookie-jar-turned-treat-jar and dropped it near his head. "There you go."

It didn't take me long to freshen up and grab my notebook. The parking places on the square would be full at noon, so I decided to walk.

Along the way, a pickup truck slammed on its brakes and avoided hitting a van by a fraction. My pulse leapt, and I thought about Axel's wreck.

Had Verity disguised herself and followed one of us to the coffee shop in Waco? Jake insisted we hadn't been followed, and I believed him. Had Verity tailed Axel and seen the exchange after I arrived?

I stopped walking.

Axel's research notes.

Had I hidden them well enough?

How far would Verity go to get the potential incriminating evidence from me? Even if she found the folder of information, there was one more copy with Axel's attorney. Would the lawyer open the notes if Axel remained alive? Or did he have to die?

Different scenarios came to me. If Verity thought I was the only person to have the evidence against her, would she come after me? The anger she displayed earlier made me think it was possible. She might still go after Axel, because it made sense, he wouldn't give me the only copy. The only variable I expected she hadn't counted on was the secret copy in the attorney's possession.

So, Axel and I would be her targets. Axel was going into hiding. That left me.

I increased my pace. Standing on Main Street might be a dangerous move if Verity thought I was the only person to have a copy of the research that could put her out of business and possibly in prison.

Chapter Fifty-Four

"Hi, Sophie." I placed the vase of flowers near the cash register. My heart raced, but I was safe in the bakery now. Verity couldn't hurt me here. "How's your day going?"

Tara Thompson waited on two firemen. Tara's curly dark hair was pulled into a bun, and she wore gloves as she sliced rye bread for their sandwiches.

"Emma, what a nice surprise. Thank you for the flowers. They're very cheerful."

"You're welcome. I'm meeting Matt and Jake for lunch. Do you want to join us?"

"Probably not. Lunch is always busy. That's why I scheduled Tara to work with me. What would you like?"

"Jake wants the daily special, and I'll have the chicken salad sandwich on wheat with fruit."

Sophie nodded. "Turkey avocado on sourdough with a side of Southwest salad for Jake?"

"He said if you make it, he'll eat it. So, yes."

"You know he's a regular. He's always so supportive and kind. I'm glad you two are dating."

My face grew warm. "Thanks. Me, too."

"Green iced tea for you? Regular ice tea for Jake." She rang up my order and gave me a significant discount. I paid, then left her a big tip.

I claimed a table for four in the back corner and pulled my notebook from my turquoise polka dot jute bag.

Matt appeared and tapped the table with his knuckles. "Hey, Emma. I'm going to order, then we can chaw for a bit on the case."

"Sounds good." I made a list on a clean sheet in hopes of not forgetting anything I wanted to share with the police chief.

"Is this seat taken?" Jake pointed to the empty chair next to me.

I smiled. His sparkling eyes didn't inspire me to think about murder. Walks in the park or picnics by the lake would be more fun to consider.

"Emma, you okay?"

"Hey there." My voice squeaked.

He gave me a quick kiss. "I'll wash up first."

"Okay." My heart was all aflutter. Jake had kissed me in public. Sure, it was more of a peck, but still, our lips touched. If a rose smelled sweet, no matter what you called it, then it made sense a kiss was still a kiss, by any other name.

"Jake Hunter must be close by, if your dreamy expression is anything to judge by." Matt's words ended my romantic musings.

I inhaled deeply. "Well, yeah. Is it okay for him to join us?"

"I'm aware you two are working together. No problem."

I met Matt's gaze. Something had him in a better mood than usual. Maybe it was the fact we were in Sophie's Bakery.

Jake joined us carrying a tray with our food and drinks. "Sophie was about to bring our order and passed it on to me instead. Which one is mine?"

"Turkey avocado sandwich and the salad is yours."

We got situated, then Matt's Cobb salad arrived.

Halfway through our meal, the police chief pulled his notepad out of his shirt pocket. "What do you know?"

"I spoke to Anthony Daniels, the creator of Good Life." I caught him up to speed on everything I knew. "Can you talk to the police in Waco and see where they are on the investigation into Axel Roberts' accident."

"Already have. The woman driving the van insists it's her fault. The police over there checked her front fender, and the damage matched Axel's vehicle, where he was T-boned. Give up your theory the accident was linked to Verity."

This information made it seem like Axel's impression of a man driving was mistaken, and maybe the female van driver had worn a ball cap. "Okay, but Verity was in the coffee shop when Axel handed over his research notes on Verity and her business. How do you explain that?"

"Where are your notes?"

I glanced around the bakery to make sure Verity wasn't around. "In my office at home. I need to have a better hiding place."

"Don't you think I should see what you've got? It may or may not be relevant to my case. I need to assess the situation, and it'll be easier once I read the files you've got. Then, I can get a better handle on the situation. Will the file prove Verity has broken the law? Or is she just an unscrupulous business owner? Lastly, is there any evidence she might be involved in Houston's murder? Emma, it's imperative I get those notes."

"Let me tell you what I know. Jewels of Texas is the name of her business. She's set up at Lutz Antique and Vintage Market, and I saw her today. It was more than we ran into each other. She came after me. Twice." My pulse accelerated, and I took a deep breath. "Matt, I'm telling you that she wants my copy of the file, and she didn't ask nicely. In fact, it was more of a threat. Thank goodness I had my dog with me."

"It sounds like I need to question her again. Sooner rather than later." He ran a hand down his face. "But I need your notes."

"You should be able to find her at the antique market. I passed her on the way to the back tent where Anthony Daniels set up his booth." I waved at Tess Carranza, who entered the bakery. "Riley Bliss is going to be tough to question. She ignored me when I reached out to her, but Anthony's wife will try to make a connection."

Matt raised his hands to stop me. "Wait, Riley Bliss?"

Jake said, "Is she the one who claimed that Good Life ruined her life?"

I nodded. "The very one. She trusted Houston and invested heavily in his company. Then, the drink didn't help her lose weight, and he wouldn't give her a refund. It sounds like she's depressed. But the thing that gets me is the long-term poisoning. Matt, did you learn anything from the hair strand test?"

"Yep. Someone has been sneaking arsenic into Houston's body for over sixty days."

That was big news. "Does that change your list of suspects?"

Matt crossed his arms. "Maybe. We're still testing items from his kitchen. Was it as easy as the culprit sneaking into his house and spiking his coffee, tea, sugar, or whatever? Or did he have a place he came to daily, and his drink or food was spiked there? For instance, did he come here every morning for coffee, and Sophie spiked it so he got a little arsenic every day?"

Sophie had been delivering an order to the table behind Matt. She turned on the three of us. "Chief Young, are you accusing me of murder?"

Matt's head jerked back. "Oh, no, Sophie. Never. I was, you know, just making an example. I'm not accusing you of anything; even if you had the strongest motive, I would never consider you a suspect."

Hmm. I watched my friend's reaction.

One side of Sophie's mouth lifted in a half-smile. "That is very good to know."

The two gazed at each other, and Jake nudged me with his foot under the table.

"Chief Young, do you have any updates on Houston Turner's murder?" Tess stopped by and ruined the moment with her question.

Sophie walked behind the counter.

Matt blew out a puff of air. "I'm working on it day and night, Ms. Carranza. Is there anything you'd like to share with me?"

"As a matter of fact, I do have something you need to see." She sat in the vacant chair and leaned forward. "There are books on poison in the library. Most are reference books and never leave the building. If you need to check out one of the books, let me know. I'll make it happen for you, Chief."

"Poison? What makes you think the murderer used poison?"

"Come now, it's a small town. Probably the only people around who don't know how Houston died have been sleeping under a rock. You come on by when you're ready. I've got the reference books sitting in my office just waiting for you. I hope you're considering Nick Jones. The exterminator probably knows more about poisons than anybody else."

"Ms. Carranza, for years, you've believed Nick murdered his first wife.

We have a thick file on your visits and reports. But I don't think there's a motive for Nick to have murdered Houston. Still, I thank you for pulling the books on poison for me."

"You're welcome, Chief. I'll be expecting your visit."

Before Matt could reply, Sophie returned with a white paper bag and a paper cup. "Tess, here's your salad and sweet tea. I hope you enjoy your lunch."

"Thank you. I'll be back tomorrow for my Friday special." Tess stood and adjusted her Vera Bradley purse on her shoulder, picked up her lunch, and walked out of the crowded bakery.

I looked at Sophie. "She has her own Friday lunch special?"

"Oh, yes. Reuben sandwich and German potato salad with sweet tea." Her gaze flitted from me to Matt. "Let me get you a refill."

"I'm good, but thanks."

"Okay." Sophie stood there as if unsure what to do next.

Matt said, "Emma, would you be willing to look at the library's reference books for me? If I know Tess, she's already marked the pages she'd like me to pay close attention to."

There was a lot to accomplish before the day was over, but if it'd help solve the murder, I'd be happy to help. "Sure."

"Thanks." Matt stood. "Sophie, mind if I ask you a question in private? I know you're busy, but it won't take long."

She looked around. There was a long line of people waiting to order. All the tables were full, but she nodded. "Come back to my office. We can talk there."

They left us alone, and I looked at Jake. "He sounded adamant about me turning over Axel's notes. If there hadn't been so many interruptions, he probably would've pushed harder. After my trip to the library, I guess I'll turn them over before he resorts to confiscating them."

"Matt may be sweet on Sophie and all that, but he'll circle back to wanting to see your notes. My suggestion would be to collect them first, then make copies at the library. Then you can turn it all over to him at once. Do you mind if I tag along?"

"Why?"

"Except for dropping in on the Nelles, I've got the afternoon off. I'm also curious about Axel's information."

"Then I'd love for you to join me. Let's skedaddle before Matt gets back."

"I couldn't have said it better myself."

Chapter Fifty-Five

J ake and I made a quick stop at my bungalow and collected Alex's file. I carried my jute bag inside and put the file in there in case Verity was spying on me. I didn't like feeling paranoid, but she had spied on Axel and me in Waco. It could happen again.

Once we were in the library, I breathed easier. Tess led us to her office. "Take your time. I'll be here until closing. If you have questions, don't hesitate to ask."

"Thanks, Tess."

How had Tess known which poison had been used on Houston? I sat in the librarian's chair at her desk and sorted through the stack of reference books. Arsenic. Bookmarks were placed in each book on the pages on arsenic.

Jake got comfortable across the desk from me and started reading the information Axel Roberts had given me.

I retrieved my notebook and began reading.

"Listen to this. Contaminated groundwater looks to be the leading cause of arsenic poisoning." I clicked my pen and jotted down the fact. "I guess that's a possible way for Houston to have gotten the poison in his body over a period of time."

"True, but neither one of us believes groundwater is how he got it in his system."

"You're right." I skimmed the page until an interesting tidbit stopped me. "I've never heard of arsenicosis, but it means arsenic poisoning. If we rule out groundwater, how was he poisoned for at least sixty days? Who sees him the most?"

"His sister and niece worked for him at the restaurant and with Good Life. There are also other employees to consider. Houston led more than a few women to believe they'd lose weight and make money by selling the drink. Did he have a romantic relationship with one of them?"

"Not with Paula, and it'd be hard to imagine he did with Riley Bliss, but there could be someone else." I went back to reading the reference book.

Jake finished Axel's file and moved to the copier. "It was nice of Tess to offer for us to make copies."

"Yeah, I don't think she was Houston's biggest fan, but she and Paula are friends. She wants to help prove Paula is innocent."

Jake hummed as he made copies.

I watched his movements. It was a beautiful spring day, and there were lots of fun ways to spend the afternoon. Fishing, running, playing golf, hiking, or even going to the batting cage. Instead, he'd offered to come to the library and help me solve Houston's murder.

He glanced at me. "What?"

"Why did you decide to go to the police academy after you got out of the service?"

He crossed his arms. "I've been blessed all my life. I enlisted in the Marines to help others. It's the same reason I decided to be a cop. It's just on a smaller scale. I want to protect people in their hometowns. It probably sounds corny, but I like to help others."

"It doesn't sound corny at all." It sounded heroic.

He turned his attention back to copying the pages from Axel.

I took a minute to text Star Daniels. **Hi Star. This is Emma Justice. Would you ask Riley if she and Houston had ever been involved romantically?**

"Don't forget to check on the cat."

"Bluebell. Right. Cowboy didn't react well when we found her."

"That was different. She'd invaded his territory, uninvited."

My phone rang. "Oh, this is Star Daniels."

"Mind if I listen? Then you won't have to repeat everything."

I nodded and swiped the phone. "Hi, Star. I'm here with Jake Hunter, a friend of mine. He's helping me investigate the murder."

"Oh, hi, Jake." She sounded as friendly on the phone as she did in person. "Howdy."

"I thought it'd be easier to call and tell you about Riley than to send a text. She didn't want to talk about Houston on the phone. She doesn't live far away, so I went to her house. She's in bad shape. Seriously depressed. Houston snowed her about Good Life. She truly believed she'd lose weight and feel better. I saw pictures of her before Houston, and she wasn't obese. In my opinion, she was more like pleasantly plump. She invested heavily with Houston's company, and she had visions of them running the business together, falling in love, and having babies one day. She admitted they never dated, but there were a lot of innuendos and promises of a future. Her mother was at the house with her and walked me to the car after our conversation. She said Riley had barely gotten out of bed for weeks, and there was no way she could've murdered Houston. The parents take her to counseling every day. If you ask me, the mother would be more likely to murder Houston than Riley. But I don't believe Mrs. Bliss had time. Her focus is on helping Riley get better."

My eyes watered. "Poor girl. Thanks for checking. I'll remove her from my list."

"Glad I could help. Just a little note of warning, on my way out of the market today, I noticed Verity had closed her booth. Not sure if it was for lunch or something else, but you all best be careful."

"Thanks. You too." We ended the call.

Jake crossed his arms. "Where does this leave us? You're ruling out Riley Bliss, which is perfectly understandable."

"Can you imagine how worried her parents must be?"

"I dare say they're beside themselves. It's a terrible thing Houston did to those women. Where are we on suspects? We've ruled out Coop Henderson and Shelby Penn. What about Elijah Barnes?"

"I think he's innocent. If we end up with no suspects, we'll circle back to him."

"Paula and Brett are innocent." When I didn't reply, Jake came closer to the desk. "What's wrong?"

"Paula has a strong motive, and she was angry, but you're right. She's innocent." She'd survived marriage to Nick Jones. If she'd planned to murder anyone, wouldn't it be Nick?

One of Jake's eyebrows quirked up. "Seems like it. We can add her to your list of only look at if we rule everyone else out."

"Okay. Now that I've met Anthony and Star Daniels, I can't imagine either one of them is guilty. Anthony has a beautiful, young wife who adores him. He's crazy about her. When you meet him, you'll soon see that he's all about love and peace."

"But he argued with Houston, right?"

"Yeah, but I picture it more of a respectful debate. Anthony's got a pretty good life, no pun intended. He wouldn't throw everything away by attacking his business partner, no matter how mad he got. Of course, this is only my opinion." I leaned back in the librarian's chair and crossed my legs. "Are Miranda and Leigh the only two suspects left?"

"Don't forget Verity Candor."

I shivered. "She's scary, but how would she poison Houston when she travels so much?"

"There's something strange about her, and I think we should leave her on our list of suspects. Axel's notes prove she's up to something shady. He proved that she lied about her jewelry. What would be the worst-case scenario?"

I considered his question. "She could get sent to prison for her crimes?"

"If Axel came up with evidence against Verity, it's possible Houston did too." Jake began to pace in the office. "The two of them were close and discussed business. Maybe she divulged something she'd done, and it wasn't ethical. Maybe it wasn't even legal. So, Houston tried to blackmail her. She could lose her business, her van, and her freedom. Was the information so bad that she'd stoop to murder?"

"We're coming up with lots of possibilities, but we don't have evidence. I think it's time to deliver the notes to Matt."

"Did you finish reading about the poisons?"

"Nothing is jumping out at me. If Houston was poisoned gradually, how was it administered? From what I've read so far, it's hard to absorb arsenic through the skin. It's tasteless and odorless, so it is easy to administer in food and drinks."

"We need Matt to tell us if arsenic was given to him long-term, or was it a different poison. Maybe he drank the arsenic the day he died." He raised his hand to stop my question. "If this happened, did Houston treat his killer so badly that they decided he had to die immediately? And what did Houston do to speed up the killer's timeline?"

"All very good questions." I drummed my fingers on the desk. "Is it time to divide and conquer? I should probably dig a little more. If I finish before you do, I'll just walk home."

He shook his head. "No, stay here where it's safe. I feel like we're close to figuring out the mystery. We should stick together."

It wasn't like I needed a man to protect me on normal days, but this wasn't normal. It made good sense to have a partner, watching my back. "Gotcha."

Jake laid the original green accordion folder on the desk. "This is yours. I'll take a copy of the file to Matt's office. If we're lucky, maybe he'll share more. Then I'll come straight back here. Please, promise me you won't leave."

"Safety in numbers. I understand, and it'll take me longer to go through these books than it'll take you to talk to Matt." I tapped the copied papers. "Stuff those in the back of your jeans and cover it with your shirt, in case Verity is lurking around."

"Will do." He folded the papers in thirds and stuck them in the back waistband of his jeans.

"Looking good there, Mr. Hunter."

Jake gave me a quick kiss and disappeared.

I returned to my research. It was time to learn more about how Houston was murdered.

Chapter Fifty-Six

"It turns out there were two poisons in Houston's system." Jake's eyes twinkled.

I jumped up from the desk in the librarian's office and crossed the room to where Jake stood by the door. "Man, I wish I'd gone with you to see Matt. Tell me what you know."

"Their theory is the arsenic was given to Houston on Saturday. The long-term poison turned out to be digoxin."

"The pharmacy dispensed digoxin to heart patients. It's not as popular as it used to be, but there are some people who still take it." I needed to be careful not to say if I knew who took it because of the HIPPA laws. One of Houston's good qualities was his desire to support local businesses, and he came to our pharmacy. I knew he didn't take digoxin, but legally, I couldn't discuss anything related to his prescription profile. "There's nothing else I can say about Houston and his medication."

Jake winked. "Understood, Sunshine."

"If we're down to Miranda and Leigh as our primary suspects, how did they get digoxin into Houston? And where did they get the drug?"

"Both good questions." He crossed his arms. "Let's flip the question. What else would show up in Houston's body, presenting as digoxin, but it's really something else?"

"I know this." I closed my eyes. They burned from exhaustion. I needed coffee.

"You okay?" He touched my elbow.

The answer hit me. "Yes. The foxglove plant's botanical name is Digitalis purpurea. Oh, Jake. I saw a foxglove plant inside Miranda's house on the day of visitation. Also, there was a foxglove plant in Star's booth."

"Didn't you rule out Star?"

"Yeah, but I can't ignore the plant." I didn't want it to be Star, but had she killed Houston to protect her husband?

"Don't jump to conclusions. Is it possible a friend brought the plant to Miranda's house as a sympathy plant instead of a flower arrangement?"

"It happens sometimes. A small juniper bonsai, a memory tree, a basket of foliage plants, and a peace plant are a few options to replace the traditional condolence flowers."

"Okay. That's good to know. We're not making wild assumptions, but do we believe it's a coincidence that someone just happened to give Miranda a foxglove plant when her brother had slowly been poisoned with digoxin?"

"No, but what gets me is the arsenic. Matt said it was in his system for sixty days, but also there was a bolus dose on Saturday."

"Hold up. Bolus?"

I nodded. "Yes, one big dose. Today, Matt told you digoxin was in his system. It's possible Houston used another pharmacy, or maybe he got it from a mail-order pharmacy. Matt needs to see if there is a legitimate reason for digoxin to be in his body. It'd probably be easier to ask his doctor if Houston had heart problems. Give me a second."

"What are you doing?"

I found the app on my phone for drugs and drug interactions. "It's just a hunch."

Jake stayed quiet while I searched. "Here we go. Arsenic can decrease the excretion rate of digoxin."

Jake rubbed his jaw. "Chemistry isn't my strong suit."

"The digoxin built up in Houston's body while somebody slipped him arsenic. I can talk to Bill, he's one of the pharmacists I used to work with, to make sure this is right."

There was a rapid knock on the door, and Tess entered her office. "Y'all, there's a woman at the front desk demanding to see Emma. She claims to know you're here."

"How? My car isn't in the parking lot."

Tess shrugged. "She's insistent. Her name is Verity Candor."

My heart sank. "She's the one we suspect followed Axel the day I met him."

"What do you want me to do?"

I straightened my shoulders. "I'll talk to her, but Jake would you wait in here for me?"

"I'd feel better going out there to face her with you."

"You'll probably intimidate her."

"Fine. I'll look at these books." He plopped down into one of the chairs. "If I hear a commotion, I'm coming out there."

Tess said, "Don't worry. I can raise a ruckus if necessary."

I exited the office with Tess. Sure enough. Verity stood at the desk, waiting to pounce. Her fists were clenched, and she swayed like it was too hard to stand still.

Tess moved between us. "Ladies, I'll have to ask you to remain civil. If you don't, I'll be forced to call the police."

"Of course." I clasped my cold hands together.

"Sure." Verity frowned.

With her back to Verity, Tess winked at me and left us alone.

"Shouldn't you be running your booth at the market?"

She raised a fist, then let it drop to her side. "For a long time, I've been excited to come to Lutz Antique and Vintage Market, and you've ruined it for me."

"That's not true. You came after me, demanding papers you claim Axel Roberts gave me."

"I know he gave them to you."

"How?" My heart raced.

"I just know." She took a deep breath and held her hands out. "Look. I don't enjoy all this negative energy. Can we call a truce?"

"Sure, but you should know something. Axel did give me some papers, and Police Chief Young has them in his office now."

Her eyes widened. "Fine. I have nothing to hide."

I doubted her words were true.

She pulled a bracelet from the pocket of her holey jeans. "This is for you. It's a quartz energy stone bracelet."

It was time to show grace. "Thank you. It's beautiful." I slipped it over my right hand, and it settled just above my wrist. "Did Houston have one of these?"

"He had something similar." She stepped closer to me. "He had some health issues and was willing to try different things to feel better."

Had anyone else been aware of Houston's health problems? "Had he felt bad for long? Is that why he created Good Life with Anthony Daniels?"

"Yeah, but he didn't tell many people about his health. He wanted to maintain the appearance of being strong and powerful."

"That makes sense. Who do you think killed Houston?"

"At this point, I have no idea. I don't know you people well enough to figure it out. Houston and I were friends who discussed business mostly."

"Verity, did you kill Houston?"

"I wouldn't confess to you if I did, but it wasn't me. I have no motive." Her tone sounded defeated.

"Okay. So, are we good? Are you going to quit threatening me?"

"I never threatened you."

Even my dog knew she'd threatened me, but I'd let it drop. "You didn't answer my question, Verity."

"Don't worry about me. I'm going to blow this town and never come back."

"Wherever you go, life will be easier, if you are honest with people."

"Sounds like you read the things Axel was accusing me of. Did you consider he's the liar, and I'm innocent?"

"No. I'm sorry, but Axel was very believable."

"Think about it." She brushed past me, bumping my shoulder as she walked out of the library.

Tess hurried over from where she'd been watching at the table of local authors. "Emma, are you okay?"

"Yes, but that was super weird. I need to get Jake so we can find Chief Young. He needs to know what happened." Why had Verity hunted me down? Not much had been accomplished by our conversation. Although she did learn Matt had the paperwork about her business. The news seemed to defeat her.

On my side of the equation, I'd discovered she planned to leave town. It was better than nothing.

Chapter Fifty-Seven

Jake and I returned to Lutz Antique and Vintage Market to speak to Matt. We found him settling a dispute between a woman selling pottery and a man with an out-of-control mutt.

"I guess we should stand back until this is resolved." Jake spoke near my ear, and his breath tickled my neck.

"You're probably right, but if we see Verity getting away, we should interrupt Matt."

"Definitely."

The man with the dog handed the woman a credit card, and Matt watched a transaction take place before heading our way. "You can't allow your dog to break nearly five hundred dollars of handmade pottery and expect to walk away. What's up with you two?"

"I'm sure you haven't had time to study the notes I brought you from Axel Roberts, but Verity told Emma she's planning to leave town right away." Jake crossed his arms.

"Why?"

"She has tracked me down at the library this afternoon, demanding the evidence Axel collected on her business. She wanted the information and found me—"

Jake cleared his throat. "Ah-hm. She followed you."

I met Jake's gaze. "Right. She followed me to the library, and that was the third time she confronted me. I finally told her you have the papers, and she's wasting her time with me. Also, she said Houston had some health issues. Have you had time to ask his doctor if Houston had a heart condition? It would explain the digoxin on the toxicology report. Also, arsenic decreases the excretion rate of digoxin. That could be the reason—"

"I'll investigate it. Anything else pertinent?"

"Verity gave me this bracelet and admitted that Houston bought healthy jewelry from her."

"I was about to look for her when the dispute broke out at the pottery booth. Where is Verity set up?"

I gave him directions to the tent where she'd arranged her jewelry. He contacted an officer with orders to find, and stakeout, Verity's van. "Thanks for the tip." He hustled away in the direction I'd indicated.

I faced Jake. "There are a lot of lies and confusion swirling around Verity. Her instinct to run when faced with business problems makes me think she's not her killer. If she murdered Houston, why is she still in Lutz? Wouldn't she have taken off on Saturday?"

"I see what you mean. Your experience with her has been focused on retrieving Axel's file on her. She hasn't seemed concerned about Houston's murder."

"Or else she's a good actress, pretending to focus on the files and business and not the murder." Jake rocked back on his heels. "So, what next? I'm running out of ideas."

"If we're seriously down to Miranda and Shelby as the strongest suspects, let's visit the BBQ Hut food truck." He reached for my hand, and his warm grip comforted me.

"Great idea."

We wiggled through the growing crowds on our way to the food area. The sight of a white enamel French bucket stopped my steps. "Wait, Jake."

"Do you see Miranda? Or Verity?" His grip tightened on my hand. "And I haven't forgotten you mentioned Star Daniels has a foxglove plant."

"Sorry, no. I want that bucket." I dragged him with me to the booth. "Oh, there are old milk bottles too."

"Yeah, like you put flowers in at Anytime Coffee."

"Right." It pleased me more than I cared to admit that he'd paid attention. The price on the bucket was acceptable, but the bottles were too expensive.

Usually, on the first day of an event, there wasn't much bartering. By Sunday, the vendor would probably sell them for a song. I bought the bucket, and to my surprise, the gap-toothed lady running the booth offered me a deal on the milk bottles.

She said, "No offense, but they aren't my favorite. Fred, my old man, insisted we bring them. He'll be happy to hear they sold. Do you want a bag?"

"How about if we wrap them in paper, and I'll carry them in the bucket?"

"I like it." She used newsprint packing paper and wrapped each bottle with care. Once the six bottles were protected, she fit them into the can. "Thank ya kindly."

"Thank you." It took two hands to carry the bucket. "Maybe I should've asked for a bag."

Jake reached for my haul. "I was going to offer but didn't know if it'd offend you. My sister is always telling me how women can do most anything a man can do."

I handed him the bucket full of milk bottles. "Hey, I don't mind accepting a nice offer. The crowd is picking up."

"Yep, but hopefully, Miranda has time for a quick chat."

To my delight, there were quite a few empty tables. Shelby delivered barbecue nachos to a couple with three kiddos. We paused until she finished handing out napkins.

"Hi, Shelby." I waved, and she veered our way. "How's it going?"

"Good, but from experience, I know it'll get busier each day of the event."

Jake said, "How'd you get out of school?"

She shrugged. "Uncle Houston pulled strings for me to have an excused absence, and he told the tennis coach I'd miss the matches today and tomorrow. I decided Momma needed help, and I already had the excuses in place. So, why not? Ms. Justice, I'm surprised you don't have a booth here."

"One day I hope to, but most people are shopping for home furnishings. They've come from all over Texas, and flowers probably won't travel well."

"Are y'all hungry?" She adjusted the hair clip that held her hair back.

"Always." Jake pushed his Oakley sunglasses to the top of his head.

"I'll meet you over there, but Momma can take your order. I need to clear some of the tables. The event has staff to keep the area clean, but they have other duties, too. Sales are better when the dining area is nice." She walked to a nearby table and began bussing it.

We walked to the food truck. "Shelby is truly amazing. I bet she goes far in life."

Miranda stood at the order counter, wiping down the surface. "Hi, guys. What can I get you?"

I pulled out my credit card. "Your largest glass of sweet tea with lemon and a small order of beef brisket sliders. Jake, this is my treat." It wasn't quite suppertime, but I hoped placing a good order might make Miranda more willing to talk.

"Thanks." Jake winked at me. "Miranda, I'd like your brisket and sausage Frito pie."

"What about a drink?"

"Lemonade, please."

I handed the credit card to her. "Have you heard any updates on Houston's murder?"

"Probably no more than you." She frowned and shoved my card into her reader. Her mood shift was dramatic. She'd gone from taking our order to looking like she'd prefer to smash the card reader in my face than take my money. "Houston was a hard man, but he was my brother. I loved him. You know?"

"I understand. I have a brother myself, but he's an optometrist in Irving."

"I've never met your brother. Didn't even realize you have family."

"Wyatt is my brother, and I have a sister. We're not tight like your family." It was as much my fault as it was theirs. "Did Houston give jobs to other members of your family?"

She hammered the little credit card machine with her fist. "Nah. My siblings wouldn't put up with Houston. We can't all be the boss. I didn't mind him telling me what to do, but it wasn't easy watching Shelby work for him."

I couldn't let her mood deter me from asking more questions. "Who do you think knows enough about poisons to kill him that way?"

She ripped the receipt off and slammed it and the credit card on the counter. "Nick Jones comes to mind. You're part of the mystery reading book club. Maybe it was one of you. Paula is in the group, right? And she was married to Nick. Seems like she's a logical choice."

I added a tip and signed my name. "Logical. Yep. Paula and I have been friends, but how well do we ever know another person. I'll think about your suggestion. We'll just sit over there."

Jake and I got settled at a nearby picnic table. Jake sat next to me and placed the French bucket on the table. "I think you struck a nerve."

"Yeah, I'm glad she couldn't wrap her fingers around my neck, or I might be a goner."

"Nah, I wouldn't let that happen."

I leaned against him. "Thanks, but Celia probably wouldn't approve of me counting on your protection."

"Aw, now. You faced down Willow Moore's killer all by yourself. Just consider me part of your buddy system, when it comes to confronting potential killers."

"Y'all talking about Uncle Houston's killer?" Shelby stood at the end of the table with two drinks. "Momma said the sweet tea is for Ms. Emma, and the lemonade is for Mr. Hunter. It won't be long until your food is ready."

"Thanks, and we were discussing the murder. It's sad that Houston was poisoned. He didn't even get to see the killer coming. Verity Candor claims your uncle didn't feel well for a while. I was going to ask your mom what she thought."

Shelby crossed her arms and swayed back and forth kinda like tennis players do when waiting for a serve. "It's possible. He'd been coughing a lot and thought it might be allergies. Then there was the time he thought he had a stomach bug and almost passed out. He finally chalked that episode up to dehydration. When he described his symptoms, I tried to research what might be wrong with him. People always suspect the worst when it comes to unexplained health problems."

"Those symptoms could be related to certain poisons." I didn't say arsenic out loud. "I heard you're taking organic chemistry in high school. Have you learned about poisons?"

She reached into her apron pocket. "Are you accusing me?"

I shook my head. "No, but I thought if you knew much about, say cyanide, you might have learned symptoms of different poisons. Did you and your uncle ever consider he might have been poisoned?"

"No, but he was sick for weeks. Maybe for months. I don't think his sickness had anything to do with poison."

"Okay, but looking back on Houston's conditions, do you think it might be related to poison? I've never taken organic chemistry, and you probably know more than I do."

"My teacher didn't go into much detail, but we did learn there are poisonous plants all around us, and we should be careful."

"What kind of plants?"

"You probably know this because you grow flowers. My teacher said lantana, foxglove, Lily of the Valley, and, oh, there's another popular plant. It's more of a bush, but I can't remember what it's called." She placed little plastic cups on the table with lids. "These are some new barbecue sauces we've been trying out. Momma's been playing with recipes."

"That sounds fun."

Shelby snapped her fingers. "Oleander plants. If I had a dog, I wouldn't let it near an oleander bush. Let me see if your food is ready." She left us alone.

Jake said, "At the rate we're going, Bluebell will be spending the night at the vet clinic."

"At least she'll be in good hands. Are you sure you don't want to adopt her?"

"I don't think Paige will allow it. Whenever I decide to move into a house, I'll have pets. For now, it looks like the cat is all yours, Sunshine."

Movement caught my attention. "Uh, oh. Here comes Miranda, and she doesn't look happy."

"Yep. It looks like she got her tail stuck in a crack."

I took a big ole gulp of my tea, dreading the confrontation.

Chapter Fifty-Eight

You've got some nerve accusing Shelby of poisoning Houston." Miranda slammed my plate on the table so hard the brisket sliders nearly slid right off.

"Calm down." If Miranda was innocent, she needed counseling for her anger issues. "We didn't accuse her. I was asking for information. I never took chemistry in high school, and I thought Shelby might be able to help me figure out something."

Miranda placed Jake's paper plate of food in front of him with less force. "Why? For your investigation?" She used air quotes.

Jake said, "Wouldn't you prefer for Houston's killer to be caught?"

"Not if it means you'll get an innocent girl sent to prison."

"We don't believe Shelby poisoned Houston." Jake placed his hand on my back. "Emma heard something interesting earlier today."

"What?"

"Verity Candor—"

Her eyes narrowed to slits. "The jewelry woman who got Houston all twisted up over his Good Life business."

I swallowed hard and took another drink. "Yeah, her. She said Houston hadn't felt well for some time. That's what we were discussing with Shelby. Did you notice any health concerns with your brother?"

More people flowed into the eating area. "He complained about a cough and sore throat, but he often complained about his health. If you ask me, he was a bit of a hypochondriac. I need to get back to work. Enjoy your food." She stormed away.

Jake chuckled. "Hopefully, she didn't mean eat dirt and die."

"No way I'm eating dirt today, especially when I have the option of eating brisket." I didn't like Miranda's tone, but she was serving food from her business, and no matter how angry she was with me, she wouldn't risk losing her business by serving tainted food. After my first tentative bite, I glanced at Jake. "Mine tastes okay. What about your food?"

"Delicious." He wiped his chin with a paper napkin. "What'd you think about Shelby's comment concerning the barbecue sauce?"

"What do you mean?"

"Miranda's been trying out new barbecue sauce recipes. I wonder why, if BBQ Hut is a successful business."

I took another drink of tea. "Always room for improvement or growth?"

"Could be." He took another bite.

"Or possibly she was bored and wanted to get creative."

We finished eating in silence. Was there a clue in the barbecue sauce? I took my little bun and tried the variety of sauces. "One is sweet. One is spicier than I like. The last option is smoky."

"You've piqued my interest. Let me see what I think." Jake tried each sauce. "I agree with your analysis."

My stomach clenched. "Hey, we just tried three sauces. What if, and this could be a leap—"

"Keep going."

"What if Miranda had Houston try each new recipe? And what if the recipes she gave him had a little bit of arsenic?" I scrolled on my phone. "Don't forget arsenic doesn't have a smell or taste. That's the reason people don't realize it's in their drinking water."

"I think you're onto something. Let's say you're right. Why would she slowly poison Houston? Also, why give him a lethal dose on Saturday?"

"Especially after she'd been playing a long game of poisoning him?" My thoughts were getting confused. What was I missing?

Jake crushed his napkin into a ball and tossed it onto the empty plate. "We need to talk to Matt."

"I'll text him." I ignored a feeling of nausea. It was probably from the stress of the murder. Or maybe trying the different barbecue options hadn't been so smart, even if the experience helped me think of a way Houston may have been poisoned. After finding Matt's contact information, I sent a brief message.

Jake cleared our table. "You finished with your tea?"

"I'll keep drinking it." Maybe it'd help calm my stomach. "Do you feel okay?"

"Yeah, I'm fine. You?"

"It might not have been a good idea to try the different sauces. Thank goodness you're okay. That means the food was safe."

My phone vibrated with a reply from Matt. **Meet me at the entrance.** "Is that Matt?"

"Yes, he can meet us now." I stood and reached for the French flower bucket. Not two steps later, pain ripped across my abdomen.

I dropped the bucket.

It clanked on the concrete.

Sweat burned my eyes, making it hard to see. Somehow, I managed to dart to a large trash can and vomited. I was too sick to care about the embarrassing scene.

Jake held my hair back. "Okay, baby. We're going to get you help."

When I caught my breath, I glanced at him. "Someone poisoned me."

"I've already called for help. Can you walk to that table?"

I considered my symptoms. Could there possibly be anything left in me? "Yeah."

Matt appeared. "EMTs are behind me."

Was this how Houston felt Saturday? I backed away from the trash can and collapsed onto the ground.

Chapter Fifty-Nine

The next thing I remembered was waking up in the Intensive Care Unit of the closest hospital. Machines beeped, and the room was dark except for a light over the sink.

"Sunshine, it sure is good to see you." Jake squeezed my hand.

"Was it poison?" I met his brown-eyed gaze. Lawsy, he was handsome, and I probably looked like death warmed over. My body ached like I'd been run over by a Mack truck, but I was alive.

"Arsenic. Just like with Houston."

I closed my eyes. "How?"

"It was in your tea. Thankfully, I didn't toss it."

My jumbled thoughts exhausted me. "So, who?"

"Shelby brought the drink to you, but Miranda prepared it. Matt's talking to each of them. Separately."

"What time is it?"

He glanced at his watch and yawned. "Four o'clock Friday morning. Sophie drove to Waco and brought Abby back to Lutz. She didn't want your daughter to drive by herself. They're sleeping at your house, but Abby wants to see you. Sophie does too."

"Sophie will be too tired to work, and Abby has final exams." Selfishly, I wanted to see my daughter and my bestie, but I understood they had other issues to deal with.

"Nah, Sophie mentioned Tara Thompson would be in charge today. Katie Paxson is in town and can pitch in."

"Katie's in college. I think you met her a while back. That's real nice of her to work. Why don't you go home and get some sleep?"

" I'm good. When Sophie and Abby get here, I'll run to my place and catch a nap."

"Shoot. I never picked up Bluebell."

Jake chuckled. "Don't worry about the cat. Have you decided to give her a home?"

"She needs someone to care about her." If there weren't people watching out for me, I might have died from the arsenic-laced sweet tea.

"I'm proud of you, Sunshine."

I drifted to sleep before I could reply and slept until a nurse arrived to check my vitals.

Jake stood. "While you're not alone, I may go look for a strong cup of coffee."

"Jake, the cafeteria is open, and their coffee is usually pretty good. Don't drink the sludge from the vending machines, though."

"Yes, ma'am. I won't be long." Jake winked at me and left us alone.

The nurse said, "Emma, I'm Sally Davis and will be with you until noon. Normally, I get off at seven, but a friend asked me to cover part of her shift. Jake, your boyfriend, and I have had quite a few conversations about your recovery. We'll go over everything before you leave."

"Thanks."

The nurse commented on my treatment for the arsenic poisoning. She also gave me tips on recovering faster. "Thank the good Lord you didn't have a seizure or need a trachea tube. You're lucky someone got you here so quickly."

"Blessed. Definitely blessed." My eyelids felt heavy.

"I expect that's right." She checked the beeping machine and felt my wrist. "Sometimes, I prefer to do things the old-fashioned way. We've got IV fluids here with drugs that should help you get back to normal in no time."

"Is my purse here by any chance? I'd like to run a brush through my hair."

She found my bag in the little closet and handed it to me. "Here's a toiletry package with a toothbrush and toothpaste. You're not ready to walk to the restroom yet, but I can help you brush your teeth."

"That'd be wonderful."

It only took a few minutes to do a bit of grooming, and my mouth felt wonderful after brushing and rinsing in the little pink plastic dish.

Nurse Sally patted my arm. "I didn't help so you could spruce up for that fine man, but it seems to me when we feel clean, we feel better in general. Get some rest now, and just push this button if you need anything. There's also a button on the bedrail. If you push it, I'll be here straight away."

"Thank you, Sally." My eyes drifted shut as she left me alone.

I wasn't sure how long I dozed before the soft swoosh of the door opening woke me. "Jake?" It was still on the dark side in my room.

Tennis shoes squeaked on the tile floor. It didn't sound like Jake's tread.

Shills covered my body. I reached for the remote control on the bed tray to call for a nurse, but before I could grasp it, Miranda snatched the device and tossed it across the room. It landed with a soft thump on the vinyl recliner, and a sense of doom settled over the hospital room.

Chapter Sixty

"Miranda, I thought we were on the way to becoming friends." She'd trusted me to give her daughter a ride to work. I'd been in her home. But I also believed she might have murdered Houston. She probably spiked my tea earlier with arsenic.

"Friends don't accuse each other of murder."

I grasped the bedrails. The blood pressure machine's beeping grew faster. No surprise there.

"You look amazed to see me, which tells me you knew Chief Young was going to question Shelby and me." She removed the lanyard she always wore. It was just like Shelby's.

"I was too sick to accuse anyone. Did you try to poison me?" With my cold fingers, I gripped the bedrails tighter. Wait. There was a panel with a call button for the nurse.

"Yes. I poisoned you just like I did Houston. Why couldn't you have died as easily as he did?" She hissed.

"I don't know. I'm sorry, Miranda. The police will understand how badly Houston treated you. They'll probably take it easy on you. You can say it was self-defense."

"Nice try, Emma. Nothing ever works out for me, but at least I can get rid of you." Quick as lightning, she slipped the lanyard over my head.

My hands flew to the polyester strap to prevent it from strangling me.

Miranda leaned over the bed and pulled to tighten the strap around my neck.

I fought back with all the strength I could muster. I couldn't let go of the lanyard with my hands to call the nurse. With my knee, I kicked toward the panel, hoping to hit the right spot.

The keys attached at the bottom clinked together.

I turned my attention to the keys.

There. Just like on Shelby's lanyard was a personal safety alarm.

I twisted and jerked my knee toward Miranda's jaw. It connected.

She groaned, and her grip relaxed a smidge.

While taking a deep breath, I yanked on the device. It came apart. The alarm blared. A strobe light went off.

Miranda slapped my face. "You jerk. You ruined everything." She fumbled to put the pieces of the alarm back together.

The door burst open.

Jake raced in, followed by Matt. Jake pulled Miranda away from me, and Matt took over and dragged her into the hallway.

Jake found the two parts of the alarm and put them together. "Emma, are you okay? I never should've left you alone."

Tears of relief rolled down my cheeks. "I'm fine now. She poisoned my tea. Not Shelby."

He lowered the rail and joined me on the mattress, taking me into his arms.

"You're safe now."

"There'll be none of that in my hospital." Nurse Sally had returned. "I see you're doing all right despite whatever that wicked woman tried to do to you."

"She tried to kill me." My voice was raspy, and I worked to control my anger. "Make sure the police chief knows."

"You got it. I'll be right back, so behave yourselves." The door closed behind her.

Jake planted a swoon-worthy kiss on my lips, and I gladly participated.

"Knock knock." Sally's voice ended the kiss.

Jake moved away but kept his focus on me. "I don't want to push her good graces."

"That's right, sweetheart. I need to make sure your girlfriend is okay." She began checking tubes and numbers on the beeping machine.

"I'll sit over there and behave, but I'm not letting Emma out of my sight again."

"Can't say that I blame you. In case you aren't aware, Blaze Davis is my son. He was questioned about Houston Turner's death, and that's Houston's sister talking to the police chief. There's another thing I know. You solved Willow Moore's murder." She stopped her movements and glanced at me. "All this leads me to believe Miranda Penn is behind her brother's murder, and she tried to prevent you from proving it, by poisoning you."

Jake said, "Blaze Davis? Isn't he the farmer who hired Eddie Hayes to work with him at the farmers market on Saturday? He was Eddie's alibi."

"That's right. Privacy laws prevent me from telling him that I'm your nurse, but this is some story." She touched my face. "Looks like she slapped you good. I've got a cream that might take the sting out of it. Come here, Jake. You can actually see the palm print. You might want to take a picture right away, in case it fades before the police get to it."

"You bet I do, and I'll make sure Chief Young does too." Jake snapped a picture. "Be right back."

I smiled at Sally. "I appreciate all you're doing for me."

"It's my life calling." She opened a drawer on her nurse's cart and retrieved an ointment jar. "Your doctor allows me to use this when I think necessary. It's a standard order on your chart."

"I trust you."

Jake returned with Matt.

Matt turned on the ceiling light. "If you don't mind, I'd like to take pictures of Emma's face to add to my case against Miranda Penn."

Sally said, "There's some bruising on her neck. You might want to snap pictures of that, too."

The police chief leaned close and took pictures of my face and neck. "I think that'll do it."

I reached for his arm. "Matt, do you have enough evidence to convict Miranda?"

"We're working on it."

"She admitted that she poisoned me, but we weren't having a nice little chat. I think she confessed to killing Houston, too. She asked why I couldn't die as easily as he did. At least she said something like that."

"Working to prove that, too." He turned on a lamp at the side of the bed and snapped a few more pictures. "You focus on getting better. I'll handle the case."

The next few minutes were a whirlwind of activity, and then I was snoozing again. Nurse Sally assured me my body needed the rest after all I'd been through.

When I woke up again, Sophie and Abby had squeezed into the room and sat next to Jake.

"Oh, Mom. You liked to have scared me to death."

"I'm sorry, honey."

She hugged me and then shook her finger at me. "No more trying to solve murders."

"We did solve the murder. Jake and I were down to Miranda or Shelby, and it was always hard for me to believe Shelby could've murdered Houston."

"Looks like a good time to slip out. Y'all be nice to Emma." Jake gave me a kiss. "And please don't leave her alone."

Sophie crossed her arms. "Don't you worry. We love Emma, too."

My face grew hot as an August sidewalk.

Love.

We'd never spoken the word.

I didn't hear the rest of their exchange, but Jake left me alone with my daughter and my best friend.

There were so many questions still needing answers, but first, I needed to assure Abby and Sophie that I was fine.

Chapter Sixty-One

Saturday morning, the doctor released me. My bloodwork was acceptable, and I had an appointment scheduled to meet my regular doctor on Tuesday.

Jake drove me home but refused to discuss the murder until I was comfortable in my gathering room.

He opened the front door for me and waved me into my bungalow.

"Home sweet home. Except for when I first moved in with Abby, I don't believe it's ever felt this good. I can't believe Cowboy didn't greet me. I suppose Abby's walking him."

"It's always good to have a place to hang your hat." Jake grimaced. "Forgive my clumsy wording. I'm glad you're home."

"Surprise!" Abby, Sophie, and Matt welcomed me into the gathering room.

Cowboy barked and ran to greet me.

"Hey, boy. I sure missed you."

His tail wagged. I doubted dogs could smile, but it felt like he smiled at me.

"You're such a good boy."

With a gentle touch, Jake nudged me. "You need to sit down. One of the conditions from the doctor was that you'd rest."

"And drink plenty of fluids, take Vitamin B supplements—" Oh, that sounded so rude. "But you're right. I need to take it easy."

I moved to the blue chair, with the plan of sitting back and propping my feet on the ottoman. Cowboy had other ideas. He wedged himself between me and the footrest. "Oh, you sweet boy. Were you afraid I wasn't coming back? I know Abby and Sophie took good care of you."

Meow.

Jake chuckled. "Your cat's here."

"Oh, my. How's Cowboy adjusting?"

Abby said, "I asked my psych professor how to introduce the cat to Cowboy, and it worked."

I quirked an eyebrow at her.

"Okay, there was a short adjustment period, but the dog doesn't go berserk when he spots the cat. It's possible Cowboy recognizes Bluebell is recovering from an injury."

I rubbed Cowboy's ear. "Or lost souls feel a need to stick together. Either way, Matt, what can you tell us about the case?"

Jake sat near me, and Abby and Sophie sat on the loveseat. We all grew quiet.

Matt plopped down on the white, slipcovered chaise lounge, then moved to a wooden Shaker rocking chair. "If I sit in that thing, I might pass out from exhaustion."

Sophie stood. "Let me fix you a fresh cup of coffee."

"Thanks. Maybe later." Matt rubbed his hands together and leaned forward. "I haven't notified the press yet. The decent thing to do was inform you all because of the work you did on this case. Miranda Penn has been arrested for the murder of Houston Turner. You were on the right track with the barbecue sauce. She spilled her guts in hopes of a lighter sentence. She also detailed how cruelly he treated her and Shelby. It was a sad situation, but murder is never the answer."

"I agree. Did she add a little arsenic to every bottle of barbecue sauce she had Houston try?"

"Nope. It was digitalis, but the doctor said Houston didn't have a heart problem. There was no prescription for digoxin."

"Did it come from her foxglove plant?"

"Exactly." Matt nodded. "Miranda's original intent was to make him sick enough to forget about Shelby. After a few weeks, the situation wasn't any better, so she began adding arsenic."

Jake said, "It sounds like she had implemented a plan to slowly poison her brother in order to protect her daughter. What happened last Saturday to change things?"

"It was the final straw for Miranda. I'm sure you two know all the puzzle pieces, but here's how Miranda explained the situation. She and Shelby had been working to buy an older car for Shelby. They'd met their end of the bargain, but Houston changed the terms. He originally said after Shelby worked for six more months, then he'd sell the car to her. Shelby was upset, and Miranda didn't trust him to not change the agreement a second time. Then Houston took away Shelby's phone. He expected her to work his Good Life booth at the farmers market, model, and waitress for him all last Saturday, without a phone. Once all her work was done, he'd return the cell."

"I remember you found it under his body."

"Right."

"Miranda saw red. She dipped into her supply of arsenic—"

Sophie leaned forward. "Who keeps a supply of arsenic on hand?"

Matt sighed. "Not many everyday people have arsenic, but she had a sneaky hiding place in her food truck."

My heart leapt. "I went through her truck Saturday when you questioned her. Why didn't I find it?"

"Because she hid it in a barbecue rub. You see, the arsenic powder she used was kept in a small, blue glass bottle. She kept it under the little sink in the trailer."

"But I didn't see it there."

"Slow down. She hid the vial of arsenic in a three-pound jar of brisket rub. As Houston escalated his control over Shelby, Miranda began to consider taking more drastic measures like a whooping lethal dose of arsenic in addition to the small daily doses. Emma, may I return to my story?"

"Yes." I squeezed Jake's hand, surprised at my lack of energy.

Matt's smile made me feel like he wasn't mad. "So, Miranda took her little bottle of arsenic and added some to a bottle of Houston's health drink. Sometimes, she added fresh fruit to Good Life and blended it for him like a smoothie. If Houston was going to be seen in public, he asked her to put it back in the original bottle so people would see that he drank Good Life."

"Well, that's pretty devious." I could picture Miranda going through the moves as Matt told the story.

"So, when she told her brother they needed to talk in private, she also promised to bring him a smoothie. He agreed. There was nothing suspicious in her actions, because she'd made him so many drinks in the past. They met in the field of clover behind the food trucks. He drank the smoothie, they discussed him not being so hard, and Shelby, he refused, and when he keeled over, she allowed him to die. Shelby is completely innocent."

"I'm so glad she wasn't involved in the murder plot." I stroked Cowboy's head.

Sophie said, "What about the jewelry lady?"

"Verity was a friend and business associate of Houston. Axel's notes provide evidence of how Verity has lied about her jewelry. I'm holding her as long as possible and hope to get the information to the state in time for them to file fraud charges against her. She stole money and lied to people, but she didn't murder Houston."

Jake said, "And Axel Roberts? Was she involved in his accident?"

"I don't believe so. For as smart as Axel is, he's a bit paranoid."

I sat straighter. "Paranoid might not be the best word. Verity did follow him and spied on us. She also tried to force me to give her the research notes. Being anxious over a legitimate situation doesn't mean being paranoid."

Matt frowned.

Sophie stood. "How about I fix us coffee? I brought over a butter kouchen and a cinnamon kouchen. And in case you feel the need for protein, there's also a spinach quiche staying warm in the oven."

My stomach tightened. Not ready for that. Sally had warned me to eat simple foods until my body had recovered. "Kouchen for me, please, and maybe green tea."

Abby squealed. "Oh, no. I've got to take my psych final. The professor agreed to let me come to Lutz as long as I agreed to take the exam online this morning." She gave me a quick kiss. "I'm glad you're okay, Mom."

CHAPTER SIXTY-ONE

"Me, too. Thanks for coming home." I gave her a hug; then she ran upstairs.

Matt stood. "Let me help you, Sophie."

Jake and I were left alone. He situated himself on the ottoman so our knees touched, and we gazed into each other's eyes. "How do you feel?"

"Happy. Tired." My emotions were all over the map. "Mostly blessed to be alive. If you hadn't been there to get me medical help, I could've died like Houston."

"Shh, shh, shh. Let's don't think like that."

"There are so many people who will be relieved to know Matt caught the killer. Paula, Brett, Leigh, Axel—"

"I'm sure Matt will notify them as soon as possible. It's not our job, mostly because he said he has a few more loose ends to tie up."

I yawned. "Man, it's too early for a nap. Let's go to the kitchen."

On cue, Cowboy strutted to the back of the house.

Jake laughed. "He's a growing pup, and he's smart. Once you said kitchen, he was off."

I laced my cold fingers with Jake's warm ones. "I'm missing the farmers market today. Oh, do you know what happened to the French bucket and milk bottles?"

"Sophie said they were on the front porch when she and Abby got here the other night. I think she and Cowboy bonded while you were in the hospital."

"That's nice. Abby always wanted a pet. Too bad I waited until she was away at college."

Sophie appeared. "Are you strong enough to come to the breakfast room? Everything's ready, but I can bring it here."

"Nope, I'm good."

She stepped closer and whispered, "Matt asked me out on an official date, and I said yes."

"Yippee." I was happy for my friends. It was about time for them to realize how good they'd be as a couple.

She sashayed out of the room.

Jake said, "Most of the town wanted to be here for your homecoming, but Sophie told them you needed to rest. Let's eat, then you should take a nap."

"I hate to sleep a beautiful day away."

"There will be lots more beautiful days ahead. Give yourself a break. You solved another murder in Lutz, and the entire town owes you a debt of gratitude." He hugged me. "I'm glad you're alive and safe."

"Thanks. Next time there's a murder in Lutz, I won't do anything by myself. Guess what? We were together when Miranda poisoned me. If you hadn't been around, I might have died. Your quick actions and suspicion about being poisoned probably saved my life." I swallowed hard and tried to shake off the near-death experience. "It's a good thing we were partnered up. You're my hero, Jake."

"Nah. I left you to get coffee from the hospital cafeteria. You had to fight Miranda off in your weakened condition."

"Technically, I did have to fight for my life, but you arrived in the nick of time. I'm glad you were there."

"There's a simple solution to your dilemma of working with a partner or not. Avoid solving any more mysteries. But if you can't stop yourself, I hope you'll always call me."

I smiled and leaned into Jake. "There's nobody I'd rather have at my side."

"Yee-haw." He kissed me until Cowboy returned and slipped between us.

I looked into Jake's brown eyes. It was going to be fun getting to know the man better. Whether there was another murder to solve or not, I looked forward to having Jake in my life.

About the Author

Jackie Layton is the author of cozy mysteries with Spunky Southern Sleuths. Her stories are set in Texas, Georgia, and South Carolina. She lives on the coast of South Carolina where she enjoys walks on the beach and golf cart rides around the marsh. Reading, gardening, and traveling are some of her favorite hobbies. She always keeps a notebook handy to write down ideas for future stories. Be careful what you say around her because it might end up in a book.

SOCIAL MEDIA HANDLES:
   https://www.facebook.com/JackieLaytonAuthor
   https://www.facebook.com/Joyfuljel
   https://twitter.com/joyfuljel
   https://www.pinterest.com/jackielaytonauthor/
   https://www.instagram.com/jackielaytonauthor/
   Bookbub: https://bit.ly/37RqGQ8
   Sign up for Jackie's newsletter: https://bit.ly/2WOPe42

268

Also by Jackie Layton

A Low Country Dog Walker Mystery Series:
Bite the Dust
Dog-Gone Dead
Bag of Bones
Caught and Collared
A Killer Unleashed

A Texas Flower Farmer Cozy Mystery:
Weeding Out Lies

An Organized Crime Cozy Mystery:
Clutter Free